Cauvery Madhavan was born and educated in India. She got her first taste of writing while working as a copy-writer in her hometown of Madras. In 1987 she moved to Ireland, arriving on St Valentine's Day – and despite the Irish weather has been in love with the country ever since. She lives with her husband and three children in beautiful County Kildare.

Paddy Indian

by

Cauvery Madhavan

Dear Aruna,

thank you for this amazing
cover.

much love.

Cauvery.

For Aruna
both lots of
love & thanks AB

BlackAmber Books

Rosemary

Published by BlackAmber Books Limited
PO Box 10812, London, SW7 4ZG

First published 2001

1 3 5 7 9 10 8 6 4 2

Typeset by RefineCatch Limited, Bungay, Suffolk

Printed in Ireland by ColourBooks Ltd

ISBN 1–901969–04–5

For my parents

Acknowledgements

This book was conceived and completed at the Anam Cara Writer's and Artist's Retreat in West Cork. To Sue Booth-Forbes and Maire L. Bradford, my soul friends, for filling me with confidence and for your love, help and advice — my gratitude immeasurable.

Thanks also to my friends Karen Donnelly, Rita Ryan and Marie Carbury, for willingly being subjected to the manuscript at various stages. Your encouragement was crucial. To Breda and James McHale for the generous loan of peace and quiet. To Emer and Andrew Hatherall for making sure my children still had a life.

To Prakash for your unwavering faith in my dream and to Sagari, Rohan and Maya for driving me mad and helping me to keep my sanity, all my love, always.

CHAPTER ONE

~

Dublin, 1989

THE SEAT WAS so damn cold. His thighs shrank away
from it involuntarily as he sat down. Over the next few
months, Padhman would come to realise that there was
nothing like a cold toilet seat to really wake you up in the
mornings.

That first morning, he mulled over it for a while as he
sat there, buttocks flinching from the plastic seat, elbows
on his knees and his chin cupped in the palm of his right
hand. I could rub it down with a towel, he thought. I'll
keep one for that purpose, tucked away in the S-bend of
the pipes. He bent to peer under and behind the toilet.
Damn! No S-bend, not even a bloody U-bend. Just a short
straight pipe that took the sewage out of the small bathroom and down the pipes on the outer wall of the house.
A hot water bottle might do the trick but then it would
have to be moved around to get the whole seat warm.
Tricky job, as it could fall in.

Padhman shifted his chin to the palm of his left hand
while with his right hand he palpated the soft folds of
his abdomen – the result of all those farewell bashes. A
hundred sit-ups every morning. I'll be rid of it soon, he
promised himself. He strained and unexpectedly farted
long and loud. That was all that remained of Air India's
incessant feeding on the eleven-hour flight. Would have
sounded (and probably smelt) different had he flown
British Airways. But his cousin Shrini had only just been

1

appointed Manager, Air India Madras – and would Amma, his mother, have let such an opportunity for a free upgrade to First Class pass by?

'Of course, nobody needs to know that it is an *upgrade*,' she had said to Appa. 'I can send some fish pickle to Kittu in London and Sumi wanted hand-smocked frocks for the girls . . . apparently Marks and Spencer's sell them, but they cost an absolute fortune. Your sister should thank God we, or shall I say *I*, found a girl like Sumi for Kittu. Underwear is what Marks is meant for, and Sumi knows that.'

Appa said mildly, 'The boy is going to Dublin, you know, not London.'

But Amma had ignored her husband, and the fish pickle, triple bagged and triple sealed, now sat in his hand baggage, along with a half-dozen hand-smocked frocks, at the bottom of the stairs.

'Upright, son. Don't forget, always keep your bag upright.'

His suitcase was enormous. Never thought I would ever have travelled with one of those 'Dubai-returnee' type of suitcases, Padhman reflected as he looked around the bathroom for a mug. But Amma had bought it in Singapore Plaza and when Raman, the driver, informed her that the newly purchased suitcase would not fit in the boot of the car, she did something quite unheard of. She told an astonished Raman to put the suitcase onto the back seat and she sat in front. In front! In the passenger seat with the driver beside her! Raman understood. Amma's doctor son was going away and these were exceptional circumstances. He drove all the way home with his wizened body pressed as far into his door as he possibly could. The distance he kept showed his respect.

That last week Amma had spent packing and repack-ing. Systematically stuffing the suitcase, arguing with her husband that there was no use having a nephew who was Manager of Air India if a few kilos of extra baggage were going to be a problem. Appa gave up; he usually did.

Padhman had by now scanned the whole bathroom. Of course there was no mug – he had known that all along. But Padhman had always found that dawdling on the pot was relaxing. Now that he thought about it, he recalled Amma telling him that she had packed two new plastic mugs for him.

'They are right on top,' she had said. 'Just unzip the case and there is one on the right and one on the left. Be careful as the one on the left contains the lamp I bought for you – a small silver Lakshmi Velaku – and the one on the right has the wicks and a small bottle of gingely oil tucked inside it.'

Appa had tsk-tsked in mock horror. The sacred essentials packed in humble bathroom mugs! Amma had been predictably indignant. The mugs were brand new, she bridled. The silver lamp was well protected that way. It would get bent, knowing how airlines threw bags around, and as for the gingely oil . . . well, the mug was ideal to contain any spills. No, Amma could not be accused of doing anything to offend the gods. If only she could see me now, thought Padhman, as he wiped himself with toilet paper.

'This is the first and the last time, Amma,' he said aloud. 'I will unpack the mugs later today. It will always be soap and water for my pure Indian arse.'

Forty-five minutes later he was dressed and ringing the bell of number 33, three doors down. Renu opened the door.

'Hi, Pads,' she said. 'Never seen you suited and booted before. Sunil!' she yelled in the direction of the kitchen. 'Padhman is here.'

Padhman followed her into the sitting room, which was identical to his. In fact, the entire house was identical to his – carpets, curtains, even down to the horrible framed pastoral scenes on the wall. Renu saw him looking around and laughed.

'Thirty-four and thirty-five are exactly the same too. He owns four in a row, our landlord. Michael Lally is his name. Sunil has paid the advance for you, Pads, but you'll see Lally himself at the end of the month when he comes to collect his rent.'

Sunil walked in, toast in one hand and cup of tea in the other. 'Hey, bastard, want some tea?'

'Three months in the West and already cursing in English?' Padhman teased him. 'I never expected you to lose your cultural identity so fast. And bastard, when I said fix me up with a house like yours, I didn't think you'd take me literally!'

Renu looked annoyed. 'I thought you might both have left the cursing behind in India.' She smiled sarcastically. 'However, if that's what makes you two feel grown up, I'll leave you to it. Will I make you a cup, Pads?'

'You'd better take up her offer, for the next time you come over you'll be making it yourself,' said Sunil. 'Renu's been on this "I'm not your slave" kick ever since we arrived.' He ducked as she tried to swat him on her way out to the kitchen.

'Just keeping him in his place, Pads. Tea or coffee? Make up your mind.' She headed out of the room.

'Coffee, please, Renu,' he shouted back as he looked at his friend. 'You are a lucky bastard, you bastard.'

Sunil nodded, finishing his cup. 'Yes, she's the best thing that ever happened to me. Look, we'll leave as soon as you have had your coffee. Hey, don't sit on that sofa . . . the springs will skewer your arse. I'll be back in a minute – got to get my tie and bleep.'

4

Padhman didn't sit at all. The net curtains fascinated him. You could see out but no one could see in. Just perfect, if you were a gentleman flasher. You could flash in peace. Ideal for the shy flasher, too. Hang on – if no one saw you, would it be classified as flashing in the true sense of the word? He was just warming up to the debate in his head when Renu walked in.

'Pads, do you know how to make coffee?'

He took the cup from her. 'Yes, and I can manage tea as well.'

'Don't forget that you don't have to boil milk here. Listen, shall I pick up a few things for you from town? I have a driving lesson this morning and the instructor is a really nice old man. Sometimes he gives me ten minutes or so at the supermarket and then drops me home. He is a widower with three daughters in three corners of the world – America, Australia and South Africa. He is so lonely, he would talk all day if I gave him the chance. Old people are very lonely here, Pads. You'll meet many at the hospital. Half their problems would be solved if they had someone to talk to.'

Sunil came downstairs noisily, two steps at a time.

Padhman put his coffee cup on the mantelpiece. 'I'll take you up on your offer, Renu.'

'And what offer is that?' said Sunil, fixing his bleep onto his belt. 'Don't buy him anything,' he advised when Padhman explained, and when Renu turned to look at her husband in surprise and annoyance, he very simply said, 'He might be on call this weekend, so he won't be around to cook.'

Renu shrugged. 'Well, you will need stuff eventually, Pads, and when you do, get Sunil to give you a hand, won't you? You'll need a lift to the shops at the very least. Why don't you eat with us tonight?' Then, as an afterthought, or was it a warning, wondered Padhman –

5

she added, 'I think I have finally mastered the art of cooking rice.'

Sunil was quiet as he drove out of the estate. Padhman let him be. The net curtains were numerous and he wondered once again at what went on behind them. Net curtains were far more intriguing than plain curtains, he decided. Curtains shut you out totally, while the net curtains had a come hither quality about them. He suddenly realised that Sunil was looking at him curiously.

'Bastard, not homesick already, are you?'

'No.' Then to his own surprise Padhman added, 'Just a bit nervous. What's the hospital like?'

'Just remember the Professor is God, the Registrar is merely God's locum and the nurses are there just for your pleasure. There now, does that make you feel better?' Sunil grinned.

Padhman found he could only manage a weak smile. 'It's been a tough three months preparing to come here and you've had a head start on me, here in Dublin.'

Sunil shook his head, laughing. 'Oh, so it's sympathy you are looking for. Go on, tell me about it, I'm all ears. Did the whole lot of them turn up at the airport? Remember what we called them – your "Jilted Juliets". Bet your Amma gave them short shrift. And I bet they didn't stay around long once they bumped into *her*. How are your folks anyway? I miss your mother and our sparring sessions. She took to Renu surprisingly well, but then I am not the son and heir apparent, so I suppose it was OK for me to have had the "loove-match" as she always put it.'

When there was no response from his passenger, Sunil stopped talking. Then he carried on a bit impatiently: 'Pads, are you all right?'

Padhman nodded. Sunil suddenly looked concerned.

6

'Bleep me if you need anything during the day. It's an easy number ... 1979, the year we joined medical college.'

Padhman nodded again. What a time for the jetlag to strike! The first day of the rest of my life, he thought dramatically. The last three months had been ... well, how could one put it? They had been spent coming to terms with the fact that with his internship successfully behind him and at last deemed a fully qualified doctor, it was time to start again, at the bottom of the heap. This time he was setting out to be a *proper* doctor. One with lots of letters after his name.

CHAPTER TWO

~

PADHMAN ALWAYS KNEW he was going to be a doctor. He hadn't always been sure if he wanted to be one, but that question never arose – except occasionally in his own head, but he always managed to dismiss it. When his grandfather, Professor Sheshadhari Anant OBE, had retired as the Professor of Obstetrics and Gynaecology and Head of Department at Madras Medical College, Appa had dutifully followed in Grandfather's footsteps. Come to think of it, Appa had never stopped doing his duty. Padhman often thought his father deserved a title like Grandfather's. Professor Sriram Anant *DHD (A). Did His Duty (Always).* Or Professor Sriram Anant *FCF (OC). Family Comes First (Of Course).*

Appa had gone to medical college and survived, despite being Professor Anant's son. He had even survived winning the President's Gold Medal in his final medical year. It had been a harrowing time for the family. The Tamil papers had picked up the story and had cried foul, and each day brought new accusations. By the end of the week, the Government was forced to call for an enquiry into the allegations. The enquiry took three months to set up and four months to draw its conclusions. Appa was proved to have been a worthy winner, and Grandfather's good name was finally restored – not that this was of any interest to the newspapers which were, by then, wrapped up in the latest shenanigans of that rising new film star M.G. Ramachandran and his latest leading lady. Appa himself was in Glasgow by then, dutifully studying for his FRCS.

The following year was a good one for both Grandfather and Appa. The Royal College of Edinburgh honoured Grandfather with a Fellowship in recognition of his work and research in the area of infertility and his contribution to the understanding of the subject. The conferring of the Fellowship only confirmed what hundreds, no it must have been thousands, of couples in South India knew. They and others, some having travelled from as far as Singapore, Burma and the Middle East, knew that Professor Anant had the touch. Every morning for thirty-six years, a queue would form outside the house. In the early days, it was the horse-tongas and the rickshaws that would pull up and disgorge their fares. Sometimes it would be a daughter and mother combination. The daughters always less communicative, awkward, and the mothers full of hope. You'd know the daughter-in-law and mother-in-law pairs straight away: the wretched look of failure scurrying behind desperate determination.

Grandfather always asked the same question of them. 'Do you sleep with your mother?' Or, 'Is it your mother-in-law who shares your bed?' And then to add to their consternation he would say, 'I am not surprised you haven't conceived.' He'd send the women packing with instructions to return with their husbands. And they did always return, the men trying not to look ashamed (the fault lies with her, the look always said) and the women doubly ashamed for themselves and for their husbands. When they came back as a couple, Grandfather was a kind and compassionate doctor, a skilful clinician. The proof lay in the dozen or so boxes of choice sweets that would be delivered every day, personally, by delighted new parents. Sometimes, they would bring their newborn with them and ask Grandfather to bless the child. He hated the idea, but knew how much it meant to the couple and he would go through the motions. Most couples, overcome with gratefulness, would try to touch his feet in obeisance, but Grandfather had a horror of that.

Over the years, he had perfected the art of avoiding this by retreating behind his desk in time or shaking hands with the husband just as he was about to make a lunge for his feet. Sometimes, if the couple looked as if they might be persistent in their attempts to touch his feet, he would climb up a four-runged stepladder that was kept in a corner and pretend to root around for a learned journal from the shelves that lined the consulting room. Grandfather deserved that Fellowship.

It was a good year for Appa too. After all the fuss and ceremony in Edinburgh, Grandfather came to Glasgow and a week later attended his son's conferral. They had returned to Madras together, taking a long BOAC flight via Paris and Aden to Bombay, and then travelling by train to Madras. After a brief two-month respite (during which he played the dutiful older brother while Grandfather arranged the marriages of his two younger sisters), Appa had got straight down to the business of following in his father's footsteps. He started by joining his old college as a Reader in Obstetrics.

Grandfather's practice continued to grow in reputation and numbers. Over the ensuing years, the marked change was the way people arrived. There were fewer tongas and rickshaws. Auto rickshaws shrieked up to the gate carrying patients and then, having dropped them off, made sensational U-turns to the other side of the street. There the drivers waited, squatting on their haunches and smoking beedis. They were guaranteed a return fare from Grandfather's clinic. Later on, a lot of patients began to arrive in cars. Some had chauffeurs, who would lean against the parked cars in groups, gossiping about the sexual inadequacies of their employers. For why else would they come to this famous doctor?

Four years later Appa was appointed to the post of Assistant Professor. 'Esteemed son of an esteemed father' was how the Tamil papers put it. Appa had built up quite a reputation of his own at the hospital and the offers started rolling in. Marriage offers, that is. Grandfather initially vetted them and Grandmother then researched the background of the various 'probables'. Amma was the first 'suitable probable' that Appa was approached about. Grandfather prepared the ground. She was the daughter of a Diwan – a titled person – and an only child. She was finishing her Masters in Music at Presidency College in three months' time. The girl had been brought up with traditional values and had nothing but respect for her elders, Grandfather went on. None of that mattered to Appa, who was looking at the studio photograph that had been placed on the centre table. The walnut frame was itself framed in silver filigree. The frame surrounded a cream silk mount, which held inside it a photograph of the most beautiful girl he had ever laid eyes on. She looked slightly anxious – the photographer must have caused her to do so, Appa thought tenderly. Grandfather was moving on to her lineage when his son, by then fully smitten, burst out, 'Yes, I will marry her. But I don't want this photographer near the wedding and I want this photograph to remain here in the house.' If Grandfather was surprised at the strength of his son's feeling he didn't show it. He and Grandmother just thought they had done their job well.

Grandmother died suddenly in her sleep, barely a month after the wedding. No one could have anticipated the profound effect it had on Grandfather. He had loved her intensely, deeply. Their partnership had been perfect. No one else would have particularly thought so. But it

11

was. For weeks he shut himself up, inconsolable, in his room and with instructions to Appa to take on his patients for a while. Appa did his duty. And Amma did hers.

As a doctor, Appa was turning out to be his father's equal, and married to Amma he soon realised that he was pretty much invincible in every other respect. Amma surprised all in the house with the swiftness with which she established her authority. The young bride not only looked after her husband and father-in-law, but also took on a household that supported eleven other people. The first thing Amma did after the funeral was to take her mother-in-law's silver key bunch and hook it firmly into her sari at her waist. It was a very symbolic gesture and no one questioned who was the new mistress of the house. In later years, Appa often teased her about her inseparability from her keys and she always gave the same reply.

'Would you go to work without your stethoscope?'

In those first weeks, when Grandfather closeted himself away, Amma made sure that the household and clinic staff knew it was business as usual as far as their work was concerned. Appa never failed to be amazed at how much she had picked up from Grandmother, about the day-to-day running of the house and the clinic, in that short space of four weeks.

Amma spoke to the watchman and the gardener. She reminded the gardener that her mother-in-law's favourite jasmine bush was to be looked after as always, and told the watchman to be careful about the roses once they came into bud. The urchins, she warned him, would surely try to steal the ones that bloomed close to the gate. She spoke to the driver, Raman, the very first time she went to the vegetable markets to shop. She told him that she would always pay for the petrol when it was filled as needed. The running account with the petrol station would be stopped.

The driver was disappointed, but she had anticipated that and told him that he could eat his lunch with the rest of the household staff from that day on. She had shrewdly realised that it was easier to have him on the premises, eating a free lunch with the rest of the staff, than to have to hang around waiting for him to come back from wherever he decided to go for his lunch. This way she could have him eat early if she needed to go out in the afternoon and if she came back late from a morning's outing, he would still be able to eat. Amma had told the cook that the driver was to be fed every day, and in addition was to be given a serving of the non-vegetarian dish cooked for lunch. That was a satisfactory arrangement on all sides.

As for the cook, Amma made very few changes to start with. Not wanting to cause any further distress to her father-in-law, she instructed the old cook to carry on as Grandmother would have expected. The two young maids were nieces of the cook, and of all the servants in the house, they were the ones most upset by Grandmother's death. The day before she died, she had summoned them and told them that she had in the white envelope in her hand, tips left for the two of them by guests and relations who had travelled to Madras for the wedding and who had stayed in the house.

'It is a lot of money,' she said. 'There are nearly twenty rupees for each of you, but you have both worked hard and you deserve it. I haven't told your aunt about it because if I do, your father will come to know of it and . . .' She did not have to complete her sentence, for one of the girls butted in, panic in her voice.

'Please don't tell him. He will only use it at the arrack shop and . . .'

The elder sister, with her face buried in the palms of her hands, finished the story that Grandmother was so familiar with.

'. . . He will beat us all up. After that much arrack, he could kill us all.'

Grandmother gave them five rupees each from the envelope. 'Tell your father this is what you got as tips, and the rest I shall put into a bank account that I am going to start for each of you. When that good-for-nothing father of yours decides to marry you off, there should be enough for a pair of gold earrings for each of you.' Grandmother shooed them away affectionately as they tried to touch her feet, for the girls were both grateful and surprised, that anyone should have their welfare at heart.

'It's your hard work in this house that keeps your mother's kitchen fires burning. Left to that father of yours . . .' Grandmother shook her head as she walked out of the room. The two sisters had wept bitterly at the funeral and Amma noticed them quietly lay a large marigold garland on Grandmother's body and touch her feet respectfully. In the following days, they went about their assigned tasks, one dusting, sweeping and wiping the rooms and the other washing, drying and ironing the clothes and later, in the afternoons, both together giving their aunt, the cook, a hand cleaning the kitchen. They remained quiet and subdued for the next two weeks until Amma sent for them one afternoon. Amma knew when they walked into the room that they both had something to say. When they saw the white envelope in her hand they both burst into uncontrollable sobbing.

'She was like a mother to us!' wailed the elder girl.

'You haven't told our aunt about the money, have you?' wept the sister. 'Oh God! If Father finds out, he will drag us out of here by the hair. He gets drunk, you see, and he would kill us for keeping the money from him!'

Amma was not surprised by the intensity of the terror felt by the two young maids. Their story was not uncommon. The jobs they had were just a temporary haven, until their father arranged their marriages to men who, in all likelihood, would do to them what their father did to their mother. Numerous pregnancies, drunken beatings and a lifetime of poverty and drudgery lay ahead. Amma calmed the maids down and told them that Grandmother had written their names and the amount of cash inside on the cover of the envelope, and had marked it with the words *Canara Bank*. The girls nodded their heads together vigorously like clockwork dolls and Amma eventually managed to get the whole picture. Separate accounts were opened for them, and with Amma as the joint account holder, the sisters knew their father would never be able to lay his hands on that money.

Amma worked through the rest of the staff systematically. The two maids at the clinic, the ayahs, looked after the two large waiting rooms, the two patients' toilets and the consulting room with its little anteroom. Amma frequently walked from the house across the cemented courtyard to the clinic during the day. She would spend a few minutes talking to Miss Angela, the receptionist. Miss Angela never said much to anyone. The phone never permitted her to have a long enough exchange that could be deemed a conversation. She had perfected the art of conveying what she wanted to say to the patients, the staff, to Amma, Appa and even Grandfather, in short two- or three-word bursts.

'Mrs Swami? Your turn . . . in, in!'

'Mrs Nathan . . . you forgetting bag?'

Or: 'Ayah . . . take sample.'

Even when she wasn't on the phone, she remained painfully brief just in case.

'Ayah! Toilet door . . . close.'

And to Amma when she saw her coming into the clinic, 'Madam . . . everything tip-top.'

After that routine greeting, Amma would make small talk with the two nurses as they walked in and out of the anteroom. While they weighed patients and took blood pressures, she would briefly enquire if Appa had had time for a cup of tea and would remind them, as she always did, every day in the years to come, to send the watchman across to let her know when Appa was seeing his second last patient.

For Appa, it very quickly became one of his most comforting constants in life. Amma would wait in the cool inner courtyard of the house, sitting on the large divan, her feet tucked up neatly under her. He would stretch back on the old planter's chair, opposite the divan, and put his feet up on one of the chair's extra long arms. The glass of buttermilk that Amma had placed there, he could reach for with his eyes closed, and he would keep them closed as he brought the glass up to his lips. Amma seasoned it with something different every day. Sometimes a little grated ginger and fresh coriander, sometimes curry leaves and mustard seeds. Other days he would smell the ground almond and honey as he brought the glass up to his lips. He would sit there slowly sipping, secretly looking at Amma through half closed eyes. She always looked back at him. This became a ritual with them. Appa and Amma . . . it was as if they silently recharged each other.

Four months after Grandmother's funeral, Grandfather announced, at breakfast, that he was returning to the clinic. Before Appa could say anything, he asked him to ring Mahesh Patel & Son, the architects.

'I want another consulting room added on to the clinic. Ours will be a joint practice from now on.' Appa was pleased, but it was what he had expected to happen in the course of time. Appa knew his life had been mapped out and he was not going to deviate from the course.

CHAPTER THREE

~

MAHESH PATEL WAS an old friend of Grandfather's, and the latter had shared his pride on the day Mahesh Patel Architects had become Mahesh Patel & Son. The two men had been bridge partners for nearly eighteen years. They played at the Gymkhana Club, twice a week, in the Gentlemen's Lounge. On Thursday evenings, each had an early dinner at home and then they would head for the Club, where normally at least three rubbers would be played – unless, that is, Grandfather was called away to attend to an emergency. This was very rare, as his assistant Dr Muthu, who naturally was on call every Thursday, knew that the normally kindly Professor had a very caustic tongue if dragged away from his game for anything but a true emergency. The Club was very accommodating of their distinguished member. Looking around on any given evening, one could count at least a dozen members whose pregnant wives, daughters and daughters-in-law had been attended by Grandfather. It was routine for his bridge table to have the only phone extension in the Gentlemen's Lounge, placed on a low stool by his chair.

On the rare occasions it rang, everyone at the dozen or so tables in the room would look up from their game and listen to Grandfather on the phone to Dr Muthu. They would look away queasily when Grandfather's voice echoed across the mahogany-panelled room.

'Have her waters broken, Muthu?' Some would wonder perplexed when he said, 'She's only four centimetres? Call me back when she is six.'

The fathers and husbands who had laboured through it before, would shake their heads from side to side and look back at their cards sagely, making the situation truly perplexing for the uninitiated. If Grandfather ended the conversation with: 'Well, Muthu, I know you can handle that. Tell the family I will see them in the morning,' the tables would all return promptly to their games. They hated the odd time when matters went beyond Dr Muthu's capabilities. Grandfather would then say, 'All right, Muthu, inform the theatre staff and tell the family I'm on my way.' This was particularly annoying for the Gentlemen's Lounge because they were always left in the dark about the conclusion. Reluctantly pushing back his chair, and with a quick apology to his table, Grandfather would be gone, down the grand marble stairs, with barely a wait at the magnificent arched portico. One of the bearers would have preceded him by half a minute and shouted to the driver to bring the Professor's car. Sometimes an excited shout of, 'Driver! Emerr-jun-cy!' would make the bearer feel he had done his bit for the poor unknown woman. At the very least, the Professor would remember the bearer's quick thinking and the generous tip on the following Sunday would reflect that.

Amma was in her bedroom at Appa's desk, writing to her father, when the maid came in and said, 'Periayyah says to come down, Amma.' Then, as if to fortify Amma with the details of the situation downstairs, she added, 'Two visitors have arrived. They look like Hindi-karans.' And then, looking at Amma directly in the eye, she giggled and whispered, 'The lady is all dressed up – like for a wedding.'

'Where is Ayyiah?' Amma enquired of the maid.

'He is with Periayyiah and the gentleman. They have all gone into the clinic.'

'Is the lady downstairs all alone?' said Amma with urgency in her voice.

And realising that she obviously was, Amma interrupted the maid, with instructions to run down and ask the lady what she would have to drink and also to tell her that Amma was on her way down. Amma then freshened up quickly. As long as anyone could remember, freshening up for Amma meant a quick wash of the face and copious amounts of Cuticura powder, from the long orange tin, vigorously shaken around and over her upper body. Appa, when he wanted to annoy her, would gently thump her on her back and the rising cloud of powder would have the three men in the house, Grandfather, Appa and Padhman in raucous splits. The subsequent pacifying of her hurt feelings was, in itself, a ritual expression of their love and adoration for her.

Amma went down and met her best friend Nimmi that day. Mahesh Patel's daughter-in-law Nimmi was lonely, and yet her in-laws and husband of a year, Raja, fussed over her and she lacked for nothing. Mrs Patel senior lived in her own world. She was a very religious woman and spent much of her day in prayer, ensconced in the little prayer room, not far from the kitchen of the Patel house. From that vantage point, she was able to receive a steady stream of things that she needed for her daily prayers and keep a close, but somewhat dispassionate, eye on the comings and goings in the house which, not unlike the Anant home, had more servants than family. When Amma visited Nimmi, she would invariably be greeted by a delicate, silvery voice that came from somewhere down the inner hall.

'Beti, ask them to put on the fan for you. Nimmi will be down soon. Sometimes if she has oiled her hair before her bath, it takes her a bit longer.'

Then Amma would hear her ring the little puja bell

and the silvery voice would return to reading from the *Baghavad Gita*, the rhythmic incantations an appropriate background to the gentle pace of the Patel household. Amma often deliberately chose to sit on a cane chair, near the doorway to the inner hall, from where she could see down the corridor into a sliver of the prayer room. From there she would watch the servants emerge from the kitchen and approach the ornate door of the room, stooping slightly in unconscious obeisance as they came closer to the door. On a little brass plate kept specifically for the purpose, they bore ghee for the lamps or freshly rolled wicks. Sometimes Amma would see them standing at the doorway with a pile of richly coloured, washed and ironed silk cloths, which the old lady would then drape around the silver idols of her beloved Krishna and Radha.

Amma was surprised at the unceremonious ease with which these devotions would stop and household matters would be attended to when required. If the dhobi turned up, one of the servants would appear with piles of dirty clothes. The dog-eared laundry book would be passed into the prayer room, while in the hallway, the dhobi separated the laundry into small piles: saris, shirts, linen and a separate bundle for things that needed to be starched before being ironed. Then the dhobi would call out the items in the piles and the cook, watching carefully, would repeat the name of the item to his mistress in the prayer room. The old lady would date and write down the list, often adding a short description of the item, which the cook would initiate. The dhobi might say, 'One blue shirt,' which the cook after a brief glance would translate as 'Aiyyah's blue shirt, which he wears for bridge,' and what might eventually be written down was *blue stripe (Nehru collar) shirt*. When the man had worked his way through the piles, the previous pages of the book would be checked to see if any items were still to be returned.

20

Then, even as the cook was helping him to gather all the clothes to be tied into a bundle, Amma would see a petite hand reach out and ring the silver bell and the reading from the Book would resume. Looking on, she always felt that these 'interruptions' were actually parts of an unbroken rhythm that made up the daily goings on of a well-run household.

Amma herself ran Grandfather's home, which she very soon began to consider her own, with a near religious fervour. She never envied Nimmi for having no responsibilities enforced on her. She would often recount her afternoon with Nimmi to Appa, adding at the end that her friend's restlessness came from not having to think about anything or anyone else's welfare or needs. Nimmi was a visitor in her own home. On that occasion, Appa remarked, rather flippantly, that what Nimmi needed was a child. 'She will have the baby demanding responsibility from every orifice.'

The opening of the new consulting room was a simple affair. Mahesh Patel and his wife, who naturally had organised the ceremony, welcomed the selected few guests, while Grandfather and Appa sat cross-legged on the bare floor of the freshly painted room, opposite the pujari, who took them through the brief ceremony of prayers, explaining the rituals as he performed them. Amma, Nimmi and Raja Patel stood behind the pujari and, while some of the guests stood beside them, others stayed outside in the shade of the veranda, peeping in occasionally as if marking their presence to the deity. When it appeared that the ceremony was about to come to an end, Amma and Nimmi discreetly left in the direction of the house, to supervise the last-minute arrangements for the vegetarian meal that was to be served.

The day ended on an auspicious note with a short, sharp burst of rain. That rain was the catalyst that was to seal the lifelong friendship between Appa, Amma and Raja and Nimmi Patel.

Grandfather had insisted that the Patels wait for the rain to stop before they left. It was in that brief delay, that the Tokyo trip was planned. Grandfather knew that Appa had been under a great strain since Grandmother's death. He wanted Appa and Amma to have a break for two weeks. Appa was to attend a scientific meeting in Manila at the end of the month and Amma was to accompany him on that four-day trip.

'I will be away on work too, in Tokyo – yes, about the same dates. The travel agents have to get back to me,' said Raja.

'Is Nimmi going?' asked Amma.

'Shouldn't let him go alone, Nimmi,' teased Grandfather.

Appa slapped Raja on the back, grinning. 'Remember what happened to the hero in *Love in Tokyo*?'

That settled it. Raja Patel said he would ring the travel agents the next day, and three weeks later, Appa and Amma flew on from Manila to meet up with Raja and Nimmi in Tokyo. It was to have been a carefree two-week holiday, but it wasn't. Amma and Nimmi both suffered with nausea and terrible biliousness from the first day and stayed in their rooms. Appa and Raja made occasional forays into the hotel lobby and at one point, even took a short stroll together, window-shopping. On the third day the ladies seemed to be better and the four breakfasted together in Amma and Appa's room, after which Appa and Raja went off to book a Tokyo city excursion. On their return, they found their wives as sick as ever. Amma had put the toilet seat down and was sitting on it exhausted. When Appa walked into the bathroom she directed him with her eyes to look at the sink. It was full up with the half-digested remains of her breakfast.

'It won't go down, the sink is blocked,' she said and burst into tears. 'You will have to clean it before you ask them to send a plumber or these Japanese will think we Indians are very dirty.'

Half an hour later the hotel doctor was in the rooms, very concerned, taking samples and specimens. He returned the next day. It was a moment he was to recollect often and savour for ever.

'Both?' said Appa and Raja in unison. 'Both of them are pregnant?'

Appa and Amma held hands. Raja cried tears of happiness and Nimmi consoled him.

CHAPTER FOUR

~

'TO OUR BEGINNINGS . . . to Tokyo,' said Sunil, raising his glass of Guinness and pushing the second glass across the kitchen counter towards Padhman.

'To Tokyo, you gobshite.' Padhman cast a mischievous glance at Renu. 'No comment, Mrs Patel?'

Renu refused to be baited. 'Very clever, Pads. A week down the line and you can curse in Irish. Mmm – don't forget to tell that to the examiners at the College of Surgeons.' She stood poised at the freezer door, with a bag of peas in one hand. 'Are you planning to study or are you two heroes watching the Grand Prix?'

'It's the Japanese Grand Prix, Renu, the Japanese!' Sunil was indignant. 'How could we *not* watch?'

'OK, OK, OK. I haven't forgotten you both have umbilical connections to Tokyo and things Japanese. The reason I ask is because if you are going to watch, I bags the couch.' With that she shut the freezer door.

Padhman watched Sunil mock-protest on his knees, nibbling Renu's fingers. These two make me sick, he thought and then said so aloud.

Renu laughed and pushed Sunil away. 'I mean it, the couch is mine.' By the fifth lap she was fast asleep.

'She's always like that,' Sunil whispered. 'Says there is nothing like the drone of Formula One cars to put her to sleep. She always watches the starts though and will grumble if I don't wake her up for the finish.'

'She knows her stuff, obviously.' Padhman yawned. 'I'll do the same in a few minutes. Wake me if there is a crash.'

24

Grabbing a cushion from the couch he stretched out on the carpet. And lay on his side for a while, still watching the television. His mind wandered. Renu's dinner had not been that bad, considering that three months back she would not have known the difference between a boiled egg and an omelette. I'm being cruel here, he thought. Her mother must have given her a last-minute crash course. Renu's mother . . . now *there* was someone who could cook. It was a great pity that Renu's mother had declined the chance to send her daughter a jar of her famous pork pickle. She didn't want Padhman to have problems with Customs, she said. He could have done with the pickle this afternoon, he thought. That brought him to the fried onion, tomato and chilli-powder concoction he had eaten with bread for lunch. If only Amma could have seen him. Pathetic or heroic? She would probably have chosen pathetic. Well, Amma, you are to blame, he thought. You should have marked the preparation time on the recipe. If I had known that just the preliminaries for making a potato and pea curry would take so long, I would have tried something else. Like toast and tea. Or bumming two meals off Renu instead of just dinner. He yawned. The TV became a blur . . . the laps, the cars, they seemed to go on and on, like his first night on call.

Padhman had walked into the Doctors' Residence at six that Friday evening last week. The Res looked like a waiting room at the railway station in Madras. Eight stiff chairs arranged in a row faced a television that flickered unhealthily. Three Formica tables separated the passengers waiting in the chairs from the trains being announced on the monitor. Padhman put a smile on as he walked in. No one looked up. He sat down on the only vacant chair, the one closest to the door. He sat on the edge at first, then settled back. He closed his eyes. Shit!

Should have introduced myself, made small talk. This is ridiculous, to sit with my eyes closed. No, I'm not scared, he reassured himself. But it's a strange feeling. The only darkie in a room full of velais. Is that what they call us, he wondered. Darkies? Better than Paki, I suppose. Unconsciously he began to relax. Footsteps sounded along the corridor and they seemed to slow down as they approached the room. Padhman was about to open his eyes when a voice at the door announced, 'Takeaway from Khyber Tandoori . . . is it for here? Beef Madras with chips?'

Padhman shrank into his chair, keeping his eyes firmly shut. Oh no! They were all going to think it was for him. The bloody foreigner who can't wait to stink up the place with garlic and onions. Look – he's even eating with his fingers. Bastard darkies should stay at home till they learn how to use a knife and fork. He was about to open his eyes and deny any involvement, when the chair next to him was scraped back and someone headed for the door.

'That's mine, and about time too. They'll be calling me into theatre any minute now. How much?'

'Sorry Doc, Friday night and all that.'

Padhman felt exhausted. I have to open my eyes, he thought. Better to get it over with. Or maybe I should wait till the Beef Madras and chips are eaten. Yes, he decided. Better to wait, or his neighbour might feel obliged to offer him a share. In his mind, Padhman ran through the conversation.

'Oh, you're awake! I was hoping you'd taste some of this curry – you know, tell me if it is the "real" stuff. Ah, go on, there's plenty. The Khyber is better than the Rajdoot, you know. The Rajdoot buggers don't serve chips with their curries. There you go, try that. Oh Jesus – no, wait! It's bloody beef . . . I mean, shit. You know, Holy Cow and all that.'

26

I must be going mad, thought Padhman. If I don't open these eyes they are going to get welded shut and I will be left talking nonsense to myself for the rest of my life. The Beef Madras actually smelt quite good. OK, Pads, he said to himself. On the count of ten. One, two . . . he could hear more footsteps approach, lighter ones this time. He reached ten and opened his eyes, blinking and adjusting himself in his chair, trying to pretend he had just woken from a short nap. The yawn that he forced out surprised him with its genuineness and length and he looked up towards the door. It was the Orthopaedic Registrar. She looked tired. Padhman instinctively got up and was about to offer her his chair, when he simultaneously realised that no one else had even cared to look up. I'm not an arse licker, but I'm an ass. Yet I can't suddenly sit down again, can I? So he kept going, getting up and walking out of the room, giving her what he thought was an efficient nod. *I'm an ass, I'm an ass, I must be an ass* was his silent refrain. He wandered aimlessly around the hospital for a while, trying to find an explanation for his self-conscious behaviour. He concluded it was nothing to do with the Irish. In fact, it was those bastard English! After three hundred years, the only thing they left Indians with was an inferiority complex.

He ended up in the canteen where a cleaning lady was stacking chairs at the far end.

'Too late, luv, too late,' she called to him across the room. 'Wait till I see now, she's just after taking the sandwiches in. Is it tea you're wanting?' She walked towards the kitchen area, still talking. 'They've all gone, it's only Mary and the new lass left now, and they're finishing up. It's past six, don't you know? On call, are you?'

Padhman sensed sympathy.

'I haven't eaten the whole day,' he said to her as she disappeared through the stainless steel doors. The doors swung to and fro but they were out of sync. Padhman stared at them as they flapped drunkenly back and forth, until the swings got shorter and shorter and they finally stood still. Through the glass panels set into the doors, he could see a corridor. It was empty but for a large kitchen trolley on which sat rows of salt and pepper cellars, white vases with red plastic carnations, and dozens of little bowls with sugar sachets, all arranged neatly. Why should the vases have to go in? What did they refill them with every night? Was he supposed to wait here for the cleaner to return? He really was hungry now and he looked up at the large plastic clock on the far wall. It was six twenty-five. I'll give her five minutes, he decided, but in the event he didn't even have to wait that long as she reappeared through the doors almost immediately.

'Mary will sort you out. Take a chair from that lot and sit yourself down. I must lock the doors now or they'll all be wandering in.' She slammed the huge entrance doors to the canteen, bolted them and walked back to where she had been stacking the chairs.

Padhman felt he had to say something.

'We had to stack our own chairs onto our desks at the end of the day when I was in school.'

She had her back to him and did not reply. Where was this Mary dame anyway? Here he was, starving, and the cleaning lady wouldn't talk. I should have thanked her, instead of feeding her trivia about my schooldays, he thought. He watched her stack the chairs and clean, systematically and thoroughly, around the tables for what seemed to be an eternity.

'This is all that I could manage for you, luv,' said the woman who came through the swing doors, walking towards him with a brown tray. 'There was no coffee left so I brought you some tea. Therese says you haven't eaten all day.'

She put the tray down on the table in front of Padhman and stood back. The cleaning lady was drawn to them immediately.

'Mary,' she said as she walked towards them, raising her eyebrows heavenwards. She was acknowledged with similarly raised eyebrows from Mary. Padhman instinctively knew that the two women had just said all that had to be said to each other, about him.

'Almost done, are you, Therese?' asked Mary.

'I'll be finished soon, just that last corner to be done. Sean's giving me a lift home today.'

Both the women fell silent and watched Padhman. He had begun to butter the two slices of brown soda bread that accompanied a plate on which two halves of a boiled egg sat, covered with a yellowing mayonnaise. Where the mayonnaise had flowed off the eggs and on to the plate, it had dried up and cracked. Padhman thought it looked vaguely familiar – like the parched earth that featured in that ad on television. He had watched it last night, the one for the Irish Relief Agency's appeal for the Third World. He tried to forget that image as he dug the fork into the egg, but somehow his actions seemed to mirror the ad. The bent, anxious set of shoulders, the camera panning to the futile digging of the scorched earth. With his mouth full, Padhman looked up at the two women and smiled. He thought he had done his best impression of the grateful Third World farmer. They seemed satisfied with his efforts and after watching him for a few minutes more, both went their own ways.

Three hours later, Padhman walked back from Casualty into the Res again. He ignored the two people slumped in their chairs in front of the TV and headed for the tiny kitchenette at the end of the room. He was starving; the egg mayonnaise seemed a distant memory. He stood at the doorless entrance to the kitchenette and looked in.

Amma would weep if she knew he had to scrounge for a cup of tea in this filthy kitchen, he thought. Actually she wouldn't. She'd be furious. No, considering it was past midnight and he hadn't stopped working since seven this morning, she would be bloody *furious*. The kind of furious that would make her immediately tuck the loose end of her sari, her pallav, determinedly into her waist. Once she had done that, Amma could sort anything out.

'And they call *us* dirty foreigners. You are Padhman, aren't you? Sunil and Renu were at my place the night before they picked you up at the airport.'

Padhman turned around to face an outstretched hand and a dark, pockmarked face.

'Manoharan – they call me Harry. I'm doing ENT.'

Padhman laughed and shook hands. 'I *was* Padhman. I now answer to Paddy.'

'Did no one tell you that you need vaccinations before you travel into that kitchen? I was going to phone for a pizza. Want to split a Deep Pan?'

Padhman nodded enthusiastically. Manoharan headed for the phone at the other end of the room while Padhman walked back to the chairs and sat down.

'Not vegetarian, are you?' Manoharan had his hand cupped over the mouthpiece.

Padhman shook his head, mouthing, 'No chance.'

Manoharan looked at the person sitting a few chairs to the left of Padhman. ' Hey, Niall. Pronto Pizza – do you want to order?'

Niall was mesmerised by the game show on the television. A few nights earlier, Padhman had had his first introduction to *Love Boat* and its leering host. Niall's fixation was understandable.

'Look, sunshine, we're getting extra chillies on ours so you won't be able to bum a slice off us,' Manoharan warned him.

'Can always pick them off, Harry. I can always pick them off.' Niall had not taken his eyes off the screen. It was the last, decider round and it was called *Touch Me-Feel Me*. The host, tight-trousered Anton Frazier, was at his embarrassing best. He goaded the contestants along as they felt up various body parts, in a line-up that was made up of volunteers from the audience and of course the contestants' partners. Innuendo transformed fingers, knees, noses and shoulders into imagined sexual objects. By the end of the round, Frazier was practically orgasmic, the losing contestants sulked, and the winners simulated sex, fully clothed, in time to rhythmic clapping from the audience, on the massive waterbed that was the prize. In fact, the first time Padhman watched *Love Boat* he was totally hypnotised, and when the phone rang he was distant and vague, trying to sound enthusiastic at hearing Amma's voice, while at the same time wondering how on earth a thumb could be mistaken for a penis.

Manoharan joined them, sitting down between Padhman and Niall.

'Pepperoni and double chilli coming up,' he said, and then looking at the television he mock-saluted Frazier. 'The Squashed Scrotum strikes again.' With Niall joining in, he sang the closing lines of the show's signature tune. 'Looo . . . ve . . . boat . . . aaahh . . . aahh . . . aah . . . what a ride.'

They ended their duet with high fives and Manoharan turned to Padhman. 'You've met Niall? Well, you have now. Great guy to know. My social life is kept alive by his rejects.'

Niall grinned and proffered his hand. 'He's taking the piss out of me, don't believe a word of what he says.' Then, shaking Padhman's hand vigorously he added, 'Padhman . . . not short for Padhmanabhan, is it? From South India, aren't you?'

Padhman warmed to him instantly. Where was the short apologetic laugh and the summary dismissal of his name, accompanied by that stock standard excuse 'I'll never remember that!' or the variant 'I'm not great at foreign names.'

Padhman's face must have registered surprise because both Manoharan and Niall laughed.

'I went to South India for my elective year, spent six months at a rural women and children's health centre near Madurai and six months at the leprosy centre in Chidhambaram. My mother's eldest brother is a priest out there,' Niall added in explanation.

'Don't ever curse the bastard in Tamil. He can swear as good as any cheyri porukie, but I have to say that the Irish accent dilutes the effect a bit.' Manoharan laughed, slapping Niall on the back.

'Poda myir! Have you ever heard yourself say "gob-shite"?' Niall countered. He looked at his watch. 'Pronto Pizza my arse. They must be waiting for the chillies to come from India.'

Manoharan was triumphant. 'I've ordered one for you as well. *Without* chillies.'

'You mean I'm going to have to pay to eat this pizza?'

'That will be a change, won't it, Dr Fahy? *Gobshite*!' Manoharan picked up the remote and started flicking through the channels.

Padhman had found the whole conversation bizarre. A Tamil-speaking Irishman? But the banter was comforting. There was something to be said about the reassuringness of hearing people curse in your mother tongue. Reassuringness? Yeah, thought Padhman. Wrong English maybe, but it does the job. The pizza arrived and the three young doctors ate in companionable silence.

CHAPTER FIVE

~

'I'VE NEVER SEEN a more ugly, flash car,' said Renu the first time she saw it. 'Always fancied yourself as Batman, did you, Pads?' She opened the door of the Celica. 'How is one supposed to get in?' She shook her head disapprovingly at her husband. 'Don't tell me you encouraged him to get this. Do I get in bum first or what?'

Sunil grinned. 'Now you see what I had to give up when I married you — all aspirations of ever owning a great car.' He waited till his wife was in and then flicked the front seat back into position, before getting in himself.

'Are you ready, Robin?' Padhman revved the engine a bit and looked at Renu in the rearview mirror. 'What about you, Catwoman? Where can I drive you both to?'

'How about Gotham City?'

Padhman meowed. 'Does she scratch too?' he asked Sunil.

'Ever wondered why I look so worn all the time?' Sunil turned around and grinned at his wife. 'You look quite comfortable there actually.'

'Hmm . . . It's not too bad, but I can't move my legs and I'm sunk so low I can hardly see out. Well, are we ever going to move, or is this car just for show?'

'She complains all the time as well. Don't know how you put up with her, Sunil.'

'Listen, you bastard, stop creating trouble. Let's ask the lady where she wants to go.'

'OK, Renu, serious now. Where to?' Padhman

33

suddenly couldn't help revving the engine once more as he waited for her reply.

She winced. 'Christ! You guys haven't grown up. Stop making that bloody racket and let me think.'

'Language, my darling, language,' Sunil tut-tutted.

Renu ignored him and looked at Padhman instead. 'Are you planning to buy me a pastry and coffee at our journey's end?'

Padhman laughed. 'Yes, ma'am. So where to?'

'Driver, Enniskerry polam! Step on it,' she ordered in Tamil and waved her hand imperiously.

'That's a good way off,' Sunil protested immediately. 'It's in Wicklow!'

'No, no, Enniskerry it is,' said Padhman. 'One needs a longish drive to truly appreciate this car.'

Sunil snorted and the Celica growled out of the estate. Padhman soon felt ensconced in a happy glow. Appa and Amma had financed the car. He was thrilled when they had called to say that one of Appa's patients who had a business in Singapore was going to send Padhman a 'parcel'.

'Yes, Padhu. A *parcel*,' Amma had repeated.

'What of?' Padhman was curious.

'Oh, look, I'll hand you over to your father.' Amma sounded annoyed.

'Padhman, have you thought of buying a car as yet?' Appa asked him. 'Mahesh was mentioning that you go to hospital with Sunil. How do you manage? It must be very difficult when he is on call. This *parcel* from Singapore should be with you in a few days.'

It suddenly dawned on Padhman that they were transferring funds out of India, via Appa's patient. Amma's cloak and dagger euphemisms! She was paranoid about phones being tapped.

'It's not like we are criminals, you know. If we can

afford it, why can't we send money to our son? Foreign exchange rules should not apply to *genuine* cases like us,' Amma had said to Nimmi, who wholeheartedly agreed.

'I was hoping to buy one in a few months' time, Appa, but it can wait.'

Amma interrupted on the extension. 'It'll make life easier, son. You have the exams coming up. Are you studying?'

That had settled it. For the two weeks before the money arrived, Padhman and Sunil bought every auto magazine on the shelves. Padhman even went to the Eason's bookstore on O'Connell Street to make sure that they had not missed any.

'The pleasure is in the anticipation,' Sunil had tried to explain to Renu.

'It's my first car, Renu – not Appa's, not Amma's, not Grandfather's. This one is *mine.*'

'This car is mine, mine,' he said aloud, speaking his mind as he waited for the lights to turn green.

Both Sunil and Renu burst out laughing.

An hour and a half later they sat, ready to order, at a café table in the open-air central courtyard of the Strawberry Rooms in Enniskerry. It had been a pleasant enough drive through the late summer countryside. Renu had dozed off while they were still negotiating traffic in Dublin. Sunil was in a nostalgic mood.

'Do you remember how we persuaded old Raman to give us driving lessons in your grandfather's Chevy?'

'Yes, poor Raman. He was in tears at the airport when I left. Must ask Amma to show him photographs of this car. I sent some photos home recently through Venkat. He's gone to Coimbatore for two weeks, the poor bastard. He should be in the process of getting married. In fact, today is the twenty-seventh and we are five hours ahead,' Padhman looked at his watch before concluding, 'which means he will be a married man by now. Tied to some poor girl he has never even met.'

'The Radiology Venkat or the Venkat at the Mater?'

'I didn't know there were two,' Padhman replied. 'I'm talking about the Radiology Venkat, but who is the Venkat at the Mater?'

'He was two years our senior. Don't you remember Venkat Palaniswamy? His father was a Congress MP. Oh, come on, Pads, he was a real pain in the arse. He organised all that horrid ragging the year we were Freshers.'

'What – that bastard is here in Dublin? Whatever for?'

'To get the letters after his name. What do you think we are all here for?'

'His father could have bribed anyone to get any letters he wanted, and right up his arse if he so pleased! What is he doing at the Mater anyway?'

'Nephrology. Pads, that's the turn we need to take, the one signposted for a mile ahead . . . yeah, he is the Nephrology SHO. The bastard has come down to earth. He stopped telling people who his father was, when they started asking him which trade union he represented!' said Sunil, laughing.

'Oh, don't look so blank, Pads,' Sunil continued. 'Congress . . . Congress of Trade Unions? I mean, it would be the rare Irish person who would know of the Congress *Party*. They all knew it for the one week after *Gandhi* was released in the cinemas. Then we went back to being the country that Mother Theresa lives in.'

Padhman was rather surprised by Sunil's outburst. 'Since when did you become the proud "Son of India"?'

'You have to agree, Pads. We knew much more about the Irish before we came to Ireland than they know about us Indians.'

'Go on, you're not serious. OK, show me an Irishman who can't wax lyrical about Tandoori Chicken.' Padhman slapped Sunil on his thigh and chuckled. 'By the way, do you know our landlord Michael Lally loves Vindaloo?'

'Poda myir!'

'And they can say Poda myir too.' Padhman laughed loudly. 'You know Niall Fahy in ENT? You should hear him curse in Tamil. The bastard would put us all to shame!'

'Nothing could put you both to shame.' Renu had woken up just as they turned off the dual carriageway. 'I love this part of the drive.'

Padhman watched her yawn and stretch in the rearview mirror. She smiled back at him.

'I'm ready for my tea now, Pads. When you get to the village, there is a sort of village square. Park there. The tearoom is just on the left-hand side of the road as you drive in.'

They ordered toasted sandwiches, a chocolate almond torte for Renu, a slice of carrot cake for Padhman and tea for three, after which Renu disappeared back into the main tearoom, in search of the toilets. Sunil followed a minute later.

'Keep an eye on her bag, Pads,' he said as he pushed his chair back.

Renu returned soon, but did not sit down. She strolled around, looking at the stoneware pottery and terracotta artefacts that were displayed on wooden ledges around the four walls of the courtyard. When she had finished, she walked slowly back to the table.

She sat down and relaxed back in her chair.

'This is the life,' she said contentedly. 'If only Sunil had no exams, phone calls to India were free, we had a maid, someone came to do the ironing, it rained only three times a week *and* I pass my driving test on Monday, life would be purrrr . . . fect.'

'Is it this Monday? You mean the day after tomorrow?'

'Yep. Why, is there something happening on Monday?'

'No, I just remembered you got your test date soon after I arrived and at that time, the test was six weeks away. It's flown, these past six weeks.'

'Six weeks and the Casanova is still lying low,' Sunil joked as he rejoined them. He looked at his watch. 'Where's the tea? They're taking their time,' he said impatiently.

Renu sat up in her chair. 'I won't be sharing my cake with you, Sunil, so if you are getting hungry, you'd better order some for yourself. It's not funny, Padhman. He always does it. "I don't want, I don't want" and then when mine arrives, you just watch, he'll take a bite, "to taste" and then "just one more" and then he'll have the cheek to say "save the last bite for me".'

Sunil was holding his stomach and laughing with tears running down his cheeks. 'Watch it, Pads. She is just about to say it is all a matter of principle!'

'Of course it is,' said Renu. 'When I order a cake, it is to be able to eat the whole thing, not just to get a taste of it in between you demolishing it. Stop laughing, will you. It isn't *that* funny.'

'It's a matter of principle, Renu,' Padhman sniggered

'What is? Oh, never mind.' Renu looked at the two of them, now pretending to stifle their laughter, and then after a few seconds she slapped her forehead and smiled. Sunil blew her a kiss. She looked back at him and for that brief moment she had eyes only for him.

There it was again, thought Padhman. Those moments between them fascinated him. They were short and intense but they had a foreplay-like quality. He watched, but as always it was fleeting, private and it passed just as he was getting uncomfortable about eavesdropping on their unsaid conversation. He envied them. Stirring his tea thoughtfully, he tried to think if there was anyone in his brigade of Jilted Juliets, as Sunil was wont to call them, with whom he could ever have shared a meaningful glance? Or a meaningful anything, for that matter. He sipped his tea and thought hard.

Sonal could have been a possibility, until she chose to go to Cornell, to do a Masters in International Economics. He could picture her even now, addressing delegates at the World Bank, her breasts resting casually on the lectern, and she herself unaware of the effect on the male delegates in the front row.

And there was Annie ... Padhman smiled without knowing it. Amma would have thrown a fit, the kind that was always preceded by the words, 'Being broadminded is one thing, but ...' And that would be followed with 'Annie Ewart? But she's Anglo-Indian!'

Yes, he thought. Annie had been a possibility. He wondered if she was still in Cardiff. He looked up at Renu. She might know. In fact, she would be sure to know, he reasoned with himself. Renu's sister and Annie had been in Pre-University together – Stella Maris or was it Ethiraj College? He wasn't too sure.

'Did Prabha go to Stella Maris or Ethiraj?' he asked.

'Christ! Your mind wanders, doesn't it?' Sunil was taken aback.

'My parents wanted Ethiraj, but she managed to go to Stella Maris in the end.' Renu pushed the remains of her chocolate almond torte towards Sunil.

'Prabha would have been devastated if she couldn't wear her precious Levi's to college. Jeans were banned in Ethiraj – in fact, they still are, I think. But this is not about Prabha, is it, Pads?' Renu was looking at him carefully.

No, he thought. This is not about Prabha, God no. This is about the last three months. About being so bloody lonely and out of my depth. Well, socially anyway.

This is about not being a somebody and this is about how pissed off I am having to study every free minute of the night and day. This is about just being impulsive.

'Is she still in touch with Annie . . . Annie Ewart?'

'Annie, Annie, Arse of an Angel. You bastard, I always knew you had the hots for her.' Sunil waggled his fork knowingly. He had scavenged all the big crumbs from Renu's plate.

'Before I answer, tell me this first. Did you guys have a name for me?' Renu sounded dangerous.

'Before I started going out with you or after?'

'I didn't ask you, Sunil, I asked Pads.'

'Look, you girls had names for us as well.' Padhman tried to be diplomatic.

'Out with it!'

Padhman grinned and said nothing.

'Are you going to tell me or what?'

'Or what?'

'Well?'

'This was before that Summer Regatta, before you and Sunil . . . Ask *him*, Renu, why don't you?'

'Darling, I've never called you anything but mine.' Sunil was grovelling.

'*Is* Prabha still in touch with Annie?' repeated Padhman, trying to return to a safer topic, adding, 'I did ask first.'

'Are you going to tell me what name I was called?'

Padhman realised Renu was not going to be fobbed off. 'You won't kill the messenger?'

'Let me hear it first.'

'Randy Renu.'

'That's pathetic, truly and utterly pathetic.'

'True, true. Oh now, don't give me the daggers, Renu!' protested Sunil. 'I meant it was true – truly pathetic.'

'Yes, and I believe everything you say.'

'Oh, come on, that's unfair. You wanted to know and anyway, all that was years ago.'

'That doesn't mean you guys weren't a bunch of pigs.' Renu was all set to sulk.

'Is she or is she not?' Padhman interjected.

Renu and Sunil turned together and looked at him in disbelief.

'Shit you two! That's not what I meant! I mean is Prabha in touch with Annie or not? Look – is anyone going to answer or am I going to grow old and die not knowing?'

Renu forgot her sulk. 'You're going to love this, Pads. Prabha spent Easter with Annie in Cardiff. Annie was meant to go to London actually, to stay with Prabha. They had been planning it for months. Annie's studying choral music or something very "high funda" as Prabha would put it. Wonder what she's planning to do with it though?' Renu paused, picking up all the cake crumbs, getting them to stick to each other by squashing them with the tip of her index finger. She was about to put them in her mouth when she changed her mind and scraped the tiny crumbs on her finger onto the side of the plate.

'All she could do if she went back to India, would be to teach.'

'I think we should be heading back,' Sunil yawned.

'Wait, Sunil, let me tell Pads why Prabha went to Cardiff.' Renu looked at Padhman and started laughing.

'It wasn't funny when it happened, but Prabha's flat-mate, I think she is also doing graphics at St Martin's College of Art, a year above her though . . . anyway, three days before the Easter break she revealed that she was lesbian. Prabha just couldn't handle it and panicked. They had been waxing each other's legs the day before that! Talk about running away from the situation! Prabha ended up practically fleeing to Wales. By the time she got back to London after Easter she had worked the shock out of her system, although it was a bit awkward to start with. Prabha is not prejudiced, you know. Just didn't know how to handle it. Anyway, what's this Annie talk about? Prabha had a great time with her.'

Padhman didn't say much. 'Just that I might give her a ring, if you can get me her number from Prabha.' That's not too bad an explanation, he thought to himself. In fact, it sounded quite straightforward.

Padhman enjoyed the drive back. This was great, just great. He would have needed a car when Annie came to Dublin and he had one now, just in time. He must familiarise himself with the roads. He was quite sure there was a Bank Holiday coming up in October. He was already feeling better. Four weeks to organise her trip. She would surely come. Bloody visas might be a problem.

'Are you coming over to study tonight?' Sunil was looking at him. 'I'll call you when we are finished with dinner. Bring the MCQ papers that Manoharan lent you. Shall we do those tonight? Oh, by the way, Pads, did I tell you that I got the '87 edition of *Bailey and Love?*'

'No studying for me this evening, Sunil. I'm going to have an early night.' Padhman knew Renu was looking at him curiously. He avoided catching her eye in the rear-view mirror and drove back to Dublin on an inexplicable high.

CHAPTER SIX

~

THE LAST TIME Padhman had seen Annie Ewart was eighteen months ago, in Madras, at the New Year's Eve dance at the Gymkhana Club. The first time he had seen her was lost to memory, but the first time she had come to his attention was years back, at school, during the furore about her black bra. Annie's famous black bra. She had been sent home from school for wearing it.

'Mrs Ewart? No, no, nothing is the matter . . . what? No, Annie is not sick. It is her . . . er . . . uniform that is the problem. You see, her class had Games today. Oh yes, yes, she is in her white T-shirt and skirt. Please wait a minute.' The Headmaster was at a loss for words. The office boy was called and sent running to fetch Annie's class teacher. When she arrived, the Headmaster picked up the phone and after a hurried, 'Mrs Ewart? Sorry for the delay. Mrs Banerjee will speak to you . . . No, no, Annie is *not* sick . . . Yes, I know, Mrs Ewart, but Mrs Banerjee will explain.' He handed the phone to the class teacher, mouthing agitatedly, 'Can you explain?'

The Headmaster would never have known about Annie Ewart's black bra had it not been for Annie herself: the boys in her class were quite emphatic about that. If she hadn't burst into tears at the end of the lunch break, the Headmaster, who was supervising the painting of the boundary lines on the basketball court, would never have walked across to find out what the fuss was about and therefore, the boys concluded, Annie would never have been sent home.

Padhman remembered the Headmaster's discomfort well. It was probably one of the few occasions that the Head must have regretted democratising the school. Padhman and four other Senior Prefects sat alongside the half-dozen teachers whom the Headmaster had volunteered onto his pet project, the 'School Forum'. Opposite them sat the Head himself and Sunil Patel, the Head Boy. It had been a difficult meeting for the Headmaster.

'A circular will be sent to parents advising them on appropriate er . . . underwear to be worn. Perhaps the teachers would have a word with their classes. Yes, Mrs Banerjee? The boys? What about them? Oh yes . . . oh no, the girls only.' The Prefects and the Head Boy showed their mettle. Straight faces right through the crisis. As for Annie, she got a pre-planned standing ovation from the boys when she walked into her class the next day. She was about to burst into tears again, but then, on second thoughts, she stuck her now white bra-clad chest out and took a bow. Mrs Banerjee's arrival interrupted the laughter and the second, but this time, spontaneous, ovation.

Two years later, Padhman was sitting next to Sunil in the fourth row of the school's small, but brand new auditorium. They were both a little self-conscious: the transition from school student to alumni was not easy in the first few years and matters were not helped by the fact that Sunil had been addressed as 'sir' by the ushers from Class Four or that the normally autocratic Raghu, the Headmaster's clerk, had accosted Padhman and, clasping his hands in his own, had said, 'Becoming great doctor, heh, heh, just like your grandfather and father. Not forgetting us, OK Padhman, saru?'

'Do you think the bugger was looking for a tip?' Padhman was curious.

'Keeps him in cigarettes,' said Sunil. 'He used to smoke

stinky beedis when we were in school, remember? But now he wants to be like the Marlboro Man. No, don't laugh, Pads, he actually told me that. Do you remember all those *Time* magazines that used to be neatly stacked in the Headmaster's waiting room? Years of arranging and rearranging them and the back covers finally spoke to poor Raghu.'

Sunil stopped talking for the lights had suddenly dimmed in the auditorium and there was a great collective ssshh-ing. The Headmaster appeared at the lectern in the corner and began the introduction to the investiture ceremony of the newly elected student body. The School Forum was now a well-established institution.

'He's greying . . . and balding,' whispered Padhman.

But Sunil's mind was elsewhere. 'What a set of asses got elected as Prefects!' he hissed 'The Headmaster should have exercised his veto. Gita Shekar and Preeti Swami! And can you imagine Bhaskar Rao as Head Boy!'

Padhman gave his friend a sidelong glance. 'Ass yourself. Poor Sunil, standards have fallen since we left, haven't they?'

Sunil sshhed him. 'Shut up, you pisser!'

Bhaskar Rao, the new Head Boy, then introduced Annie Ewart who was going to sing the school anthem. The audience rose to their feet, the ex-pupils joining in and singing with a gusto and pride of the sort they had never exhibited while in school. But the joint effort barely lasted a minute. Annie Ewart's voice was one in a million, the voice of an angel. Hers was a voice that you listened to, not accompanied. When she finished on a gloriously high note, Padhman remembered turning to Sunil and saying, 'Fuck, can she sing!!!'

He remembered it, all right. The lights came on a few seconds later and four heads from the seats in front of them turned around almost simultaneously and Padhman cringed as one of the parents, for row three had been reserved for the PTA, said, 'You couldn't be ex-pupils of this school. Or perhaps you have forgotten what you learnt here. Try that again with "She sings beautifully" or maybe you need re-education.'

Padhman had broken into a sweat and was grateful for the lights that had been dimmed again for the start of the light entertainment being put on by the Junior School.

Annie always managed to get me into a sweat, thought Padhman, as he reached out to switch off the bedside light. He stayed awake, watching the instant pitch darkness turn slowly to shadows. Soon he was able to see around the room clearly. How many years had he been doing this, this staying awake long enough to be able to see in the dark? Grandfather had showed him how to do it. Padhman smiled as he remembered that horrible hot summer and the dreadfully itchy chicken pox. He had slept with Appa and Amma for two weeks and then declared himself too scared to go back to his own room and his own bed. Grandfather had coaxed him with promises to show him a trick that would help him see in the dark. The seven year old's curiosity got the better of him and, with Grandfather sitting by his bedside, he reached out and switched off his reading lamp.

'Keep your eyes wide open, Padhu. Can you see how dark it is?' Grandfather was holding his hand.

'It's black dark.'

Grandfather had laughed and squeezed his hand. 'Yes, black dark. But here's the trick. If you keep your eyes open for just a while longer, the black dark will turn to grey shadows and now Padhu, make sure your eyes are still open . . . look around. You've got it, you've learnt the trick! Look, you can see me!'

Padhman could see more than Grandfather. He could see the trainset and the bookshelves and even make out the book titles. Why, he could see as far as the door where his schoolbag sat, packed and ready for the next morning.

Sixteen years. And I still wait every night for my eyes to get accustomed to the dark before I finally close them. Imagine explaining *that* to Annie.

CHAPTER SEVEN

~

MONDAYS WERE THE shittiest days. This one was
going to be no exception. Padhman was standing at the
kitchen window, eating his breakfast, having been drawn
there by the incessant rain. He looked out at the circular
clothesline, now collapsed and twirling hopelessly in the
wind. An optimistic Irish joke. Padhman turned to the
sink and rinsed bits of marmalade and toast crumbs off his
fingers. As he fetched his bleep and tie he wondered again
about the newsagent. He couldn't remember if the shop
opened this early, but to his satisfaction the shutters were
just going up as he pulled up outside. He held the door
open for the dour-faced Mrs Fogarty who owned the business. She barely managed a smile as she shuffled past him,
her fingers hooked onto the straps that bound two heavy
bundles of plastic-wrapped newspapers.

He followed behind her, shaking out his wrists, vainly
trying to get rid of that awful cold-dampness that came
from holding the grimy aluminium door handle; it
seemed to have been carved out of ice itself. Mrs Fogarty
shuffled along and when she reached the newspaper racks,
just dropped the two bundles on either side of her feet and
then, without actually stopping, and as if no longer
weighed down by the heavy ballast, proceeded at a brisk
pace to organise herself and get the shop ready for the
steady stream of customers that she knew would come, as
she was the only corner shop in a three-mile radius.

Padhman wasted no time either. The fact that there
was only one sort of Good Luck card helped. He wondered

what Renu would make of the black cat with a horseshoe around its neck, frolicking on a bed of four-leafed clovers. Sitting in the Celica in front of Renu and Sunil's house, he inscribed the words *To Renu* and then under the printed *Best of Luck* he added *Hope you pass the test* and he signed it *Pads*.

Renu was touched that he had remembered.

'My parents called to wish me luck. I didn't think anyone else would have remembered, or even known. Will you have some tea?'

He hesitated. 'Won't get parking at the hospital if I stop now.'

Should he remind her about Prabha and getting Annie's number? Padhman suddenly felt a bit guilty. That's what this Good Luck card was really about. He had hoped that somehow, seeing him might have jogged her memory about the previous day's conversation. It's now or never, he decided.

'Oh, I thought Prabha might have rung to wish you luck.' Then turning away from the door he casually added, 'Better go. I bet Sunil's taken the last parking space. See you, Renu, best of luck again.' She just waved and then closed the door.

Padhman felt a bit deflated as he drove off. He was still trying to talk himself out of what he knew was an illogical state of mind, when he turned into the hospital. The staff car parks were full and Padhman swore loudly as he drove around the maze that was the hospital grounds trying to find an empty spot. They didn't know how to treat doctors in this country. Come to India, you sorry bastards. We're backward, but we know our doctors are gods incarnate.

He squeezed into the first vacant place, reversing over a well-faded single yellow line. Locking up, he glanced around, noting with satisfaction that there were at least eight other cars parked over the same yellow line. Strength in numbers, he thought just as he noticed, amongst the offending eight, a bright red Mini. Maura Higgins's Mini. As he got closer he spotted the infamous *Nurses do it patient-ly* sticker across the rear windscreen of the car. The slogan had been the cause of a prudish attempt at disciplinary action, a long story that Niall Fahy had summed up succinctly. 'She basically told the Hospital Board to shag off. And they had to, the interfering bastards.'

Six minutes later Padhman was in Casualty. The post-weekend smell still clung to the place and was barely masked by the efforts of the cleaning ladies. Maura Higgins was at the nurses' station with a couple of the other nurses. She smiled briefly as Padhman walked past to the doctors' room. Micheal Martin, the Registrar, was already there. Calm, unflappable and a great teacher. He looked up from the patient notes he was reading.

'Parking a bitch, wasn't it?'

Padhman nodded. He poured himself a plastic cup of coffee and sat down on the only other chair. 'Desperate, was it, the weekend?' He pointed to the notes that Micheal was scanning.

'Looks like they had the usual shite. Still, there was only the one stabbing and no, it wasn't the MacDonaghs.'

Padhman looked up as Maura Higgins walked in.

'Ready? We've got three pussycats and one angry tiger out there. That's just to start with.' She was smiling as she handed out the files, three to Padhman and one thick one to Micheal.

Padhman walked towards the cubicles. Maura Higgins followed him into the first and drew the curtain close around the bed. She handed him the file. A toddler lay fast asleep in its mother's lap and the mother herself was sitting awkwardly, half-on half-off, the examination trolley. She stopped the clearly audible argument that she had been having with what appeared to be the father of the child. He stood beside her, alternating between glowering at her and tidying the child's non-existent hair. The woman did the explaining. Jamie ('from his own jumper, God love him') had put a button into his mouth this morning. He was a clever lad ('Clever me arse,' muttered the father) because he had told his mother straight away and she, having grabbed him by the chin and jerked his mouth open to confirm the deed, saw the offending button slip further down his throat.

'I bent him over and shook him but nothing fell out.'

Maura put a hand on the mother's shoulder and squeezed it in sympathy, for she seemed on the verge of tears. The child slept through the ensuing examination and when Padhman suggested that the best course of action would be a detailed examination of the child's bowel movements for the next few days, to confirm the inevitable excretion of the button, the father exploded.

'That's a load of shite, that is!'

Padhman cheered up instantly and the rest of the morning flew along.

It was three in the afternoon when he bumped into Sunil and his mind turned to Annie again. Sunil was ecstatic. Renu had called to say that she had passed her driving test.

'We're getting a Chinese takeaway to celebrate. Renu has ordered that you join us for dinner.'

Padhman needed no further persuasion. This Monday was turning out to be not so bad after all.

Padhman stopped off again at Fogarty's Quic-Pic on the way back home. Mrs Fogarty was cleaning the tiny deli counter and the refrigerated display cabinet. She looked at him from the corner of her eye and flicked her head sharply in acknowledgement. Padhman headed for the rear of the shop. He needed bread. All that remained in the three brown wicker baskets were a couple of loaves of brown soda bread. He hated soda bread. It was so close-textured and he always felt that it congealed into unpalatable little lumps that stuck to the roof of his mouth the minute he took a bite. He stood there for a moment wondering what to do. The only other thing that he had planned to buy was orange juice and so he headed for the chill cabinets. He picked up two cartons and then, having spotted in the adjacent freezer cabinet an intriguingly named *Choconut Ice Heaven Supreme (Suitable for Vegetarians)*, added it to his basket and headed for the till. Mrs Fogarty gave him a short, or was it a sly smile, as she double-wrapped the dessert, before putting it into the plastic bag along with the orange juice. Padhman felt he had to explain.

'Dinner with friends. They are celebrating. She passed her driving test.'

Mrs Fogarty slammed the till shut and gave Padhman his change. She tapped the Heaven Supreme sharply with her index finger and said loudly and very slowly, 'Keep . . . in . . . freezer,' and then waited in anticipation, to see if she had been understood. Padhman looked at her. He had had many one-way conversations with Mrs Fogarty. Most of them had been explanations of some sort, all prompted by either her single raised eyebrow or a nearly imperceptible tut-tutting. Sometimes an ever so slight drawing back of her breath or even the way she turned the item in question around in her hand before putting it into the bags, would leave Padhman with the feeling that he just had to say something, that he was in some way obliged to satisfy her curiosity. He had in the process told her that he needed the roll of cotton because he wanted to make wicks for the silver lamp, the Lakshmi Valaku that

52

Amma had given him. He had told Mrs Fogarty he was an only child the time he had bought Amma and Appa's wedding anniversary card, quickly assuring her that he would also be ringing them up and congratulating them on the day. Padhman had, over a period of time, confessed to being a marmalade fanatic, a starcher of his shirt collars, a good Hindu even though he was paying for a pound of beef burgers, and he had even told her of his occasional study-induced headaches the time he had bought the multi-pack of paracetamol. He looked at her now. After all that soul-baring, did she really think he couldn't speak the language?

Exasperated, he tapped the Heaven Supreme with his own index finger and answered in a similar loud and slow fashion, 'O . . . ka . . . y.'

'You . . . are . . . so . . . touch . . . ee, Pads,' said Renu in an exaggerated fashion, accentuating each word. 'Anyway, it's more likely she thought you slow – you know, as in d-i-m.'

Padhman remained serious. 'She probably thinks I dream in Arabic. The patients do. "Tell the doctor how you fell off the bike, luv. Go on, he speaks English, don't you, Doctor? He speaks Arabic only at home. That's right, to his Mam. Now luv, are you going to show him where it hurts?"'

Sunil turned around from the sink where he was washing up. 'Wait till they ask you if you speak "Er-Doo".'

'Christ! We must be the only country in the world that wallows in pride about the fact that we speak English. And only Indians would take offence so easily – you know, at the fact that others are surprised. It's typical of our colonial mentality, absolutely typical! It is what keeps our schoolchildren sweaty in pinafores and ties. Hey, do you want to take some of this fried rice back with you, Pads? And some of the ribs?' Renu was clearing up the remains of the Chinese meal.

'The flied lice and the libs? Hokay, Lenu. Me takee flied lice.' Padhman pushed the chair back, away from the table and relaxed.

'And libs?'

'And libs,' replied Padhman.

'You poor pathetic creature. Still struggling with the cooking, are you?' Renu was looking at him and shaking her head.

'I have to say that your culinary skills have improved dramatically.'

'Now that you have buttered me up, Pads, I am going to call Prabha.' Renu stopped and looked at Sunil and they both together looked at Padhman. He grinned back at them sheepishly. This caused them both to whoop and Sunil, pulling off the yellow washing-up gloves, bowed to Renu with an elaborate flourish and a salaam.

'You were right, oh mighty wife!'

'Look, it isn't anything like that. She's just great fun, Annie,' Padhman blustered but knew his explanations were useless.

'Remember New Year's Eve? We were there too.' Renu widened her eyes dramatically and then walked out of the kitchen into the hall. Padhman felt his heart race as he heard her pick up the phone. Sunil opened out the large windows behind the kitchen sink and a blast of cold air flooded the room.

'Is your father-in law paying your heating bills?'

Sunil looked at Padhman patiently. 'There is nothing worse than the lingering smell of a Chinese meal. Except, of course, the lingering smell of Indian food. I hate coming down the next morning and getting hit by that awful stale stink when you open the kitchen door. It is somehow, you know . . . Have you ever smelt Manoharan's clothes?'

Padhman laughed aloud. 'Bastard, is that all you worry about at work?'

Sunil remained passionate about his theory and carried on about airing out his jackets, cross-ventilating the house, always using the same locker in theatre and then finally, theorised about how one could always spot an on-call room that had been used by an Indian or Pakistani doctor, just by the smell. Padhman could hear Renu laughing in the hall and he tried hard to eavesdrop, hoping to catch something about Annie. He found Sunil giving him a long look.

'You're going to ask her to come over, aren't you?'

Padhman laughed. 'Did you smell that?'

'Well – are you?'

'Why shouldn't I?'

'If you are just fooling around with her, I think you are looking for trouble. If you aren't, you are in deeper shit still.'

'Because she's an Anglo?' Padhman's hackles were up.

'Bastard, I'm not your Amma.'

'Look, Sunil, she may not want to come at all.' Padhman shivered slightly.

'True.'

'I liked her, you know. She was the only girl I went out with who never gave me a copy of *Jonathan Livingstone Seagull*. Or that Khalil Gibran stuff.'

'You were intellectually matched, you mean?'

'Piss off, Sunil! I got more about the meaning of life from the *Charlie Brown Annual* she gave me. And it made me laugh.' Padhman heard Renu say goodbye and then put the phone down.

'She'll call you, if she wants.' Renu walked straight to the windows and shut them firmly. 'It's freezing, Sunil, so don't start off about the smell of stale food, please.' She shivered as she sat down on the chair, crossed her arms and slid her hands into the sleeves of her sweater. Padhman didn't bother hiding his anticipation as he looked across at Renu.

'Prabha said it would be more appropriate to pass on your number to Annie instead. You know Prabha – feminism and the sisterhood, but then, she is as yet unattached. However, she's not heartless. She said she would call Annie straight away.'

CHAPTER EIGHT

~

PADHMAN FRETTED FOR three days. He was OK as
long as he was at work in the hospital, where among other
things, a shattered tibia, a partially collapsed lung, a gan-
grenous toe and a pre-menstrual Maura Higgins kept him
going. He was in the canteen having lunch with Siobhan
Hogan and Maura, when Manoharan spotted them and
headed towards their table.

'Lunching with the Hogan-Higgins Partnership?
Padhman, you have made it.' Manoharan pulled up a chair
next to Siobhan, slid his tray on to the table and sat down.

'Missing us in ENT are you, Harry?' Siobhan laughed
and Maura moved their empty trays off the table to make
room.

'Not from what I could see at Whelan's on Saturday.'
Maura had a knowing look on her face.

Manoharan grinned. 'We carried on to Crofter's and
ended up at The Katz. Why didn't you join us?'

'And cramp your style? I noticed Niall Fahy was in
great form.' Maura was stirring her coffee with utmost
concentration.

'Maura, it was only a leaving do for Pat, you know, the
Ward Sister. She's off to work in Dubai. She'll make more
money there than all of us combined.' The thought
seemed to suddenly deflate his spirits.

Padhman noticed Siobhan trying to catch Manoharan's
eye in vain. Giving up, she turned to Maura and said, 'I
need a fag, let's go out.'

Maura was staring dully into her coffee. She nodded,

and with a brief 'See you,' both the Ward Sisters walked out, weaving their way through the maze of occupied tables and a snaking queue of nurses, doctors and porters that had doubled on itself.

'Pre-menstrual,' said Padhman, looking in the direction of the two nurses. 'She told me.'

Manoharan, who was trying hard to manoeuvre shiny and slippery boiled peas onto his fork, let them all escape back on to the plate. 'Maura told you *what?*'

'Well, she warned me actually. Yesterday.'

'Umm, that's Maura all right. She and Niall . . . the poor bugger. They were . . . Listen, before I forget, next Saturday I am organising a small party for Venkat and his bride at my place. Are you on call?'

Padhman shook his head. 'No, I'm off. I haven't seen Venkat since he got back.'

'They aren't back yet – not until next Wednesday. I'm picking them up from the airport.'

Padhman stood and put on his white coat. 'Niall and Maura – you were saying something about them.'

Manoharan waved the last pea that he had speared on his fork around in circles. He spoke with an air of confidence. 'Temporary breakdown, that's all. Normal service will resume shortly.'

That'll be Annie and me, Padhman reflected as he walked back to Casualty. But of course, he and Annie had never had a breakdown. Or a break-up. Or a normal service. Normal service!

'Can't kiss,' she told him the first time he had tried. They were parked at Elliots Beach. 'I'm singing two solos for the Archbishop at his ordination at St George's Cathedral next Sunday. Might catch a bug – my throat, you know.'

They had sat in Appa's car for a while and she had told him about the two hymns that the Archbishop had

58

personally chosen and how the first one was an old favourite of hers. After his initial awkwardness at having been rebuffed with such a watertight excuse, Padhman had slowly relaxed and then, listening to Annie, got a sense of the great honour that had been bestowed on her. He was thinking about her ambition to sing at St Paul's Cathedral in London, which at that time had seemed so far-fetched to him, when his emergency bleep went off with a piercing shriek.

He quickened his steps and could hear the distant wail of approaching ambulances as he walked into Casualty.

'RTA, three casualties,' said Maura as he walked in. 'Mother and child. And one baby.'

Padhman felt the vomit and the adrenaline rush up together. Is this why I wanted to be a doctor, or is this what makes me wonder why I am a doctor? He didn't think of Annie at all for the rest of that day.

She woke him up with her phone call. She apologised for calling so early on a Saturday and she apologised for not having called him five days ago. She still spoke with that curious lilt that any Indian would identify immediately as the 'Dingo lingo'.

'Have you sung at St Paul's yet?' Padhman wondered what had made him blurt that out.

'No, but I will,' she answered, after a short pause. 'What about you? What are you doing?'

'I'm in bed,' he replied, and then listened to her laugh unsurely. Shit, that's not what I want her to think. He mentally slapped himself on his forehead and then kicking the quilt off, jumped out of bed.

'Actually, I'm at the window now, drawing the curtains open.' It was a fabulous day as it was meant to be. The weather report was the last thing he remembered listening to on his clock radio, before he fell into a hellish sleep, in which the Hogan-Higgins Partnership cradled dead infants to sleep, while he test drove the ambulances.

'What's the weather like in Cardiff?' He tried to picture her with her brownish, poker-straight hair that she sometimes left loose to fall nearly to her hips. When she sat, she would put her hand behind her neck, gather her hair up and with a flick of her wrist, bring it all in front, over her shoulder and then let it go.

'It's miserable. Like always.'

'Catch the first flight to Dublin. It's a grand day. That's what the natives would call it.'

'I was thinking of coming across next weekend.'

Padhman couldn't believe what she had just said. If he had been in the Celica, this would have been an engine-revving moment. But what he actually said was, 'It might be raining next weekend.' This time he did give himself that slap on the forehead. She wants to come to Dublin and I've bloody put a damper on it! I'm losing it, I'm out of touch.

'Well, you come over to Cardiff then.' She was laughing.

Annie, she was uncomplicated. Padhman had nearly forgotten that he had never needed to play any games with her.

'What I meant was, come today, this weekend.'

Annie laughed again. Padhman knew that she had flicked her hair off her face with her fingers. It was an affectation of hers that he used to tease her about, mimicking her when she least expected it.

'Pads, are you free . . . what is the official word for it . . . are you "on call" next weekend?'

'Nope. Come on Friday, Annie, make it a long weekend.'

'I'll check with Renu and Sunil if it is OK. I'll stay with them.'

Twenty-four minutes later Padhman put the phone down. He looked out of the bedroom window, overcome with a light-headed restlessness, then went downstairs and looked out of the kitchen window. A large crow was trying to balance itself on the central pole of the collapsed rotary clothesline. Padhman watched it as he reflected on the long conversation he had had with Annie. She was going home for Christmas and was already excited about it. She had exams in the first week of December. It was hard to study when all she could think of was Christmas Eve. Her brother Vincent was coming home from Brisbane and she hadn't seen him for two years. She reckoned that this year, her parents' famous 'open house' on Christmas Day, at their sprawling Railway General Manager's colonial-style bungalow, would be very special. It would have to be. She had already bought four bottles of port and she was going to buy six Christmas puddings from Marks & Spencer.

'My mother has started the servants spring-cleaning already. Her Vince home from Australia, me back from Wales, vintage port, proper puddings from Marks . . . What a Christmas it is going to be!'

'What about your dad?' Padhman had not known what else to say. Such enthusiasm about Christmas was alien to him. OK, Amma and Appa had always booked him for the Christmas party for members' children at the Gymkhana Club. He could even vaguely remember a big fight with Sunil over the result of the egg and spoon race at one Christmas party. Grandfather had called them both 'young hooligans' and in his capacity as the President of the Club had urged the Member for Entertainment (who, having only recently been elected to the Committee, grinned back benignly at Grandfather, convinced that the President was only 'putting on' a great show of fairness but then, having realised that Grandfather meant what he

61

said, went on to use the story, for years to come, to illustrate the true meaning of impartiality) to disqualify both for unsporting behaviour. Padhman knew a few Christmas carols, having learnt them as a matter of routine in school, and Grandfather's Miss Angela at the clinic had always sent Christmas cake to the house during the season. All in all, Christmas was no big deal for Padhman.

Asking Annie about her dad had only made her laugh.

'Daddy would prefer to spend Christmas in the GM's personal saloon carriage, chugging down the track being pulled by "a glorious piece of our heritage" as he would put it. You know, Pads, he wept when the *Jhansi Ki Rani* was decommissioned and sold to be the prime exhibit in a steam train museum in Yorkshire.'

She was quiet for a few seconds as if thinking about her dad. Then she sighed. 'Yet he was one of the main movers behind the drive for electrification of the railways. Anyway, how are your parents?'

Padhman told her about Appa and Amma sending him money for a car.

'You mean you are still a spoilt brat?'

Padhman knew she was teasing. Or was it half-teasing? He wasn't going to take offence today. Not today. He filled her in with details about the Celica.

'I can't wait. It sounds fabulous, like a Batmobile.' She burst into a fit of the giggles.

Padhman couldn't help grinning. Renu had obviously been talking to Prabha.

'What else did the wicked sisters tell you?'

'Oh, this and that. You're a hopeless cook, apparently. But it'll be great seeing you again, Pads.'

The crow had given up on the clothesline and had flown off to sit in comfort on the felt and pitch roof of the tiny wooden shed at the bottom of the back garden. Padhman wondered for one impatient moment what it actually wanted to do. It seemed fidgety and kept looking at the clothesline, cocking its head this way and that, as if trying to make up its mind as to which angle to approach the pole from. Shit, what am I up to myself, Padhman wondered. It was one thing to be sitting in Enniskerry with Sunil and Renu feeling like a lonely piggy in the middle, and it was quite another thing to try to rekindle something with Annie. It would be great to see her again, but what was it going to amount to? Nothing, he thought to himself. And it doesn't have to amount to anything. He pictured himself saying that to a disbelieving, disapproving Renu.

'Anyway, Renu,' he said silently, 'I never actually invited her.'

Annie had of her own accord said she was planning to come. Thank God she was going to stay with Renu and Sunil. That itself gave Annie's weekend visit a respectability and legitimacy that would never have been possible if she had stayed with him. Not that it would fool Amma. But Amma didn't have to know. Of course, the reality was that Amma would find out. Find out what, Padhman? He was exasperated with himself. There is this girl I used to know and she, like me, lives abroad, out of India. We've got in touch and she is coming over and staying with common friends and that's that. There is nothing *to* find out, Amma. Padhman noticed the crow had landed on the clothesline pole again and was balanced on one leg, shifting and hopping delicately in an effort to stay upright. The bird suddenly seemed to realise that Padhman was watching and it tensed up and kept very still. A few seconds later it cocked its tail and shat. Padhman banged his fists on the window.

'Shit!' he yelled at the crow. 'Shit and double shit!'

The crow flew off with not a backward glance. Padhman watched the yellow, green and white dropping drip and slip, slowly coating the slack plastic lines that lay collapsed around the pole. It's going to dry and harden up if I don't clean it, he thought. He filled the largest pan that he had with hot water and opened the kitchen door. The grass was wet and his toes curled up and griped his rubber flip-flops in an unconscious effort to keep them dry, away from the icy cold dew.

Padhman cursed as he walked towards the clothesline. Standing on his tiptoes, he stretched across, about an arm's length, and poured the water slowly over the top of the pole. He watched it coaxing the crow shit along and realised very quickly that he had only succeeded in making matters worse. The entire clothesline was now speckled with stubborn bits of whitey-greeny-yellow. The pan in his hand still had a little bit of water in it and Padhman flung the last drops disgustedly on to the clothesline. As he turned to walk back to the kitchen, he got the distinct feeling that he was being watched and on looking up in an almost furtive fashion, he saw Mrs Ryan from next door at her bedroom window. She smiled but looked embarrassed and was about to drop the net curtain back, when she was pushed aside by her twins, who looked down at him in undisguised amusement. He realised how strange, and possibly exotic, his watering the clothesline must have seemed.

'Crow shit,' he yelled out in explanation. Mrs Ryan hesitated before nodding politely and moving away from the window, and a few seconds later the net curtain fell back into place.

Padhman shut the kitchen door and wiped his feet on the small offcut of carpet that clashed so horribly with the cheap and weary linoleum. He hated what had just happened. He hated being the fool foreigner. Like the idiot Indian that Peter Sellers had portrayed in that movie *The Party*. 'Eeejit Indian' in this case. The Ryans would be having a good laugh. Bugger them and what they thought, he decided, placing the pan upside down on the draining board of the sink. He was surprised when the doorbell rang. It rang twice, the second time as he walked down the hall to the front door.

'Mam wants to know if you'd like to borrow the hose, to wash down the clothesline.' It was the Ryan twins. 'She says she'll throw it over the fence if you do.'

They spoke nearly in unison, one almost echoing the other. Neither of them looked at Padhman directly, but peered curiously down the hall.

'What are your names?' asked Padhman.

'Ronan Ryan.'

'Roisin Ryan.'

'Ronan and Roisin, very twinny names.'

'We're twins.'

'Couldn't you tell?'

Padhman looked at them, and laughed. 'Who's who?' he teased.

They both turned their attention from the hall and looked at him in serious amazement.

'Do you not have any Ronans and Roisins where you come from?' said the girl.

'All Roisins are girls and all Ronans are boys.' Ronan spoke firmly, with conviction.

'OK, Ronan and Roisin,' said Padhman, pointedly looking first at one and then at the other, 'tell your mother that I will be glad to borrow the hose.'

Happy that they had been identified correctly, they both turned and hopped on to the low wall that separated the two front gardens and then jumped over.

Padhman went upstairs. From the bedroom he could see into the Ryans' garden, much as they could see into his. He stood there staring disinterestedly at the row of back gardens. He had a clear view of at least two and a half gardens on each side of his own. No chance of making love to Annie in the back garden then, he thought, and was startled by the direction of his own subconscious. He walked back to the bedroom and got under his new 13-tog duvet where he thought about making love to Annie. About the great unlikelihood of that happening. As Amma would have told him, good girls waited till they were married. Sunil had once, in a brave attempt to be funny, baited Amma.

'Waited till they were married . . . for what?'

She had given him a deeply withering look and he had spent the rest of that Sunday afternoon trying to mollify her, eating three helpings of the chicken biryani and then five of her legendary rasmalais. Of course, Amma also had her own ideas about how decent young men should behave. They waited as well. Oh, she was a great believer in equality, Padhman had to hand that to her. Her moral standards were applied across the board. But the problem was that Amma could never understand the difference between decent and normal. Decent and normal were not always the same thing. Especially when you were a young man. That's how Padhman justified all those half frustrating evenings at Elliots Beach. Or the bruised lips and stiff necks after two hours or so in the air-conditioned anonymity of the Emerald Cinema. Or the ninety-step climb up to the tiny cupola at the very top of the dome of the Gymkhana Club, where once you had got your breath back . . . Well, the last time he was up there he nearly never did get his breath back.

It was New Year's Eve and he and Annie had collapsed onto the dusty floor of the cupola. Annie was laughing, gasping exaggeratedly. They both peered through the tiny leaf- and flower-shaped holes in the filigreed cement wall, down at the manicured lawns far below, and at the two hundred tables at which Madras's finest sat, celebrating the New Year. The mouths of the clay ovens of the open-air tandoori kitchens, for which the Club's Dance Nights were famous, glowed an eerie, hypnotic orange and the turbaned and white canvas-shoed bearers scurried around, between table and kitchen, as if driven by clockwork. Padhman could see the table at which his parents sat, along with Raja and Nimmi Patel and a few other friends.

Annie pointed to the dance floor. 'Sunil and Renu are fed up with dancing. Isn't that them leaving the floor?'

Padhman could see them, tiny figures, weaving their way past the tables. 'The band must have stopped playing the smoochie songs. Sunil and Renu only do the slow numbers.' In fact, the band had stopped playing completely and they could hear the compère for the evening announce the start of the raffle draw.

Annie had turned around and, still on the floor, she sat with her back against the wall. Padhman watched Sunil and Renu disappear out of sight under the awnings and into the Club. He turned around and sat next to Annie. The tiny bare circular floor was littered with dried leaves that the wind had blown up from the huge neem trees that provided so much of the cool shade on the Club's lawns. There was no light in the cupola, but it wasn't pitch dark. The reflected light from the festive illuminations threw distorted shadows of the intricate filigree pattern around the curved wall. Across from them a few feet away lay the remains of a bird's nest.

Annie drew her knees up to her chin. 'It will be freezing when I arrive in Cardiff.' She doodled in the dust with her finger. 'We are going to Bangalore the day after tomorrow, my mum and me, to buy some warm clothes. Sweaters and gloves and that sort of stuff. I'll need a jacket too, but I suppose I could get that in Cardiff.' She stopped doodling and stared at the floor. 'Pads! The place is crawling with ants.'

Padhman looked down to see an army of tiny black ants, marching in one column towards the bird's nest, and another column returning from the nest, stopping for seconds'-long brief encounters with their comrades heading in the opposite direction. Annie's doodles had created little hills in the dust, over which the ants scurried upwards, undeterred.

'Don't get up. They won't bother you unless you are in their flight path.'

But Annie had already scrambled up and was dusting herself down. Her hair fell over her shoulders and for an instant Padhman couldn't see her face, nearly veiled as it was by the fine strands of her hair.

'Sit on my knees,' he said, drawing up his legs. She flicked her hair off her face and gave him a long look and then sat gingerly on his knees, uncomfortable and trying not to put all her weight on Padhman.

'Now what? You can't kiss me from my perch here.' She was smiling, teasing and when he reached out to put his hands on her waist and pull her down she was expecting it. She sat on his stomach, sort of sidesaddle, leaning back against his still drawn-up legs. They had kissed and Annie leaned back against his legs again. Padhman had reached out and stroked her breasts.

'You are nice, Annie Ewart.'

'I know.'

Coming from anyone else that would surely have been a smart, jokey answer. Coming from Annie it was just a statement of fact. That's just how she was. She had looked down at his hands that were tracing circles around her nipples.

'Do you like that?'

She nodded in reply and then, placing her hands over

his and still keeping them against her breasts, said in a voice that seemed to be breaking, 'You'll have to stop, Pads. I'm very, very . . . very, *very* ticklish.' She burst into a fit of infectious laughter. Padhman had wished then that she wasn't leaving Madras. He said it to her.

'And I can't wait – not to leave Madras, I mean – but I can't wait to get to Wales.' She was still sitting on him, leaning against his legs. She was quite different from any of the other girls he had ever persuaded to come up to the cupola with him. In fact, she had needed no persuasion. She hadn't worried if anyone had seen them go up and she hadn't pushed Padhman away mid-kiss to say that they had been there long enough. They had kissed and he had touched her and all of it had been without any hungama . . . so natural and effortless.

Recalling all this, Padhman found he was hot under the duvet and he flung it back. He sat up in bed for a few minutes, with his hands crossed behind his head, leaning against the headboard. Directly across from him, on a narrow table against the foot of the bed, lay Bailey and Love's *Textbook of Surgery* on top of a pile of other medical textbooks. Padhman looked away to the window, contemplating the choices he had. It was tempting to stay in bed all day long, aimlessly thinking about Annie, but he really should be studying. Perhaps he could stroll over to Sunil's and go through a couple of anatomy chapters. Renu tended to indulge them with coffee and toasted sandwiches when they studied together. He could hose down the clothesline to start with and then decide what to do with himself. It was nearly time for an early lunch. Perhaps he could walk to Fogarty's and get himself a frozen pizza . . .

He realised that he had dozed off in mid-deliberation only when the phone rang and he woke, slightly disorientated, wondering fuzzily if it was still today. By the time

69

he had put the phone down, having agreed to meet up with Manoharan at Whelan's, Padhman was wide awake and mentally trading off the evening ahead with what he hoped would be a productive afternoon of concentrated studying. He'd start right after lunch. And after he had hosed down the clothesline.

Once I start studying, I could keep going till six or even until seven, he thought determinedly, guiltily.

CHAPTER NINE

~

WHELAN'S WAS MUCH larger than he expected it to be. The pub occupied a very narrow, V-shaped corner site formed by two major roads that merged to become one of the principle routes into the city centre about a mile away. It was a cavernous establishment, obviously running a good bit down the length of both the streets that it fronted. He walked in rather self-consciously and stood as casually as he could at the bar. When the Guinness had been placed in front of him, he raised it to his lips and from that relatively camouflaged position behind the pint glass, he turned to look around. The two men at the end of the bar looked up, held their glasses and raised their chins. Padhman smiled and nodded, a single sharp nod. This put him at ease straight away, his own ability to follow and reply in the unspoken Irish and the fact that the communication was being directed at him in the first place.

He put the glass down and looked around again, this time with purpose. Manoharan was nowhere to be seen. There was obviously more to the pub than the dozen or so tables that the eye could see, for Padhman watched the bar staff and customers emerge and disappear, around the corner, at the end of the very long bar counter. From somewhere around that corner came the sound of musical instruments being tuned, interspersed with occasional sound checks by a voice that needed its throat cleared. Padhman, glass in hand, followed the sound through two crowded lounges, one leading into the other, and finally into a fairly large room with a wooden dance floor and a small raised platform, on which the members of a band seemed in earnest preparation. Padhman spotted the hospital crowd straight away. There was a great deal of hand waving and a shout or two of, 'Here, Paddy!' as he walked towards the table. Fortified by the rowdy reception, Padhman smiled genially at the few heads that turned to see who the recipient of that communal welcome was.

'Hey, bastard, we thought you weren't coming!'

Manoharan was desperately distinct in a Manila-print silk shirt, the kind that well-meaning foreigners wore when they headed East. Padhman tried to shrug off the twinge of embarrassment he felt on behalf of India. A stool was requisitioned from a neighbouring table and he found himself seated beside Maura Higgins who, very dressed up in uncustomary black, was snuggled proprietarily against Niall Fahy. In fact, almost everyone looked totally out of character. Out of their uniform, the staff and student nurses sitting opposite him had lost the demure air that it conferred upon them. The two Casualty interns were obviously well on their way to being totally pissed and the Appointment Secretary's legendary chest looked even larger without her name badge pinned on it. A corona of smoke hung around the four tables that had been pushed together. As the band struck up, this time for real, Padhman wondered what sort of evening this was going to turn out to be.

'This could be your lucky night.' Manoharan had leant across conspiratorially.

Padhman then lost sight of him for a moment, as a sudden exodus of nearly all the women at the table forced both him and Manoharan to sit back in order to give way. Padhman watched curiously as they piled all their handbags on to the floor and then, gathered in a loose circle around the bags, started dancing.

'She's a real hot chick, the one in the leather trousers. She asked me twice if you were coming here tonight.'

Padhman looked first at Manoharan, who had sidled up to sit next to him, and then over his shoulder at Niall, who smiled back knowingly and nudged Maura.

'Yes, she definitely fancies you, Paddy,' Maura assured him.

'I'll let her dance with her handbag for the moment,' said Padhman nonchalantly. He stared into his Guinness. What does she see in me, he wondered. What do any of them see in us, foreign doctors with our cruelly mimicable accents and horrible ties? Would I still be as exotic if I said that I had a jealously guarded, unrivalled collection of *Beanos* (true), that I had a mother who made a great roast chicken, (admittedly with a green chilli and coriander stuffing) or if I confessed to having spent the best part of my teenage years in sixteen-inch flares, stabbing the air in a maniacal fashion? Padhman cringed at that sudden memory. His Travolta-esque efforts on the dance floor had been legendary.

Manoharan had joined the girls and the circle expanded to let him gyrate his way in and he didn't stop till he was in the centre. Manoharan was like a bird of paradise, in colour and texture. His well-oiled hair had been coiffed back and the shiny strands which fell over his forehead shook excitedly in time with the music. His face, indented as it was with pockmarks, shone now and then as the little beads of perspiration on his nose caught the light. His shirt shimmied along, releasing waves of exotic colours with every twist of his hips.

Padhman looked back into his glass. It was comforting, the pint of Guinness. Its hypnotic, swirling blackness lent itself to contemplation. One needed to pretend contemplation when the couple sitting opposite you were making soft sucking noises as they kissed. Niall and Maura were obviously making up for lost time. Padhman turned to look at the dance floor again. Manoharan was dancing only from the hips, his knees bending and flexing to the beat. He stood in one spot grinning animatedly, wiping his face with an enormous white handkerchief that he had taken out of his trouser pocket with a flourish. He showed the wet results to the women dancing around him and then balled up the handkerchief and stuffed it down the front pocket of his trousers. I bet he calls it 'kerchiff' thought Padhman uncharitably. The sight of Manoharan dancing with what looked like a codpiece gone askew irritated him no end.

'Same again, Padhman?' Niall had got up.

'I'll get this one,' Padhman said quickly. 'Maura?'

'Ballygowan, please.'

Padhman walked through the two lounges and then back into the bar as quickly as he could. He knew that he was whirlpooling into an increasingly illogical mood. It would have helped if he could talk to himself aloud. He looked at himself in the bevelled-edged mirror that backed the busy shelf behind the bar. His face, framed by a bottle of Jameson and a fake antique pickling jar, looked slightly elongated and yellow. He cocked his head to the right. His cheeks now appeared gripped between the pickling jar and the slightly dusty head of a well-stuffed pheasant. Still stretched and faded, he looked like an exhibit from The Great Dr Sorkar's Travelling Museum of Oriental Magic and Mystery. Am I a freak, he wondered.

Manoharan embarrasses me, he admitted. OK, I can handle that. My problem is that I am sort of secretly ashamed of my embarrassment. Sort of secretly? God, I'm a complicated bastard! He looked again at himself, gloomily. I should be at home studying. I really, really should be studying. He paid for the drinks that had been placed on a little round tray and then slipping off the barstool, he turned with the tray in his hand and headed back, but very unenthusiastically.

'Hey! Hang on, I'll grab a drink and follow you. They're in the back room, are they?'

I'm the only one followable at the moment, reasoned Padhman and curious as hell, he turned around. The girl he saw wasn't familiar. He waited while she ordered her drink.

'I hate walking all the way through to the back on my own,' she told him. 'Everyone always thinks you are pretending that you haven't been stood up. It's a small phobia I have.' She laughed. 'Not being stood up, just the walking past the smug, seated punters. You know, they're already with their friends – na-na-nan-nana – and you have yet to find yours. Oh, don't mind me. I'm like that – a bit odd.'

Can't imagine *you* being stood up, Padhman thought as she threw a polite marching order to him, over her shoulder.

'Here's my drink, I'll follow you now.'

With his tray in his hand, he walked to the end of the bar, where he made a show of slowing down and looking back. She was right behind him and she nodded, smiling, mouthing, 'Still here.' She was obviously from the hospital, Padhman was sure of that. He was overcome with an urge to look at her face and that lovely mouth once again. I'll lose her to the handbag gang once she gets to our table, he thought, and spurred on by that, he took the chance provided by an approaching glass-laden barmaid to step aside, tucking himself exaggeratedly against the wooden archway that separated one lounge from the next.

'Busy pub, isn't it?' he said, taking in as much of her as he could. The jet-black hair, the green eyes, the denim shirt with tiny pearl buttons, her very slightly crooked teeth and that hypnotising mouth. It was her lips

75

actually. When she talked and smiled they took up her whole face.

'Sure, you come out on a Saturday night and it's like this everywhere. It's quieter across the road at Slattery's though. No live music and it's much smaller too.'

The barmaid was well past them.

'Shall we go?' She looked amused.

'Not till I've introduced myself. I'm Padhman. Hi! I'm in A&E. The Senior House Officer.'

She held out her hand. 'Pada-man . . . Pad-man . . . mm, was that right? I mean, did I say it correctly? It's easy enough. Pad. Man. Not as tough as Harry's. Still I can say that, too. Man-o-har-ran.'

Padhman didn't know why, but he wanted her to be able to pronounce his name correctly. 'Try Padh-man. Padh . . . dhh, not Pad.'

He watched fascinated, as her mouth and lips worked around the sounds.

'How's this? Padhh-man. I'll practise, I promise. Oh, and I'm Aoife. Aoife Gorman. I've seen you with Niall Fahy in the canteen a couple of times. I'm the surgical intern.'

'Aoife. OK, after you, Aoife. They are right at the very end. Most of them are on the floor already.'

'Dancing or plastered?'

'Both varieties.' Padhman grinned happily as she walked past. He followed her, his senses lightened by an inexplicable sense of anticipation. She sat diagonally across from Padhman, squeezing neatly into the space made by Niall and Maura, when they had enthusiastically pushed up for her. Padhman looked at his watch casually. It was nearly nine o'clock. I won't look at her again till nine-fifteen, he decided.

Manoharan left the floor at that moment and returned

76

to the table, flopping down beside Padhman. The big white handkerchief came out again and he vigorously wiped his face and neck, all the while filling Padhman in on the details of the party he had planned for Venkat and his bride, the following Saturday. Padhman listened to him distractedly, trying hard not to use peripheral vision to see why Aoife had leant across Niall and why, with an elbow and a hand resting on Niall's knees, she was deep in conversation with Maura.

'Can you bring plates and cutlery? And glasses, if you can. Do you have six of everything, because if you do, the only other person I will have to ask will be Sunil. Niall has already said he'll bring a dozen . . . at least.' After a pause, as if letting Padhman mull over the mystery of Niall's generosity, Manoharan added in explanation, 'He doesn't rent.'

Padhman snapped out of his inattention when Manoharan prattled on, detailing the menu.

'Puris and channa masala. Tiwari's wife is making that. Joe and Phil – Philomena – she always makes prawn pulao. They are Goans. Renu has said she will bring tandoori chicken and Krishnan's wife said kebabs would not be a problem as long as Noorjehan Stores sells minced lamb this week. Gaja is in Glasgow for the Part One. He'll bring rasmalai and laddoos from Bombay Halwa House on Friday. Unless he fails the exam, in which case he won't turn up at all.'

'Will the puris be hot?' Padhman was salivating. 'Is she going to fry them at your place? Nothing worse than cold puris.'

Manoharan was sympathetic but firm. He had no extractor fan in his kitchen-cum-dining room, and moreover that velai-sahib Sunil would kick up a stink about the smell lingering on everyone's clothes. 'The Tiwaris eat puris or parathas every night. Sometimes aloo parathas.

Bastard, if you want to eat hot puris, the trick is to land up at their house at dinnertime.'

Padhman was gulping back the rush of fresh saliva that filled his mouth, when there was a sudden exodus of people to and from the dance floor. Most of the handbag gang had returned to the tables. Opposite him, Aoife had got up to let Niall and Maura through. Smiling at Padhman, she then sat down again. He sneaked a look at Manoharan's watch. Twelve minutes past nine. Three minutes to the deadline but then she had made him break it.

The band struck up again, this time for 'all of you in love and here tonight' and then getting a bit carried away, the crooner, a close-shaven peroxide blonde, went on, 'And for lovers near and far, far and near, anywhere and everywhere, this is for youooou.' For a while, almost everyone turned to watch the couples on the floor, some desperately clinging to each other, a few keeping a nervous distance and the confident ones just casually wrapped round each other.

Padhman looked around the tables at the watching faces. He could sense the longing on some and the brief, fleeting envy before they turned back to their neighbours, their smokes and their pints. He could feel them looking up again from their dry-roasted peanuts, as he asked and then led Aoife onto the floor. He could nearly lipread Maura.

'Don't look now, Niall, but guess who has asked who to dance?'

Niall whipped around on cue and Padhman gave him a small wave. Maura whipped him back around promptly and Aoife giggled as Padhman explained the events that had gone on behind her back. She was relaxed in his arms as they danced and talked.

'Don't you miss home? Are you from the same place as Harry? You must hate the weather.'

'Harry's from Coimbatore. Madras is in the same state . . . like you have counties. But we're a day's journey away by train from Coimbatore. What about you? Do you miss home and do you hate the weather?' Padhman, who was only teasing, watched her face become thoughtful.

'No one has ever asked me that before. Oh, I pop in to see my parents nearly every day and I actually love the weather. I know, I know, I'm odd, but then I've told you that before. There, I've confessed. Do you ride?'

'Horses?'

She nodded.

'No. Why?'

'Irish weather is best viewed from horseback. Riding on a crisp, cold morning . . . it kind of refreshes you, cleans you up inside out.'

'You mean like colonic irrigation?'

She slapped him playfully on the shoulder. 'Why don't you come riding with me? You'll see what I mean.'

'Irish weather is best viewed through a window, preferably one beside a roaring fire. What if it rains? Have you ever thought about the poor horse?'

Padhman could see Aoife rising to the bait. Her eyes narrowed very slightly as she tried to pretend that she was amused and he felt a sudden charge of pleasure go through him. He liked what was happening. He was his old self again. He hadn't lost his touch. It had been weeks, no months since he had been 'on the pull'. Maura had explained that expression to him once.

'On the pull? Oh, you know, it means when you are seriously flirting. Aahh, go on, Paddy, tell us who it is. Can't hide anything from your Aunty Maura, you know.' She had wagged the Steri-Strips that she was holding under his nose. And right now he couldn't hide anything because Maura was looking on intrigued, over Niall's shoulder, as Aoife stopped dancing and with her hands on her hips looked at Padhman.

'You on call tomorrow?'

He grinned and shook his head.

She put her arms back around his waist, this time dancing closer, much closer and looked at him mischievously. 'Padhh . . . man, you are coming riding with me tomorrow.'

'Is it Doctor's orders? I'll be the model patient.' Padhman could feel her breath against his neck. She liked him, he could tell. It struck him that she hadn't stopped to reflect on the colour of his skin before sending out those definite vibes. Shit! There I go again, he reproached himself. So bloody conscious of being a foreigner. Anyway, why shouldn't she like me? I am the original tall, dark and handsome stranger. My breath smells of Guinness, but then so does hers. Do I always have to analyse things? Why can't I just . . . just ask her where she goes riding.

'Shall we move to Slattery's?' This Aoife Gorman had got under his skin very quickly. 'To discuss this riding thing – you know, the arrangements,' he added in explanation.

She obviously didn't believe him; she wasn't meant to anyhow. 'Yes. This place is too noisy, can't hear yourself for the band or see each other for the smoke.' They laughed conspiratorially. I could have her done for aiding and abetting, thought Padhman. That's a good sign. A very, very good sign.

Slattery's was as Aoife had described it, much quieter, much smaller but nearly as crowded as Whelan's. Walking in, Padhman was convinced that every eye in the place was aggressive, disapproving of the fact that he was with Aoife. He had seen that sort of thing on American documentaries. Black men who snarled into television cameras about their sisters going out with white men. No, no, that wasn't quite the right analogy. He was thinking of the white men who hated their own, the slags who went for the blacks. The camera would then cut to white women slyly hinting about greater sexual satisfaction, while in another take, the black sisterhood nodded in agreement as one of them recounted the pleasures of being treated like a real lady by a white guy. Padhman was nearly convinced the camera was panning to him next, and he flushed under his collar. He felt foolish when, seated a few minutes later, he looked around and found no one was even looking at him. Except Aoife.

'Nice, friendly place, don't you think?'

Padhman, only just returning from where he had momentarily lapsed to, nodded and steadied himself against his pint glass. I shall pick up where I left off with her, he thought determinedly.

CHAPTER TEN

~

MY LIFE EITHER stands still or leaps forward in geometric progression, Padhman reflected. He was looking at himself in the mirror, while he tried to squeeze out the last thin sliver of toothpaste onto his brush. It was the second of the two tubes of Close-Up that Amma had packed for him and he found himself humming the advertising jingle. Why did I start that? he thought, mildly irritated. Now I'll never get it out of my head for the rest of the day. He brushed his teeth, bared the clean results in the mirror and then slicked his tongue over them the way they did in toothpaste ads. He leant over the sink, closer to the mirror and wagged his mouth this way and that. If only Aoife could see him now. He spoke her name out loud as he showered.

'Aoife. Aoife. Aoife.'

He was to meet her at her place.

'Not later than ten and Padhman, don't come in your Sunday best.' Was she laughing at him when she had said that? He tried to picture her as they had said goodnight. It had been awkward. He sensed that for her too, reality had struck. Strangers a few hours ago, they had talked and – lulled by their mutual attraction – had told each other far more about themselves than they normally would have done. Or should have done, for that matter. I don't really care, reasoned Padhman, looking appreciatively at his reflection, as he tucked his best corduroy shirt into nearly new jeans. At least one person outside India, at least one person in Ireland, knows a little bit about who I really am. He struck a pose in front of the mirror and held out his hand in mock greeting.

'I am the man from Madras. Yes, as in curry powder. I'm hot and yes, ladies, the answer to your questions is . . . I *can* set your tongues on fire!'

He loitered around in front of the mirror for a few more minutes recognising in the reflection, to his satisfaction, a part of himself that had taken a back seat for the last few months.

When Aoife opened her door to him, she groaned dramatically. 'Padhman, I said old clothes! These will get ruined.'

He followed her through the rather dark hallway of her basement apartment into a bright, warm kitchen.

'I didn't want to look like your Middle Eastern stable-hand. And anyway, you weren't seriously planning to get me up onto a horse, were you?'

'I was, and you *will* look like a stable-hand because you'll have to borrow Colm's gear. He's bound to have something lying around. Colm?' She broke into a wide grin and slapped the table as she answered. 'He's the stable-hand.'

'I only wanted to make a good impression on your grandmother . . . your Nana.' This Nana was important, of that he was sure. Padhman had gleaned that from the night's conversation. He knew that he, too, would have liked Aoife to make a good impression on Grandfather. Now, there was a bond he never would have thought he would have in common with any foreigner. Foreigners put their old people into homes. That was the general opinion in India. It was one of Amma's pet subjects.

'Let's hope Nana makes a good impression on *you*, Padhman.'

She had turned and, with her back to him, she stood watering a collection of plants placed in and around an

83

enormous Belfast sink. The last time he had seen a sink that size, it was being loaded onto the kabadi-wallah's motorised cycle rickshaw, along with two rusty Primus stoves, a heavy cast-iron table-top meat mincer, assorted lidless and chipped pickling jars, dented pots and pans and a broken down Westinghouse floor polisher. The day the replacement, a gleaming double-drainer and double-bowl stainless steel sink arrived, Amma had been ecstatic.

'Do you want tea or coffee? Yes, we do have enough time.' Aoife looked up at the large clock on the wall. 'I won't be a minute more with these plants. There are five big ones that have to be watered in situ. Put the kettle on if you want.' Padhman could hear her opening and closing doors and then a shout of, 'Bloody hell! Get me a teacloth will you, Padhman!'

There were two checked cloths with the word *Teacloth* helpfully emblazoned across their edges, hanging neatly on hooks over the sink, and grabbing them, Padhman headed in the direction of her voice. The door off the kitchen took him into the sitting room. He stood there for a few seconds looking around curiously. The polished wooden floors were well worn and an enormous sofa was the only furniture, sitting alone in front of a huge cast-iron fireplace. He could hear Aoife muttering and cursing and he crossed the room to the door on the far side, only to find himself in another darkish corridor with two wedges of light falling on it from two doors that were slightly ajar. The first, the door closest to him, was the bathroom. He could see the claw feet of a large bathtub. The door on the left was shut and the door on the right, the second one that was open, was definitely the scene of the commotion. A large plant, a trailing type, had tipped out of its pot and it was very clear, in a messy sort of way, that the disaster had struck after it had been watered.

Aoife looked irritated at her own clumsiness and taking the tea towels from Padhman, proceeded with a dramatic sigh to clean up.

'I'll stay out of your way.' Padhman stepped over the mess and headed for the book-lined shelves on the other side of the room. This must be her study, he thought. 'You can tell a person by the books they read,' he said aloud, looking at the shelves that stretched the entire length of the wall.

'Look at the desk, Padhman. You'll find on it a volume on surgical emergencies and surgical management, a concise edition on critical care, a textbook of medicine and a manual of intensive care. What does that make me? Am I a masochist, am I an insomniac or am I just a fool who became a doctor?'

Padhman looked at her curiously. If she was already unhappy barely six months into her internship she was in deep shit. But he wasn't planning to lecture her on the miseries that lay ahead, not today – and anyway, he did not need reminding himself. He turned back to the shelves. It was clear she loved books. He scanned the shelves, noting titles and authors at random. *The Flora and Fauna of Ireland.* Robert Ludlum. Frank O'Connor. Ruskin Bond. *The World of Horses.* Padhman spotted Shaw, Arthur C. Clarke, John Banville, Ayn Rand, James Michener, *Fifty Ways To Cook A Potato*, Dickens, *Gone with the Wind*, a hundred or more *National Geographic*s and Somerset Maugham. He carried on. It was almost like looking through a secret window he was not meant to. *A Shopper's Paris. The Children of Lir and Other Irish Legends. Walking in the Beara Peninsula.* Salman Rushdie. A French–English, English–French Dictionary.

Despite his obvious interest, Aoife didn't mention her books until half an hour later, when they were nearly at her Nana's.

'Well, go on then. What did my books tell you about me?'

'Hmm. That you're a – how shall I put this – a mixed bag?'

'As opposed to a mixed-up old bag?'

He grinned back at her and was about to tell her what he really thought she was, when she pointed ahead. 'That's the turn-off. The gate is set well back off the road and you could easily go past it, Padhman. Slow down.'

He obeyed and as they turned into the gates he let out a low whistle.

'Your horse lives here?'

'No, my Nana does and the horse lives . . .' She puckered up her lips and punched him in the shoulder. 'The horse lives in the stables, the dogs in the kennels and oh, we have room for exotic creatures too. Medical specimens from the Sub-Continent . . .' She trailed off laughing and blew him a kiss, but Padhman didn't know that. He was trying to catch glimpses of the house in the distance. The Celica crunched down the narrow beech-lined lane. It was windy in parts, with what looked like deep ditches on either side. He had seen that spectacular autumnal colour on enormous beeches before. He unconsciously slowed down the car as he concentrated on tracking down the sense of déjà vu.

The Viceroy's Bar – that was it! The Viceroy's Bar at the Gymkhana Club in Madras. A huge canvas hung behind the wooden bar there. It had to be huge to accommodate the enormous beeches painted in meticulous detail and – yes, it was all coming back to him – in spectacular autumnal colour. The painting was signed with the barely legible initials *HC* and the narrow brass plaque embedded into the frame said very simply *'November' by Henry Chadwick Esq.* Under the painting, fixed to the solemn wooden panelling of the actual bar itself, was another brass plaque with the words *Donated by Mrs Caroline Chadwick in loving memory of her late husband, Henry Chadwick Esq. August 1901*. Padhman and Sunil had spent every afternoon of an entire summer holiday, the year they had turned seven, learning how to swim at the Club's pool. And every afternoon, after the lesson they would perch themselves on the high stools at the Viceroy's Bar and while waiting for the triple-decker club sandwiches and milk shakes to arrive, they would speculate endlessly about the Chadwicks. They often wondered what Henry had been late for.

'Did this house ever belong to a family called the Chadwicks?' he asked impulsively.

Aoife looked at him curiously. 'The Chadwicks? My grandfather was born in this house. No, never heard of them. I'll ask Nana. Why?'

They were approaching a fork in the lane and Aoife hesitated when Padhman turned to her questioningly for directions.

'We'll drive up to the front of the house first. Then we can turn around and take the left fork here and go into the house from around the back. So take the right for now.' She leant forward, peering through the windscreen expectantly as if she couldn't wait to see what lay beyond that ochreous blaze of leaves. 'You didn't answer me,' she said, still looking ahead. 'Who are the Chadwicks?'

'Oh, it's a long story, but it's one that doesn't matter.'

Padhman wondered where he would begin explaining something like that to someone he had known for barely a few hours. On the other hand, how would he explain all this – last night, this morning and right now – to someone who had known him all his life? Sunil was never going to believe this.

They passed the last tall beech and the house suddenly came into view. The vast expanse of gravel in front of it was heavier and thicker than on the lane, and the Celica swung its behind as if it was double-jointed. As he pulled up outside the house, Padhman hoped no one behind those enormous windows had watched their slip-sliding arrival. He realised he was expected to get out of the car and he did so, looking at the house over the roof of the car, with an elbow resting on his open door and the other hand shielding his eyes from the sun. He hoped that it also hid his disappointment. It was not quite what he had expected at the end of that grand parade of beeches. Like some of the female patients in the private wing of the geriatric ward, it was a house that had passed the stage of aging gracefully and had in a cruel fashion just withered.

'I love this house.' Aoife was defensive, almost reading his mind. 'Come on, let's drive around the back and get inside.'

There was a charge of dogs across the very large cobbled and walled courtyard and Aoife berated them affectionately as they milled around, each torn between trying to catch her attention and wanting to suss Padhman out. The rear of the house looked less grim and though the wide stone steps, leading up to the olive green door, had sunk heavily on one side, the sense of decay was less obvious.

'Nana must be in the kitchen.' Aoife pushed open the door and strode ahead. Padhman followed behind, not sure if the dogs that he was at that moment tripping over, were allowed in. He could hear Aoife kissing her grandmother and as he paused outside the kitchen door, he was a bit annoyed with her for rushing ahead, instead of walking in with him. Now on his own, he was going to have to make an entrance. Moments later he reflected that it hadn't been that bad after all. The old lady had folded her Sunday paper and had slowly got up to walk across the kitchen towards him. She had her hand outstretched.

'Aoife never said she was bringing a friend.'

Within minutes the introductions were done and Padhman was sitting at the outsize kitchen table, listening to the two women discuss what he was going to wear.

'Yes, I suppose he could wear Colm's gear. It may all be a bit too small for him, Aoife. If the boots don't fit, try Eamon's.' They forgot Padhman momentarily as they exchanged information about Eamon. Eamon hadn't been in touch with Nana. He hadn't rung home for a week. Aoife's mother was going to wring his neck, she was going to give out to him. Molly had called twice to ask about Eamon. Molly had called Aoife too. And there was Monty. Monty was pining for Eamon, there was no doubt about that.

The conversation was beginning to make no sense to Padhman and he looked around the kitchen as casually as he could. He was immediately struck by the contrast between the desperate exterior of the house and the immaculate inside. Like the table, everything in the kitchen was outsize. The ceilings were way up high, the slabs of the stone-flagged floor were immense, the windows behind the pair of deep, cream-coloured ceramic sinks were door-sized, and in a huge tiled hollow that must have once been a hearth, sat an enormous old-fashioned cooker with four intriguing doors, each a different size. On either side of the hearth were shelves containing scores of books – cookery books by the looks of it. On the long, narrow mantel above the hearth and on the walls and shelves around the kitchen were displayed a fine collection of giant-sized crockery. Plates the size of the Celica's alloy wheels, enormous platters, tureens and pitchers, gravy boats and assorted copper ladles, some of them the size of a small dish. Occupying pride of place, dead centre of the mantel and directly above the cooker, was a larger than life-sized glazed fish plate. Complete with realistic fins, scales and a tail that was caught in mid-flip, the salmon looked back at Padhman with a baleful eye and pouting lips. It was beautiful and ugly at the same time. Padhman felt other eyes on him as well and he looked away from the mantel to Aoife and her Nana. They seemed to know what he was thinking.

'It's beautiful and ugly.' He was looking at the salmon again, wondering what had made him confess.

'A doctor and a diplomat.' The old lady was laughing but sounded approving. She got up and gathering her papers, headed for the door.

'Spend some time with me before you both leave,' she ordered. 'I'll be in the orangery.'

As they walked across the courtyard and through a narrow archway towards what Padhman could smell were the stables, Aoife seemed preoccupied. It was nearly mid-day but the sun hadn't broken through the clouds and a fresh wind stirred newly fallen leaves, the ones that were still crisp, breaking up heaps and making new ones. Yesterday's leaves were already too heavy and soggy and they lay in wait, innocuous little slippery traps. He had seen victims in Casualty with broken ankles and twisted tendons. Padhman shivered and pushed his hands deeper into his jacket. It was a useless act, much like hunching up one's shoulders. That fresh wind would get you anyway. He looked sideways at her. She was puffing warm breath into cupped hands. I don't really want to ride, he thought. Appreciate this weather? I must have been mad. *She* must be mad. With every thought, he hunched up his shoulders a notch more.

They were at the stables when Aoife quickened her step, making strange soothing noises and calling out, 'Bella, Bella, here girl!' Four curious equine heads poked out over four of the half doors. Aoife was nuzzling Bella in the third stable and calling out to each of the other horses by name, by the time Padhman walked past the first horse, keeping a safe distance.

'Come and meet her. Here, stroke her on her cheeks like this.' She held Padhman's hand in her own and they stroked the horse together. 'I'll get Jess ready for you. She's a pony, great with children and you'll be OK on her. I'll lead, don't worry.'

Fifteen minutes later he was astride Jess with Aoife holding the reins and riding just a step ahead on Bella. Colm's riding gear consisted of a pair of jodhpurs and a lumberjack-style quilted woollen shirt that smelt faintly of sweat and mainly of horses.

'Change in the tack room,' she had said to him, adding encouragingly, 'Turn on the electric heater.'

The heater was a rusty old one and only two of the five elements worked. The constant ticking that emanated from it was ominous, and Padhman wondered blackly how he was going to explain, first his frozen and then his exploded genitalia, to the staff at Casualty. It was when Aoife shouted out to him, that he stopped thinking and just changed, emerging out of the tack room a bit anxious, not knowing what sort of a fool he looked like. I must be OK, he thought, for she handed him a waterproof jacket and a riding hat, without any comment except to check if he had switched the heater off. He was impressed with her patience as she showed him how to mount and dismount, reassuring him constantly that Jess was a gentle and reliable animal.

'We'll go up to the top of Boston Hill. The views are great. You OK, Padhman?' It was disconcerting having to look up at her. Bella was a big horse.

They kept a gentle pace and Aoife pointed out various things of interest as they slowly ascended the hill. They stopped for a moment at the ruins of a tree-house that her father had built for her and Eamon. So Eamon was a brother, but Padhman had guessed that.

'Who's Molly? Is Eamon missing?' Padhman was curious.

'Oh, you heard us carrying on in the kitchen. Eamon is a brat and Molly is his girlfriend. He's missing a few screws in his head all right. No, no, he's not missing. He is in France with his mates. Potholing and caving.'

'And Monty?'

Aoife laughed aloud. Was he imagining it or did Jess just shake her head and snort. 'Monty is Eamon's horse. Colm is not much use with Monty. He's a strong horse and he'll behave only for Eamon or my father.'

They passed through an open gate and were now on a narrow country road that led to a very steep hump-backed bridge. Padhman clung on to Jess, convinced that the pony in her struggle up the bridge was going to accidentally dislodge him from the saddle.

'Does the poor horse have to carry me up the slope? Can't I just dismount and get on to her again?'

'Padhman, look at me. Hold yourself like this. If you keep your weight forward she'll be fine.'

They were over the bridge before he could say anything more. He wasn't really enjoying this, but he followed her instructions to turn and look to the right, down the canal bank. He noted dutifully the old Catholic Church now deconsecrated and the hundred-year-old national school by its side. Both were now family homes. Her father had studied at that school till the day he was severely caned by the priest from the church next door. That, for having shouted abuse at a man on the *Lucky Lady*, one of the many slow-moving barges that carried Guinness to the various towns along the length of the canal. Her father had protested to Nana that all the boys in the school did the same when the *Lucky Lady* passed by. They all knew that man on the boat well. He would regularly expose himself to the children as the barge went past the school. One hand on the tiller and one hand holding himself.

'Dad never went back to that school and Nana never went back to that church. Why am I telling you all this morbid stuff anyway?'

Padhman shrugged his shoulders. 'Because I'm here stuck on a horse behind you and can't escape?'

Aoife grinned back. Padhman sighed dramatically and she laughed. They had crossed back into a field and he could see for himself that they were nearly at the top of a hill. Minutes later she helped him dismount and tie Jess to the stud rail fencing that seemed to run along the entire crest of the hill, disappearing out of sight where the hill dipped towards the canal. She hitched herself up and sat on the fence. They looked out at the view together, she with her face thrust out, as if determined to take in all that fresh, cold air and he standing in her slim shelter, trying to appreciate distant County Meath, despite a nose that was dangerously close to leaking. He sniffed, in what he thought were imperceptibly short intakes and then moving right behind her, slipped his hands around her waist and into her jacket pockets. He wasn't too surprised when she lifted them out of her pockets and placed them, under her shirt, against the warm folds of her skin.

'They'll be warmer there,' she tried to explain, at the same time flinching from the cold of his frozen fingers. Padhman drew his hands back out and she looked over her shoulder at him, unsure of why he had done that and what she was to say.

'Let me warm them up first.' Padhman rubbed his hands together vigorously and blew into them before sliding them back in under her shirt and holding her around her waist. He laid his head on her back and huddled against the wind.

'I still say the best place to view the Irish weather is from a window beside a fire.'

'But then you wouldn't be cold and holding me like this.'

'True. On the other hand, there are other things I could do to you.'

'Aha. We are at a window, beside the fire, remember?'

'There is a shag-pile carpet on the floor by the fire.'

'Not a very good choice of words, Padhman.'

'Am I really having this conversation with you?'

'What do you mean?'

'Will you have dinner with me tonight?'

She nodded, still looking at the view. He moved his hands under her shirt and cupping her breasts, gently squeezed them in satisfaction. They stayed like that for a while at the fence. He, with his cheek on her back, staring at the grains on her leather jacket and at the little clear plastic backs of her pearl earrings and she, comfortable, with her arms wrapped around his from the outside.

CHAPTER ELEVEN

~

MY LIFE EITHER stands still or leaps forward in geometric progression. Was I saying that to myself only this
morning? If it was this morning, Padhman wondered,
what could describe the giant leaps between then and
now? He looked around the bedroom. His keys and wallet
lay on top of the *Textbook of Surgery* at the foot of the bed.
Yes, waiting to be unlocked, he thought ruefully. That
was real enough. The phone by his bedside had been
nudged off the hook. That was real too. The rattan shade
that hung from the ceiling was throwing very real
checked shadows diagonally across one wall. It was Aoife's
presence in the bed beside him that was a bit unreal. Her
pale pink nipples were unreal. He had said that to her and
in return she had pointed to his, laughing at how brown
they were. She had never seen such dark brown nipples.

'What about you? Have you seen pink nipples before?'

He wondered now if his answer needed to be as honest
as it had been. It was complicated, he told her. He had *felt*
nipples, but never seen any. Could she understand? He
tried to explain as best as he could, the uselessness of the
cinema and the limitations of the dark car parks at Marina
Beach. Parked cars were a beacon for voyeuristic fishermen. They would creep out of the darkness and surround
the car, leering in through the windows, hoping to catch a
glimpse of something, anything. It was a dangerous thing
to do, to park at the beach.

He told her about what had happened to Sunil and
Renu without mentioning names. When the fishermen

started rocking Sunil's car violently, he had, with considerable presence of mind, started the engine and driven off at speed. A few pairs of bare feet had been run over in the process. By a sheer coincidence, Padhman had come across two of the fishermen in the Orthopaedic Out-Patients clinic in the General Hospital, ten days later. He told Sunil he was sure they were the same bastards. Padhman stopped that story there. He had never told Sunil of the near pornographic details with which the two men had regaled the filthy, over-crowded waiting room. Padhman was sure the facts had been embellished. Renu was not that sort of girl. She and Sunil were only engaged. He paused guiltily in his thoughts. What sort of a girl did that make Aoife then? And by Amma's standards, for they applied to everyone, what sort of a young man did that make *him*? He would have easily pushed Amma out of his mind, but Aoife was incredulous.

'Couldn't you just take a girlfriend home?'

'If you were happy enough to have her seated on the sofa, making small talk with your mother – if your mother were that modern to start with, then yes. This is the first time I have lived on my own,' Padhman added.

He tried hard to explain. 'That's how it is in India. You never live on your own. You live with your parents for roughly a quarter of your life, and then with your spouse for about half your life and then when you're old or if one of you dies, you go to live with your children. Consequently, we have no unmarried mothers or old-age homes. You may be lonely, but you'll never be alone.' He repeated that to himself. *You may be lonely but you'll never be alone.* That was a nice philosophical touch, a depressing, but pithy end to his speech. He had looked at Aoife to see if she had caught the irony and therefore appreciated his wit.

Aoife, however, was on a quest. 'So where do people snog? Where do they make out?'

'They don't.'

'You didn't?!'

Padhman was not ready to admit anything of the sort. He felt handicapped enough that she had seen him cling to the pony in nervous desperation. No, he was not also going to admit that he had lost his virginity fifteen minutes ago, at the embarrassingly ripe old age of twenty-four.

'I never kiss and tell,' he said, as enigmatically as he could, and then proceeded to suck her mouth gently into his. That was a while ago and though she lay right next to him, it was, as he kept saying to himself again and again, still so unreal, unbelievable. She lay still and curled up into a ball, with her back towards him. Her skin was stretched taut over the knobbly outline of her spine and he could see she was cold. The fine, down-like hair at the base of her spine was standing up in tiny, goose bumps. Chickpea flour and yoghurt would get rid of that. That's what babies in India were massaged with, the best natural exfoliator of down. Yet there was absolutely no way he was going to tell her *that*. He knew enough about women to be aware that all talk of body hair and the related painful subjects of waxing and plucking, were as taboo as farting in public.

He reflected on the things he had just told Aoife. He had exaggerated a bit – an unconscious effort to make excuses for his own inexperience. Though inexperienced was not what he would be considered in Madras. He had had girlfriends from the age of eleven. The first, God yes, the first had been a velai – the American Consul's youngest daughter. Their entire affair had been conducted below the surface of the swimming pool at the Gymkhana

Club. He wasn't the kind of boy who would shy away from her invitation.

'Do you want to touch me?' was all the come-on an eleven year old needed.

Padhman tried hard to remember her name. Sally? Sandy? How could he have forgotten? They never arranged to meet, just took a chance on the other being there, sometimes very early on a weekend afternoon and sometimes on Movie Nights, at near dusk, before the pool lights were turned on. He would search for her tubby pre-teen chest under the Mickey Mouse float she always wore, holding on to the lip of the swimming pool's drainage channel with his other hand. She for her part, would touch him only with her deft little toes, poking and prodding him through his swimming trunks, causing him all sorts of unexpected pleasure, but quite often, pain. He would draw up his legs in automatic agony, upon which she would give him a beatific smile and just float away, leaving him to recover in his own time. It was a strange, near-silent, aquatic sexual awakening. He had never even told Sunil about it.

The American Consul's youngest daughter had moved out of Madras at the end of that year. She never had said much and she never said goodbye. She moved on with her family, to other pools maybe, in China or Peru, Padhman never did find out. She was the first and the only girl who had got to the point without any preliminaries. Even as an eleven year old, he knew that things would never be that easy again. He wondered now if her treatment of him had anything to do with, oh . . . what was the right word, this paranoia of his that surfaced now and again about white people. After all, she had never even asked him his name and she had deigned only to touch him with her toes.

As if to compensate, every girlfriend he had had since had only ever wanted to talk. Over the years he had become adept at persuading them to agree to more, but it was all very childish compared to what he had achieved in twenty-four hours with Aoife. He had held breasts and stroked nipples in the dark and semi-dark, through hastily lifted tops and unopenable bras. He had been held, he knew sometimes it was nervously, he had been stroked and squeezed, even giggled over, but then always zipped back. He had kissed very receptive lips and sucked on surprised but willing tongues, but rarely had he a chance in all the fumbling, to watch the faces, appreciate body parts or see what he was doing. Except with Annie.

Padhman felt a rush of guilt. He sat up and propped his pillow against the headboard. He drew the duvet over Aoife, covering up all distraction and then leant back against his pillow. Technically, he had done nothing wrong, he reasoned. It was all a question of timing. Or mistiming perhaps. Aoife had happened before Annie had arrived. He would speak to Annie on the phone. No, that was ridiculous. What would he say? 'Don't come to Dublin next weekend'? Shit! He smoothed the duvet cover as it lay over his waist and legs with long even strokes, trying to think straight, calming himself down.

First things first, he told himself. I haven't done anything wrong. What was I expecting from Annie anyway? We hadn't left off anywhere serious that we could pick up a year and a half later and carry on from. But on the other hand there had been the beginnings of something, again it was a question of timing. He hadn't seen her since that New Year's Eve night up in the cupola. Damn Sunil and Renu. They had arrived at the top, panting and near collapse to find Padhman trying to look unconcerned and Annie looking unconcerned. There had been a few moments of fidgety embarrassment before Padhman and Annie had vacated the cupola, with a tandoori order for Renu, a request for a beer for Sunil and a promise to find

99

and hold a table for the four of them. The evening had been tame after that and a few days later, Annie had rung to say a brief goodbye before leaving for Cardiff.

He had been lonely and impulsive when he had asked Renu to contact Annie. He had revived her for himself, reminisced about her. None of this would have happened if he had just stuck to his books. He groaned silently. Now that was a worry that was worth worrying about. The exams were in March. If he got through he was almost certain of a surgical job in July. If not, he would be looking at wasting time in ENT or worse still, killing time in Geriatrics. Killing time in Geriatrics! Sunil would love that. Padhman grinned. The answers were clear all of a sudden. Annie would come, he would take her out, show her around Dublin, and they would be friends, just friends. She would go back, he would get down to his books and he would pass his exams. Any other niggling doubts about anything to do with Annie, he would face when it happened, he thought defiantly.

What of Aoife? Almost as if she had read his mind, she startled him with a murmured, 'I hadn't fallen asleep, you know. What are you thinking?'

'About us.'

'So was I.'

'OK, you first.'

'By your Indian standards then, am I a bad girl?'

'You're a loose woman and I am an utter cad. That's by Amma's standards. Amma is my mother – that's what I call her. Now you tell me, by Irish standards, have I been a bad boy?'

'I can't think of anything funny to say, Padhman.'

'So just be honest.'

'You've been normal but decent.' She had turned around and was looking him straight in the eye.

100

He couldn't believe she'd said that. Normal but decent. Not normal *and* decent. So she could see the difference too. But he didn't have the courage ask her whether this was normal for her. Did she normally sleep with men she had only met the day before? Did decent Irish girls do normal things? Were normal Irish girls decent? Oh God! I'm confusing the crap out of myself, he thought, when all I need do is lie back and enjoy this normal but decent thing that I have involved myself in.

'Look, just forget that we only met yesterday. Pretend that we've known each other a while. You'll be less traumatised.' She was reading him like a book. No, more precisely than that, like an ordnance survey map.

'Will you be less traumatised too?'

'No,' she said, lifting herself and lying on top of him, her breasts squashed flat against his chest and her voice muffled as she continued speaking into his neck. 'No, because I feel I've known you all my life.'

It was nearly midnight when Padhman returned home in the Celica. Aoife had said she would ring for a taxi to take her home, but he would not hear of it. He noticed the lights still on in number 33. That meant Sunil and Renu were awake. They had done it to him before and so he rang their doorbell without any remorse. He wanted a coffee. He might just mention Aoife or maybe not. He waited for what seemed like ages and was beginning to wonder if, knowing it was him, since only he would call round at this hour, they were waiting for him to give up and go away so that they could carry on where they had stopped. Coitus interruptus, he thought wickedly. He heard the window being opened and stepped back from the porch to look up. Renu's head appeared.

'It's not what you think it is,' she whispered curtly. 'We are actually in the middle of a fight. Come back tomorrow.'

He was back on the pavement when he heard the latch being opened once more.

'Tomorrow, come for dinner, Pads.'

He turned back to wave, but Renu had shut the window again.

CHAPTER TWELVE

~

MAURA AND NIALL had sent a postcard from Boston. Siobhan had pinned it to the over-crowded board at the nurses' station. Maura would do that, thought Padhman unkindly. Manoharan was the source of the gossip. Maura had turned her nose up at Lanzarote, he reported. Niall would have to do better than that in terms of culture and class. If he wanted to be stuck in some pretend Irish bar, surrounded by English lager louts, well, he could go alone. Or with Manoharan.

'I left at that point,' Manoharan told him gleefully. 'When she had him by the bollocks.'

Padhman knew she was an ambitious woman – for herself and therefore for Niall too. He was consultant material and she had her feet on the ground. Most people grudgingly admitted that she was good for him and that he would become a consultant for her. Padhman was only just beginning to comprehend the snob value of Cape Cod at the end of a scheduled flight, compared to the Costa by charter.

He pinned the postcard back, noting the way Maura had twined hers and Niall's names together into a joint signature. So why am I being so protective of Niall, he wondered as he rushed off to the canteen. It was Friday. They'd spoken on the phone, but he hadn't seen Aoife since that last weekend together. Their rotas had crossed. She had tutorials to attend. Eamon was home at last and the family was going to have dinner at her Nana's. Tuesday on call had been a killer. Someone had declared it

Juvenile Asthma Night. By four o'clock on Wednesday morning, Padhman was nauseous. He was sick of the nebulisers, the fogged-up masks, the brave smiles, the pitiful gasping. He didn't want to make any more small talk about Ninja Turtle pyjamas and Barbie slippers. He wished Maura were in the ward, instead of in Boston. She had a way with angry and helpless parents. But he had survived the week and he was going to meet Aoife for lunch. She was on call this weekend. I'll bring her a Chinese tonight, he thought as he walked into the canteen and queued up, looking around to see if she was already there.

Mary, the dinner lady, had over the months now practically adopted Padhman. She winked at him as she slid two crisp Yorkshire puddings, that she had put away for him, onto a plate and then asked what he would have to go with it.

'You spoil me,' he said as he reached out for the plate. He liked her. She was a solid, no-nonsense, meat and two veg kind of person. He imagined that at her house, at her table, the carrots would never be mushy, the dog would be called Ben and the washing would always hang out to dry if it was a sunny day.

When he found her, Aoife was indignant.

'They said the Yorkshire puddings were all gone.'

'It's my Eastern charm,' he said, and plopped one of them on her plate as he sat down. 'And luckily for you, I'm the sharing type too.'

'I thought I'd never see you this week. I'm wrecked, Padhman. I'm dreading this weekend. I've got my period and the showers in the Res are filthy.'

'I'll bring you a Chinese for dinner. I'll bleep you and see how it's going and you can tell me then what you want.'

'Oh, I'll tell you now. A 35 and a 61. Now, fill me in on

this busy weekend that you have planned, this weekend of entertaining old friends and attending parties. Let me feel truly miserable.'

I don't want to be doing any of those things, Padhman answered silently. I am smitten. I love you. I am the one truly miserable. I'll be as sick as a dog till next weekend. I'm going to take you away – Connemara, Kerry, somewhere. Soon we'll have known each other for months, years. You won't be a loose woman and I won't be a cad. 'Bastard, she's here now. What are you going to do?'

'What do you think? Ride off with her into the sunset, naturally.'

Padhman tried to hide his confusion and his annoyance. What did Sunil and Renu think this was – an arranged marriage? It was an arranged something though. What on earth had possessed him to do it? It was these two . . . they had made him feel lonely. He looked at Sunil and at Renu who had just walked into the room wiping her hands on her jeans.

'Annie's gone up to her room to get some photographs to show us. Did you like the tandoori chicken, Pads? Shall I spice it up a bit more? I have thirty legs, which should do, don't you think?' She was anxious, as he supposed all the other contributing cooks were, that hers should not be the offering that people were too full to eat or worse still, the one that people would somehow refuse to take home, because suddenly they had no place in their fridges. This was what Manoharan must have meant yesterday. Mrs Tiwari's culinary prowess usually gave the other ladies a complex, he had informed him knowledgeably. But it was obviously an issue that Manoharan had dealt with sensitively, for the menu that was lined up for his party tomorrow was impressive.

Annie walked into the room waving the packet of photographs in her hand. They sat down on opposite ends of the sofa, herself and Renu, both cross-legged, like it was time for a ritual, and looked at the photographs. Padhman was weary. It was always worse when you had only yourself to blame for a situation. Even worse, when you were the only one who knew that a situation existed. Annie's attitude – no, her *non*-attitude, her lack of any attitude – had thrown him completely.

'Hi, Pads,' she had said casually as she let him into number 33.

Padhman stared at her. He would never have recognised her if he had had to pick her up from the airport.

'What happened to your hair?'

She still had the mannerism and flicked back the strands that fell over her forehead. The rest of her hair was cropped short, very short. He never knew she had such a long lovely neck. She looked stunning.

'Like Audrey Hepburn, isn't she?' Renu had walked into the hall from the kitchen. 'I'm going upstairs to get a jumper. The kitchen is bloody freezing. It's that friend of yours and his overworked olfactories. You're getting a sample of tomorrow's dinner. I'll be down in a second.'

'Why did you cut it?' Padhman persisted, as he followed Annie into the sitting room. 'It suits you though,' he added.

' It was a pain to wash, Pads. It never dried quickly enough.' She laughed happily. ' I'm rehearsing those two excuses for Mum and Dad. I really just wanted a change.' She was smiling, relaxed, sitting back on the sofa. So confident, so collected, she hadn't changed at all.

He was weary, but relieved, with the way the evening had progressed. Towards the end of the dinner Annie said that she wanted an early night. She was tired and she wanted to be well rested for whatever was planned for tomorrow. Padhman decided that he would read no more into that than was meant. The early night wasn't an

106

excuse. It wasn't because she had decided that Padhman, a year and a half later, was not really her cup of tea – and though he knew that it would be a blow to his ego, he desperately wished she did feel that way. It would serve him right and he would have atoned for this situation in that way. He was keen to get away from number 33 and go to see Aoife at the hospital as arranged. Sunil had nodded off on the sofa. Thank you, friend, thought Padhman, exhaling gratefully.

'I'll see you tomorrow, Annie.' He kicked Sunil on the shins gently, as if drawing Renu and Annie's attention to the only reason why he was leaving. 'I forgot my *Bailey and Love* in the doctors' Res. I'll have to go back to rescue it before it gets pinched.'

Annie had unfolded herself off the sofa. 'It was great seeing you again, Pads. What time do you want me tomorrow? Is it far away, Wicklow? Is that where we're going?'

Sunil opened one eye and warned, 'Bastard, don't ring our bell before ten. I mean it.'

'That's between me and Renu. What time is breakfast, Madame?' Padhman knew he was asking for trouble, but he had wanted this saying goodbye business to be light-hearted. It would be easier to walk away with everyone feeling good.

'The cereal is in its usual place. We're nearly out of milk. Get us a carton from Fogarty's.' Renu was smiling at him sweetly. Sunil's shoulders were shaking silently. Padhman kicked him a little harder on his shins and left.

On the way to the hospital from The Great Wall of China he pulled into McDonald's. He balanced the two hot apple pies with ice cream with extra chocolate sauce on the passenger seat, next to Aoife's 35 and the 61 in their neat brown paper bag. Being in love was a hungry business.

*

'Walking is a hungry business,' Annie explained to the waitress as she took down their order. Padhman watched Annie as the two women discussed the route he and Annie had just walked. Renu had pulled out the book at dinner last night and suggested *Walk No. 3: Devil's Alley, 4 Miles. Walking time: two hours. (Walking shoes required, unsuitable for families.)*

'A woman's body was found close to the waterfalls, early in the summer,' the waitress informed them. 'Do you want any bread with your soup? Yes? Brown or white? OK, I'll get you a selection. She wasn't murdered there. They did the job in Dublin and then dumped the poor thing in the glen. It's an eerie enough place as it is. Strangled, she was. Anyway, you had a good walk. Coffee or tea? Now or later?'

Annie and Padhman giggled as she left. They had talked non-stop to each other during the walk, which they completed in two and a half hours. Padhman unconsciously put aside all his anxiety about the 'situation' as he kept calling it in his own mind. He had laughed, not realising that much of it was sheer relief, when she told him about her first Welsh boyfriend and breaking up with him because she had called him an English pig during a minor argument. Relief because Annie had a love life of her own. It had made him feel better, less guilty for having dragged her over to Dublin.

Now, looking at her across the table as she thumbed through the guidebook, he felt more than a little foolish. The fact of the matter was that Annie would always have a greater chance than him of having someone madly in love with her. She was beautiful, intelligent and when you got to know her she was the most agreeable angel. He was a bit startled by his own verbose assessment of her, but as he said to himself, it was true. Having assured himself that he was no big loss to her, he felt genuinely absolved.

He drove her back to Dublin and tried to give her a tour of the city, pointing out the sights as they either crawled by or whizzed past depending on the traffic. He engineered getting caught by the red lights in front of Christ Church Cathedral, so that she could look at it for an extra couple of seconds, and then he drove down by the grey and decrepit quayside, with its crumbling buildings and windows boarded up with concrete blocks, down the one-way system, past the Four Courts and up to O'Connell Street where he turned left over the Liffey, while simultaneously urging her to look right, so that she could see down what he assured her was one of the main thoroughfares of the city. Trinity College perked her up and they went around St Stephen's Green twice because she had missed looking left, down towards Grafton Street, the first time. He realised that she was fast asleep when he turned to point out the hospital to her, slowing down as he went past the main gates.

Annie walked towards him with a can of Guinness.

'Sunil said you'd want one of these.'

The four of them had been late arriving at Manoharan's. Padhman looked around for Venkat. The men had all deviated to the side of the room furthest away from the kitchen, which was not too far, as Manoharan's flat had a small open-plan dining-room-cum-kitchen, which led directly into the sitting area. Sunil had tried to insist that everyone leave their coats in the car. Renu cut him short just as he began explaining to Annie, the only one unaware of his phobia, that the smell of Indian food was particularly partial to lingering on coats and jackets.

'Annie and Padhman are not married to you, Sunil. I am the only one who needs to freeze.'

Sunil muttered dire warnings as he parked the car. Now he was in charge of the bar that had been set up in

109

the bedroom, on the tiny dressing table. Padhman could see Renu hovering by the side of Mrs Tiwari, who was directing the traffic around the dining table.

'Is your item heated already, Mrs Sunil?'

Renu looked guilty. 'No, Manoharan never said . . . should I have? I'm sorry. Does he have an oven?'

'The oven is full. Leave it on the counter and wait. You can talk to Dr Venkat's wife.' Mrs Tiwari nodded in the direction of a huddle of women. Renu walked defiantly in the other direction, towards Padhman and Annie.

'I hate these Indian do's,' she whispered to them. 'That Tiwari female is a real bossy-boots. She always calls me Mrs Sunil. Not Renu, not Mrs Patel, but always Mrs Sunil. Just look at this room. It doesn't make a difference where we damn Indians go. All the men on one side, back-slapping each other and all the women crouched over the fire.'

That outburst didn't stop her from dragging Annie away towards the huddle, which parted just as they approached. Padhman caught a glimpse of an anxious face with a fixed smile. The bride was enduring what brides always have to, legitimate gawking and even a certain amount of legitimate pawing: strange women holding her by the palms and wrists, touching the nape of her neck and the tips of her ears, examining, admiring, envying and comparing. The last thing Padhman noticed about the bride, as Renu closed the gap again, introducing herself and Annie, was, of all things, the thick green woollen socks peeping out from her delicate gold open-toed slippers, under her very bright red and gold silk Kanjeevaram sari.

Padhman spotted Venkat and tapped him on the shoulder. They hollered greetings at each other, before hugging and slapping each other's back. Renu should see us now, thought Padhman. His had been a congratulatory back slap. He got the distinct feeling that Venkat had reciprocated with the kind of hug that one returns when one is being consoled.

'So, my friend . . .' Padhman waited, wanting Venkat to say something first, to gauge his mood before saying anything more.

'So . . .' Venkat seemed to be struggling for words.

'Yes?' Padhman felt he had to coax him along. He didn't know Venkat too well, but this was an instinctive bonding – this was what happened when all that connected you was a shared hometown. A hometown that was, oh . . . he didn't really know how many miles away, it was easier to measure distances by the flying time. That made it eleven hours away from London. Fourteen hours from Dublin. He almost forgot what he was waiting for, when Venkat replied.

'She can't bear the cold, you know. She wouldn't come out without the socks. Poor thing.' Venkat was looking in the direction of his bride. Padhman was at a loss for anything to say. Venkat and his wife had only travelled here from the apartment below.

'She has the heating turned up to the highest setting and she is still frigid, poor thing.'

Please, please don't say that to any of the velais in the room, Padhman prayed. It will be all over the hospital and we will all, all of us Indians collectively, be the laughing stock of the place. If that bastard Larkin found out, the theatre staff would be regaled with it for years to come. Padhman looked around furtively. There weren't too many velais around, but at any time they might approach Venkat to congratulate him and he would unburden himself. God! Maybe he already had. Was that why those three nurses were standing aside and laughing? They looked as if they were sharing a private joke all right. Padhman grabbed Venkat roughly by his arm.

'Don't say frigid,' he muttered through gritted teeth. 'Haven't you consummated the marriage?' It was such an old- fashioned, horrible word, and Padhman shuddered inwardly as he said 'consummated'. Venkat looked shocked at the intrusive question and then horrified at the implication.

'Of course I have. Oh my God! You mean it means . . .?'

Padhman nodded. Let him think whatever he wanted as long as he didn't use that word again. Venkat looked mortified and then relieved. He suddenly hugged Padhman again, back-slapping him with embarrassment and gusto. Padhman found himself looking over Venkat's shoulders at Renu, who was shaking her head in what he knew was disgust. Venkat soon moved on to mingle and Padhman, left with his Guinness, proceeded to relax. He watched Annie talking to Mrs Tiwari. They seemed to be getting on well. Annie caught his eye and waved to him and then making her excuses to Mrs Tiwari, she joined him at the windowsill that he had commandeered.

'Renu begged me to check on the oven situation. There will be room for the tandoori chicken in five minutes.' Annie flashed her fingers at Renu to indicate five minutes, before she turned to Padhman. 'How can you drink that foul stuff?'

'It's an acquired taste all right. You must be bored, Annie. Sorry we had to drag you to this, but Manoharan would have taken offence if we hadn't come. You haven't met him, have you? He must be around somewhere.'

'Prabha calls these "The Slice of India" parties.'

'Oh, she's a snob like her sister.'

They both laughed and as if on cue Renu walked towards them.

'What's so funny?'

'You. You're a snob.'

112

'Do you know what Pads, I'd ignore you, except it takes one to recognise one. Are you telling me that these would be the people you would socialise with in Madras? I wouldn't care two hoots about Mrs Tiwari and her bloody queue for the oven, and I bet you wouldn't count Manoharan as one of your best buddies back home. Go on. Let's see you admit it.'

She was right, though not entirely. 'Point taken, Renu, but having got to know them, I wouldn't drop any one of them. As for Mrs Tiwari, she just fancies herself as the mother hen. Look, she's calling you, Mrs Sunil.'

Renu gave him a dark look and grabbed Annie's arm. 'Come with me, Annie, that woman drives me nuts.'

Padhman headed for the bedroom. The bed was covered with an enormous mountain of jackets and coats. Sunil was holding court in there.

'Another one?' he called out as he saw Padhman walking in. Padhman shook his head. He had a feeling dinner was going to be served any minute and he was hungry. Manoharan was counting heads. He explained that it was all Niall Fahy's fault. He had waltzed off to Boston forgetting that he had promised a dozen of everything: plates, glasses, and cutlery.

'Paper plates won't do because the curries will flow off or leak through. Go and count the number of women, will you? I may have to borrow some more crockery. I may even have to ask Venkat himself to get some from his flat.' He looked a bit hassled. Padhman went back to the kitchen area and counted all the ladies. Mrs Tiwari was watching him.

'Counting heads, Doctor Padhman? You should have consulted me. Total peoples is twenty-eight. Ladies and gents included.'

Renu giggled but she had her mouth firmly in her glass of Coke when Mrs Tiwari looked around. Half an hour

113

later, nearly everyone had finished eating. Padhman and Annie had encouraged the three Irish nurses through the feast, even fetching water for them when they were in dire straits. Renu was flushed with the success of her tandoori chicken and, having been asked by Mrs Tiwari to tell all the assembled ladies the secret of her recipe, was nearly ready to forgive the woman all her past sins.

Manoharan nudged past him, an empty plate in his hand.

'Hope you ate well. Gaja brought the sweets. He passed his exams, by the way. Must tell Mrs Tiwari to put the sweets out now.' He was suddenly whispering conspiratorially, leaning closer to Padhman. 'Do you know that dingo dame? Some friend of Sunil and Renu's. I might ask her if she wants to go to The Katz afterwards.' He nudged Padhman and winked. 'Want to join in the fun?'

Padhman wasn't sure what came over him. He dabbed his lips precisely with his paper napkin and then turned to Manoharan.

'Actually she's not an Anglo-Indian. She has a Welsh father and an Indian mother. Her mother is a pure Saraswat Brahmin and her father is Lord Cardiff. She wouldn't want to go out with the likes of us. You see, she is engaged. In fact, to someone connected to the royal family.' Padhman stopped and took a deep breath. Manoharan was entirely disbelieving.

'Shall I introduce you?' challenged Padhman.

Manoharan hesitated. 'Not now, later maybe. Let me see if Mrs Tiwari wants any help.'

Or wants her arse wiped, thought Padhman. He didn't want to stay in Manoharan's house any longer. He walked up to where Annie was standing with Sunil and Renu, talking to Venkat and his bride.

Venkat, probably remembering what had passed

between them earlier, introduced his wife to Padhman in a half-hearted fashion.

'You were busy with the ladies,' Padhman apologised to her, 'or I would have come and introduced myself earlier.' She smiled but said nothing. I bet she has even forgotten her husband's name in this melee. Padhman wanted to say something more to her, something reassuring and welcoming, but he hesitated and the moment passed. He turned to Annie. 'Shall we go back to my place?' She seemed relieved and nodded enthusiastically.

'Make some excuse to Manoharan, won't you,' he said to Sunil and Renu, and taking Annie by the elbow, headed towards the door.

They were both shivery and frozen at the end of their ten-minute walk back to his house. They stood in the hall next to each other, shoulder to shoulder, with the backs of their legs pressed against the radiator, occasionally bending slightly, reaching down to press the palms of their hands against the hot metal as well. They stood like that for about fifteen minutes, discussing the bride and the food. Padhman's heart wasn't really in the conversation. He tried to blame his slowly blackening mood on Manoharan. How dare he call Annie a dingo? That nudge and that wink had made his stomach turn. But try as he might, Padhman was not able to stop the finger of blame from somehow pointing to himself. What had possessed him to make up that idiotic pedigree? Padhman realised that he hadn't actually stuck up for Annie for what she was, an Anglo-Indian. Instead, he had implied breeding, by giving her what he reckoned would be a more socially acceptable background. What a nation of bigots he came from. Fresh foreign blood was acceptable, but diluted by a hundred years or so it was sour, unpalatable. He couldn't quite look Annie in the eye, as he asked her if she was ready for a cup of coffee.

She nodded and followed him into the kitchen.

'What happened to you, *men*? Eating and running off like that?' She was drumming her fingers on the kitchen counter.

That's what gives you away. That bloody Anglo expression – *men*. Padhman held his breath, feeling rotten and really mean. Oh Annie, that's below the belt and you don't deserve it. He gripped the kettle in irritation. He was irritated with her for showing him up like this and irritated with himself for finding fault with her.

'Manoharan is a bit of a pain in the arse sometimes,' he said briefly. 'Actually, I just got fed up. Let's forget about that crowd back there. Come on, you carry the mugs in, I'm going to light a fire. We'll keep an eye out for the Patels and get them to come over.'

By now, he considered himself something of an expert at lighting a fire. Layering the fuel in the correct proportion was the key to a good blaze. The base layer of the smokeless coal, the strategically placed firelighters, the thin layer of wood chips, then the positioning of a couple of peat briquettes and finally the filling of the gaps with just the right size pieces of coal: he had it down to a fine art. Padhman leant away from the fire as it crackled and spat into life. He was glad Sunil was not there to spoil his sense of achievement. Their opinions about the other's ability to light a fire was a festering sore in an otherwise close friendship.

'Your coffee,' said Annie as he sat down on the sofa. Padhman groaned as he looked up. She had left his coffee on the mantelpiece. He huffed and puffed dramatically as he got up and then returned to the sofa to sit down at the opposite end from where Annie sat, cross-legged and comfortable.

She was looking at him directly. 'They are probably wondering why we left so quickly and without them.'

'Sunil and Renu? Oh, they'll give us a decent interval before they come back.' Padhman was staring into the fire. He wasn't quite sure where this conversation was going to go. Just when he thought the situation was under control, Annie had to state the obvious. There was still unfinished business between them. Say something, he said to himself.

'I don't know why I asked you to come to Dublin, Annie.' Sometimes he had found it was best to brazen it out with honesty.

She was looking into her obviously empty mug and she remained silent. She sighed softly and then stretched her legs out, her stockinged toes almost touching him.

'I don't know why I came either, Pads. You know how it is when you wake from a really nice dream and you spend ages in semi-conscious limbo trying desperately to get back into it?'

She had said it eloquently and Padhman nodded his head.

'That's all it was,' she said gently.

Padhman nodded again. I won't say anything more, I'll let it be. But just for the record, Annie, just for the record I could have taken you back. We could have slipped back ... back into that dream. She tucked her feet under her purposefully and with that the mood lifted, changed.

'Tell me about your job, Pads. Do you have time to study at all?'

Padhman grumbled for a while, since it was some time since he had had a sympathetic ear. The lack of sleep, clean sheets, and a hot meal when he was on call amused her and spiced up the true mundaneness of his life. He couldn't tell her about Aoife. Not this time anyway. He would tell her about Aoife when she came to Dublin the next time. He asked Annie about that.

'There is no concrete arrangement as yet. We might

117

come over to Trinity College – they have a Choir Festival in February or March. I'm not even too sure of the dates.'

They were discussing the weather in March when Padhman thought he heard Sunil's car. He got up to look out and he could see Sunil reversing into his drive.

'They're back,' he said to Annie over his shoulder. 'Shall we ask them to join us?'

'And stop them fantasising?' Annie was laughing. 'They will be *soooo* disappointed, Pads.'

He turned away from the window and headed for the door. 'Back in a minute. I'll just go and tell them to leave their violins behind.' He left the room as she put her head back against the wing of the sofa and stretched out her feet again.

When he returned with Sunil and Renu, Annie was not in the sitting room. Renu headed straight for the fire, kneeling down in front of it.

'It needs some more coal.' Sunil was looking at the fire critically.

Padhman tried not to react. 'Put a briquette on, Renu. That should keep it blazing.'

'You didn't start it with enough coal. The idea is to have glowing coals, not blazing ones.'

'Ignore him, Pads. He's doing it on purpose. Where's Annie?'

They heard the toilet flush and a few seconds later the door opened and Annie walked back into the room. She gave him no warning before she sat down on the sofa and looking at him announced, 'Pads, your mother just phoned. It was when you went to call them.' She looked a bit shaky.

'I am sorry,' she went on. 'The phone rang and I picked it up automatically. I told her you'd be back in a minute.'

'Shit!' said Sunil explosively. Padhman was appreciative of the sympathy expressed in that one word. But shit didn't quite describe the true shittiness of the situation. Padhman suddenly burst out laughing. He held his sides as he laughed hysterically, bent over, with tears running uncontrollably down his cheeks.

'Can you picture Amma's face?' he howled at Sunil. 'First the shock and then Annie carries on talking and then the . . . the shock again! She'll never believe any explanation. Renu, will you pick her up from the airport tomorrow? Amma must be packing already!'

Sunil, Renu and Annie were looking at him with a mixture of curiosity and sympathy.

Annie spoke first. 'You'll have to put her out of her misery, Pads. She probably thinks that we are living together.'

Sunil shook his head seriously. 'No, I think you are wrong there, Annie. She probably thinks you are expecting her grandchild and she is already wondering whether you will insist on the child being baptised.' With that he walked towards Padhman, his shoulders beginning to shake and giving each other a high five they collapsed on to the sofa in a further, joint outbreak of hysteria.

Renu turned to Annie and smiled sardonically. 'This could go on for a few minutes yet.' They stood at either end of the mantelpiece and watched Sunil and Padhman, slapping the arms of the sofa, all doubled up, wiping their tears and then slowly, all their hilarity spent, being reduced to two foolish-looking men sitting hunched on the sofa, with idiotic grins on their faces.

'Aren't you glad that we didn't start something?' Padhman looked up at Annie.

'You mean . . .? Why did you leave Manoharan's then? We thought . . .' Renu sounded disappointed as she turned from Annie to Padhman and then back to Annie. Even Sunil seemed to have sobered up at that realisation and he straightened on the sofa.

119

'It just wasn't meant to be.' Annie shrugged but she was smiling.

'Is anything in your life uncomplicated?' Renu was looking at Padhman with genuine sympathy. 'Annie picking up your phone, in your house, at eleven at night and you have just popped over to call Sunil and Renu to join you both. So cosy and you know . . . couple-ish. Oh, the circumstantial evidence is stacked against you, Pads. I am waiting to hear how you are going to wriggle out of this one with your Amma.'

Renu's words were ringing in his ears as Padhman dialled home. He was glad he had waited till the next morning. As he had expected, Amma had had time to give herself a talking to. She did that sometimes – talked herself into a false state of calmness, which led her to sometimes pretend disinterest when she was actually dying to find out what was going on. This was an old game they played, and Padhman stuck to the time-honoured rules. No letting out anything unless Amma gave up, broke her own rules and asked the dreaded direct question.

'We called yesterday you know, Padhu,' Amma said after a few minutes of this and that.

'I know. Must have missed your call by a few minutes. I had just popped across to Sunil's.' Here it comes, any minute now. But I'm not going to say it, Amma. You will have to ask me about her. I won't tell you what she was doing at my house unless you ask. Padhman punched the air as the expected question materialised.

'I thought that Ewart girl was studying in London or Edinburgh. She surprised me, answering the phone like that.'

That Ewart girl! Amma was well aware of Annie's name. But then referring to her like that was part of

120

Amma's strategy. It was meant to annoy Padhman and make him say more than he wanted.

'Why, was she rude?'

'You know what I mean. At that time of the night. Alone in your house. We didn't know what to say to her.'

'It was very late, yes. What were you both doing up that early? It must have been four in the morning in Madras.'

Appa answered on the cordless. 'One of those Chettiar weddings. The nuptials were at five and we had to pick up Nimmi on the way. Raja is out of town. Actually Padhu, he will be in London next week. Hasn't Sunil told you? Raja told Amma he would call you from London.'

Padhman chatted with his father, both men acutely aware that Amma was impatient to return to all her unanswered and unasked questions. Finally, it was Appa who, with his dry observation, 'Amma needs to be put in the picture, if I am to have any peace,' made Padhman relent.

'For God's sake, Amma, she was here visiting Dublin and she stayed with Renu and Sunil.'

'And?'

'And nothing. Oh, I forgot. We . . . oh my God, we had coffee together!'

'There is no need for you to talk to your mother like that.'

This was a crucial point in their tussle. Padhman recognised it from the many times he had been there before. This was where the volleys could become more sharp and intense or it could also be the point where one of them, knowing what lay ahead, backed off. Padhman unexpectedly felt a twinge of guilt. Later on, trying to analyse his reaction, he concluded that such a familiar admonishment from his mother must have made him, in a perverse kind

121

of way, feel homesick. What else would have made him make peace with Amma the way he did?

Even as he said goodbye to Annie at the airport that afternoon, he knew that his mother had not quite finished her say about 'that Ewart girl'.

CHAPTER THIRTEEN

~

PADHMAN WATCHED AS the water gushed out of the taps. Waiting for the tub to fill up he read the copy on the back of the box of bath salts. A soothing mantra, it almost seemed adequate just to read the box. The tub was a quarter full and he shook the bath salts in generously. They fizzed on contact with the water and he watched fascinated, as wave upon wave of fragrant bubbles were pushed by the flow from the taps to the far end of the tub, where they gathered and bobbed gently up and down as if unsure where to go. No wonder Mrs Fogarty was so curious. He couldn't picture himself in that tub either, he admitted. He hadn't been inclined to tell the shopkeeper that the bath salts were for Aoife. Mrs Fogarty had picked up the box to key in the price and then had abruptly put it back on the counter, while she went through the rest of his shopping. Padhman, alert to her signals, decided to dig his heels in. After all, he hadn't even told Sunil and Renu. Every passing day made it more difficult. What was he to tell them? That he was running baths for a girl he had known for barely ten days? Should he leave it to the hospital grapevine? As he reflected on how he was going to introduce Aoife to Sunil and Renu, he watched Mrs Fogarty pointedly forget to key in the bath salts. Padhman pushed the box towards her. She picked it up with an exaggerated sigh.

Padhman remained impassive, taking out his wallet and readying his money. Mrs Fogarty could be quite determined on occasion. She had obviously read the backs of these boxes when she stacked them and was determined to find out what desperate aches and what troubled body needed the ameliorations offered by the product.

'The long days are on us,' she said, and waited.

Padhman knew he was being petty, denying her a small satisfaction, but despite two more circuitous attempts, the last of which was accompanied by the slamming of the till, he remained unmoved and walked out of Fogarty's Quic-Pic victorious.

The tub had filled up rapidly and Padhman turned off the taps. Aoife had told him she would be up as soon as she had watched the weather report for the weekend. She and Eamon had volunteered to spend Saturday and Sunday with their Nana, helping her plant bulbs.

'This year she wants them in large drifts – of hundreds, she said. She threatened Eamon that if he made any excuse like last year, she wouldn't have him over for Christmas. She wasn't sure about you, Padhman. I told her it was your idea. Oh, she was happy all right, she was looking forward to meeting you again. She just wondered if you knew what was involved.' Aoife had put her arms around his waist and pinched the little bit of flab he had around his stomach, between her finger and thumb, as they stood at the door of the sitting room watching the tail end of the Friday evening news.

He could hear her now coming up the stairs. She didn't thank him for running the bath until she handed him both the glasses of wine and sank in slowly with her eyes closed, her fingers gripping the edges of the tub as if she didn't want to make an undignified splash. This is exactly like in the movies, Padhman thought and looked on fascinated. And it's all happening to me. He sat on the toilet seat, mindful that the lid tended to shift unexpectedly and watched, waiting for her to open her eyes.

'Your mother would be proud of you,' she murmured,

taking the glass of wine from him. 'She has trained you well.'

Padhman spluttered into his glass. Aghast, yes, scandalised – definitely, but he couldn't somehow see Amma being *proud* of him at the moment.

'Oh, you know what I mean, Padhman. You *are* nice. OK, it means different things in different cultures, but you are a very nice guy and she should be proud of you.'

'Running a bath for you in Ireland is like holding open a door for a girlfriend in India. Yeah, that should convince her.' Padhman was looking at Aoife make a face back at him. She flicked suds towards him but they missed and landed on the lino. He looked at them in mock horror.

'I suppose you have servants in India to clean up after you.' She flicked some more of the bubbles towards him.

'Home help, you mean. We call them servants in India, but when we Indians are abroad, we are careful to refer to them as help. Dignity of labour and all that. We are great believers in it. When we are out of India.'

'What do they do, your servants? Do you have more than one?'

Padhman hesitated. It wasn't easy to explain why a household of four people would need . . . God, he had to count them on his fingers. He didn't even know the exact number – seven if you counted the gardener and eight if you included the dhobi, who came for the laundry twice a week. She listened to him, her eyes widening occasionally as they would if she were attending some fascinating lecture on medical oddities. He meandered around slowly, telling her about his school, the Chadwicks, Sunil and Renu, dwelling for a while on the intense humidity in Madras, what it meant to be a Hindu and the reasons why vasectomy camps were held in India.

'Do you realise how much I am going to have to tell you about myself?' he said.

He tipped his glass up, shaking out the last drops of wine onto his tongue. Aoife shook her head even before he asked the question.

'I left it next to the cooker – I meant to bring it up.'

'I'll go down but I have to say this first,' said Padhman, heading for the door. 'Your mother didn't train *you* too well. Forgetting the bottle downstairs? A poor start to a night of drama and seduction.'

When he turned around to look at her as he left, she had sunk further into the tub, her eyes were closed and she was trying hard not to smile. She must have known he was looking, for she flicked a few more suds onto the lino.

'Provocative and slovenly to boot,' said Padhman, wondering if his reaction to the accumulating suds on the lino was an indication of some slave fetish that he had hidden away in the erotica section of his subconscious.

Padhman was in pensive mood as Aoife drove up past the beeches and swung her car confidently into her grand-mother's courtyard. She had listened to the radio most of the way, switching stations distractedly. The enormity of the task that lay behind his comment to her the previous night weighed upon his shoulders this morning. Where was he to start telling her about himself? He nearly felt he should make a list. He was obsessed with the need for Aoife to know him completely. She had some idea, yes. Bits and pieces, unconnected details, insignificant asides that he may have added, some fairly good insights into certain aspects of his childhood and personality, but nowhere near a complete picture.

It was a different story the other way around. Padhman felt that he knew Aoife well. She was in her own sur-roundings. He had the advantage of being able to observe her in her natural state, where every element of her habi-tat told him volumes about her. He, on the other hand, was like an exhibit in a zoo. Plucked out of his own realm and placed in a linoleum-lined and net-curtained enclosure, he felt much like a captive tiger, pacing the bare concrete floor of his cell, wishing the paying public could see him in his true glory, stalking the lush jungles totally at ease, confident and in control. Except for his clothes, his demeanour and what he told her about himself, Aoife had nothing else to go by. She could form no notions other than those based on what he told her. Will I ever be able to tell her enough? Will she get fed up listening?

'Eamon's here already.' She was looking at the mud-splattered four-wheel drive beside which she had parked.

There was another problem. Padhman continued to brood in the same vein. Her family lived against the backdrop of a living canvas; he, on the other hand, was going to have to paint in background pictures of his life for them all the time.

But he was curious to meet Eamon and, as he helped Aoife carry in the shopping they had done for her Nana on the way to the house, he said as much to her. She sounded pleased.

'Oh, you'll like each other.' She was confident. 'Anyway he is the younger brother. Traditionally it's the elder brothers who, you know . . . lynch the man who casts his eye on their sister.' She cheerfully mimed the garrotting and the hanging tongue of the victim, adding as if in consolation, 'But I've told you about my two older brothers. The one in London might come down for Christmas and Seamus in America is undecided. He and Heidi – she's German, I told you, remember – they have just bought a fabulous house and they may not be able to afford the trip this year.'

Thank God, thought Padhman as they walked into the kitchen. I'll deal with the brothers, one at a time. Aoife was right though. Eamon was very likeable and Padhman was soon at ease, heading off with him to the sheds to load the bags of bulbs onto two wheelbarrows. They made a couple of trips tipping the bulbs in little piles on the vast expanse of grassy slopes on either side of the front of the house.

'The plan is to do this today and plant along the avenue to the house tomorrow. You are very good to have volunteered. Or were you volunteered? You can confess, Padhman. I grew up with Bossy Boots.'

Eamon was smiling. Padhman was struck by how alike brother and sister were. Eamon had the same open face and green eyes. That same expressive mouth that Padhman found so very sensuous and attractive on Aoife, probably made Eamon a charmer with the girls. His hair was tousled and reddish-brown.

Padhman suddenly remembered something and laughed. He laughed even louder when he heard Eamon say: 'Aoife's a witch. She has the black hair to match.'

Padhman nodded back, a wide grin on his face. I'm sorry, Eamon, this one I just couldn't share with you, he thought to himself. That Aoife's hair was not naturally black had come to him as a shock realisation, in the midst of an intricate moment of passion, passion that soon dissipated when his uncontrollable mirth forced her to sit on his chest, threatening to suffocate him with her pillow unless he told her what was so funny. When he finally explained, Aoife didn't see the humour at first, but when she emerged from the locked bathroom half an hour later, where he assumed she had escaped to soothe her ruffled dignity, she walked to the bed, mincing her steps exaggeratedly in cat-walk fashion and then thrust her hips out at him.

'I used your razor,' she said, and then fell into bed laughing.

Padhman looked at the piles of bulbs. She *was* a witch. He was caught in her spell and he loved it.

'Where do we start?' he asked Eamon.

'We'll head back to the house and see what's keeping the others. Nana has organised for Mr Barrett's lads to muck in as well. Colm should be here too. We don't have to start without the others.' He gave Padhman a big wink. But, before they even moved, they could see Aoife headed towards them, followed by a spade- and shovel-carrying posse. She held aloft a pair of wellies.

'You'll need these, Padhman.'

'I'd prefer you,' he whispered to her, putting one arm on her shoulders to steady himself, as he slipped off his shoes and changed. The wellies were at least a couple of sizes too big for him and he wondered aloud which giant they belonged to.

'They're my dad's, actually.'

Padhman found her exchanging a glance with her brother.

'He was on the phone to Nana just now. He and Mam will be here for dinner.'

Eamon took in a deep breath. He was looking at Padhman in mock sympathy. 'An inspection visit on neutral grounds. Don't worry, my friend, Nana will maintain the peace. If I can do anything to help, sister dear . . .'

Padhman watched him duck and move behind the wheelbarrow as Aoife made a show of setting on him with her spade.

'It won't be so bad, Aoife. Dad must have checked him out in the hospital.'

Padhman was still wondering about that remark, when they trooped back to the house for lunch, about three hours later. It had been hard work and they had all quickly fallen into a rhythm, working loosely in pairs, one carefully turning the sod and the other dropping the grit and then the bulbs in and stamping the clump back into place. Rain threatened constantly and twice they stopped, looking up at the sky collectively, wondering whether the intermittent, irritating drizzle would turn to a proper shower. They had finished planting on the sweeping slopes to one side of the house, going down to the very edge of the small woods that bordered the property.

There was an appreciative murmur from everyone as they divested themselves of their boots, gloves and coats in the large utility room. Lunch smelt delicious. Padhman quickly followed Aoife into what looked like another smaller utility area, where he waited to wash his hands at the sink after her.

'What did Eamon mean about your dad checking up on me at the hospital?'

Aoife scrubbed her hands vigorously, working the soap between her fingers. Like a Masonic handshake, Padhman thought. The way doctors washed their hands was a real giveaway. He waited for her to answer and the time she was taking sent ominous signals.

'Well, I thought you might have known or guessed along the way. Padhman, I would have told you, but I was scared in case it put you off me. Anyway, Dad hasn't really checked up on you at the hospital. I only told them, Mam and Dad, about you this morning.'

'And they are coming to, how did Eamon put it, "inspect" me a few hours later? Anyway, what is it about your dad that would put me off?' Padhman was trying to keep calm. What could she be about to tell him?

'OK, see how you feel about this. Do you know Professor Gorman? Peter Gorman? Well, he's my dad. If you are still talking to me, I'll be in the kitchen, and if it makes you feel any better, I was planning to tell you this weekend. I wish I had. I should have, in the car, on the way

130

here . . .' She trailed off, her voice full of regret and walked away.

Padhman's first thought was the pair of wellies he had just taken off. He should have known who her dad was when he saw the size of them. Professor Gorman was a giant. Physically and professionally. Padhman had twice been an insignificant member of the Professor's Grand Rounds, part of the entourage following along, ahead of the interns but behind the more senior SHOs and far behind the Registrars and Senior Registrars who were themselves jostling behind a Lecturer or two. Like a brilliant comet with a progressively diminishing tail, the Professor and his procession advanced through the wards creating as much anticipation and excitement as the real thing would.

Padhman rinsed and re-rinsed his hands under the tap, giving himself some time to think. That Professor Gorman was Aoife's father was not a problem for him. He could handle that kind of pedigree. After all, he had grown up in the reflection of his grandfather's glory and his father's impeccable medical reputation. He was well used to coping with whatever consequently rubbed off on him, whether it was the unfounded envy of his classmates in medical college, the obsequious manner of the porter at the college gates, who would insist on saluting him every morning when he went through the gates on his motorbike, or the annoying and obtrusive interest that the entire Faculty seemed to take in ensuring that he turned out to be a doctor worthy of his grandfather and father.

Why was Aoife so hassled about it? She was sitting between the Barrett boys when he returned to the kitchen. They shifted places, playing haphazard musical chairs so that Padhman could sit beside Aoife.

'So what's the big deal?' he said to her quietly as the

131

conversation at the table turned to horses and Mr Barrett's chances at the Naas races the next day.

Her mouth was full and she shook her head, waving her slice of bread at him as if she were flagging down his curiosity, asking him to be patient.

'It's not a big deal, Padhman, though I know it came out sounding like that. I don't know if you will understand. It's like this: if I were my father's son it would not be a problem. Do you get my meaning?'

It was Padhman's turn to shake his head. The beef casserole was delicious and he had his mouth full. She waited for him to reply.

'You are going around in riddles, Aoif.' Sometime during the week he had shortened her name and it had stuck.

'No, I'm not. I'm trying to find the best way to say this. If I were Professor Gorman's son, no prospective girl-friend would hold that against me. But as Professor Gorman's daughter, dating me would always be seen by the rest of the medical world as a career move. The fear of being perceived like that scares most men off.'

She jabbed her fork angrily into a piece of beef. It was so tender it disintegrated and her fork made a tinny, teeth-clenching sound against her plate. Padhman listened as she hurriedly apologised to the Barrett boys, for two of the younger ones had dropped their own forks and held their hands against their ears, pained expressions on their faces. When the conversation resumed a few minutes later, Aoife glanced at Padhman briefly as they both ate. He didn't keep her waiting a second longer.

'Professor Gorman couldn't change the way I feel about you.'

This was not the way he would have planned it. This was too public a forum for such a declaration. Padhman was surprised at his own depth of feeling and he nudged her gently with his knee. When she nudged him back, he

132

knew then that this was the Sunil and Renu kind of moment that he had so wanted for himself.

Professor Gorman wanted to show Padhman his collection of antique surgical instruments. The rest of the family groaned. Millie Gorman pushed her chair back and stood up to help her mother-in-law. The dinner had been a simple one and the eating of it had been slow and relaxed, the conversation punctuated with frequent asides to Padhman, like footnotes in a book, giving him explanations or putting things in context, so that he was able to follow the drift.

Padhman watched Aoife's mother as she moved around the kitchen. She had been cordial and polite – too polite, he thought. It was an antagonistic reflex in reverse that he recognised straight away. Amma had often been like that with girlfriends that she reckoned or hoped would not last. Millie Gorman was also obviously peeved with her mother-in-law, who not only had had first viewing of Padhman, but had also failed to notify Millie of the goings on. A sub-plot in what was certainly going to be a saga. *Our* saga, he thought, looking at Aoife and it was then, just as he was wondering how soon they would be able to make a getaway back to Dublin, her house or his, that the invitation to view the old surgical instruments had been extended.

Padhman wasn't sure what to make of the collective groan that arose from the table. Professor Gorman's smile was tinged with a hint of sheepishness and Padhman knew the man had to be indulged. Anyway, under the circumstances it was hardly an invitation, more a rite of passage and Padhman followed with as much enthusiasm as he could dare show, without being seen through.

As they walked through the house, Peter Gorman pointed out the many changes that had been made over the years: the restoration of the elegant orangery and ongoing projects, like the re-plastering of the formal drawing room that was turning out to be a major challenge. As they headed into the library, Padhman was unprepared for what he saw. This library wasn't a grand name for a family collection of books. This was a library in the true sense of the word. In a room that was possibly the largest in the house, with little alcoves leading off it, was the biggest collection of books that Padhman had ever seen outside a public library. The walls were lined from floor to the high ceiling with books and the alcove to which Professor Gorman had led Padhman, was crowded with glass-topped display cases of the sort that one would see in a museum. They housed an impressive collection of old and some very old medical and surgical instruments that Padhman would have found fascinating, had he not at that moment been absorbed in watching his host, who seemed undecided as to which one to take out and show the young man.

At first, the Professor hovered over a nineteenth-century portable amputation kit. But he just ran his finger along the edge of the boxed set and seemed satisfied that the glass cases had indeed kept away the dust. He pointed out the rather grim-looking screw tourniquet that sat in its assigned space in the box, between the ivory-handled saw and the heavy pliers, and said with a shake of his head, 'That set saw service in Napoleon's battle at Borodino in 1812. The poor bastards.' Next his eyes ran over his collection of forceps, that were arranged in rows, chronologically, and then something in the adjacent case seemed to have caught his eye, for he opened it with a flourish and took out the largest exhibit, which he handed ceremoniously to Padhman.

'A double duck-billed speculum. Ingenious device, wouldn't you agree?'

134

Padhman heard himself say, 'James Marion Sims, 1813–1883, one of the first pioneering gynaecologists and his double duck-billed speculum for the examination of the vagina, in conjunction with light reflected from a mirror.'

The Professor looked at Padhman in delighted surprise. Padhman wondered if he should confess that all he had done was recite from memory the inscription at the bottom of a sepia print of a rather stern, but handsome, waist-coated and bow-tied doctor, standing formally beside accompanying illustrations of his 'double duck-billed' speculum and mirror. That print was one of a set of four prints of famous gynaecologists which hung on the wall behind Grandfather's rosewood desk, in his consulting room at the clinic in Madras. A speculum, a double duck-billed one at that, is going to shape my destiny and smooth this awkward rite of passage, Padhman thought. He gazed down in bemusement at the bizarre contraption still in his hand and as he handed it back, realised that his reaction had been interpreted by Professor Gorman as one of keen interest.

An hour later, they returned to the small room beside the kitchen, where the rest of the family sat in various states of repose in front of a blazing fire.

'You bored our visitor to death, dear.' Millie Gorman was obviously not impressed with the amount of time the two men had spent together. She smiled at them solicitously, but Professor Gorman was not fazed by the reprimand that lay behind that smile, nor by the impatience signalled by the brandy being swirled around, very deliberately, in her glass.

'On the contrary, Millie. We were marvelling at a sheer coincidence.'

As Professor Gorman enthused on, Padhman was struck by the similarity between Millie Gorman and his own mother. Amma bristled with signals and yet firmly believed that she always contained her feelings.

Millie Gorman seemed to brighten up as she listened to her husband and when she turned to Padhman, she was looking at him rather more benignly. 'Three generations of gynaecologists, that's remarkable. Normally one in the family is enough to put off any others.' Then with a very casual glance at Aoife she added cheerfully, 'Your parents must be waiting for you to return to take over your father's practice.'

'Oh, that's at least a couple of years away, I reckon, Millie. The young man has exams to pass before he can consider going home.' Nana Gorman had joined the fray.

'No doubt he won't waste any time getting them then. After all, that's what he came to Ireland for.' Millie had relapsed into her earlier testy state.

Padhman realised that the Gormans had all turned to look at him questioningly for clarification. They were each waiting for him to say what they wanted to hear.

Looking back, it had been a defining moment in his relationship with the Gormans. He remembered staring blindly into the fire for a seconds'-long eternity, his mind a total blank and then saying the first thing that came into his head.

'I miss my parents terribly.'

It was a disarming confession, and the Gormans would never have guessed how surprised he himself was by it. It had taken a simple truth to thoroughly charm them and even though it wasn't exactly the answer to their collective questions, unasked though they were, they each interpreted his declaration to their own satisfaction.

Even now, with the weekend behind him and what, from the dull tattoo drumming on the window-panes, sounded like another wet Monday morning ahead, Padhman couldn't help the self-congratulatory mood he continued to remain in. He had made a good impression on Aoife's family, though he knew that Millie Gorman was only temporarily mollified. However, in her he had found Amma's psychological double and just recognising that had, he felt, given him a huge advantage. Whereas with any other person he might have tried ingratiation, with Amma, Millie and their type, he knew that the chances of such an overt approach backfiring was very high. Not that women like them would succumb to any amateurish ambush either. Aoife had laughed at his analysis.

'I hadn't realised you were so devious, Padhman. I'll have to be more careful myself.'

'No, no, Aoif, not devious, just prepared,' he had said, giving her a three-fingered salute.

CHAPTER FOURTEEN

~

PADHMAN TURNED AND stretched out to the other side
of the bed, from where the red liquid crystal in the clock
radio poured scorn over all his thoughts and reflections. As
he took heed and got out of bed he mentally ticked off the
things he wanted to do this week. He *had* to study – and it
was going to take some effort to get back to his books. He
had a letter to write, for Grandfather, who had become
increasingly deaf over the last two years, got very frus-
trated, tearful even, when telephone conversations disintegrated into futile shouting sessions. He definitely had
to tell Sunil and Renu about Aoife, and about his weekend
at her Nana's. Renu would relish the finer details.

The phone rang as he picked up his towel. He instinctively knew who it was and got back into bed, plumping
up the pillows against the headboard as he picked up the
phone.

He paid no attention to the preliminaries as he went
through the motions of greeting and being greeted. All
he could think of was how much he really did miss them.
Amma and Appa spoke together at first and then both
became silent for the other, though when they spoke
again it was once more in chorus. Padhman could just
picture them now. Appa laughing at their foolishness and
keeping an eye on the time and Amma noting Appa's
deliberately casual glance at the clock.

'Your father's watching the clock. I had so many things
to tell you, Padhu, but with Appa timing us everything
has gone from my head.'

138

But she hadn't really forgotten anything, except perhaps, the order in which she had planned to say things. If Padhman had given it any thought since he last spoke to them, he would have guessed where Amma's thoughts still lay.

'The Ewarts are planning to migrate to Australia. Nimmi met them at the Gymkhana. Their son Vincent is sponsoring them.'

Padhman sighed silently. It was with a sense of déjà vu that he waited for Amma to make her point.

'Is she going to come to Dublin again? Padhu, we have no problem with you being friendly with her, with their daughter Annie.'

'But?' Padhman knew that he had been practically prompted to ask the obvious.

'It's your life, but you should realise that they will want their daughter to go with them. She will be migrating to Australia too. So many of the Anglos are slowly leaving India. They say Australia is full of them.'

'Amma . . .' Padhman felt like saying something scathing. Something cutting and hurtful. He felt slightly sick that he should have cause to be ashamed of his mother. I denied Annie's Anglo-Indian identity too, he admitted to himself, but that was me speaking to Manoharan in his currency. Why did I do that? That makes me as guilty as Amma and her ilk. Does Appa never have an opinion about such things? Grandfather has so many Anglo-Indian friends. Bernie and Victor Clark. The De Mellos. They still remember his birthday every year. Eugene Donaldson. Wendy and John Price. All these were dear friends of the family. But what if Appa had wanted to marry one of *their* dear children? Through his irritation and confusion, Padhman tried to refocus on what Amma was saying.

'You will have to do the exams, you know – with the

Australian Medical Board. Things are tough for Indians. Australia is quite racist, they say. Think of . . .'

Appa interrupted. He was laughing. 'Amma has you married and settled in Sydney already.'

But Padhman's annoyance was not placated by his father's jesting. He recognised the good cop-bad cop technique that his parents had used on him ever since he could remember. I'm too old for this. I have a job, I've left home – I'm a bloody doctor, for God's sake! I saved two . . . no, three lives last week. What was it Eamon had said on Sunday? That he counted to ten when his mother 'got on his case'? But as Padhman exhaled slowly, he realised that Amma had annoyingly and predictably moved on. Now she was saying something about Grandfather.

'You haven't written to him for a month, Padhu. We have had to tell him there is a postal strike on.'

'Amma, Annie Ewart doesn't have to go to Australia. People don't have to live where their parents live.' Padhman could hear the sullenness in his own voice.

Amma was never one to back down in the face of a threat, implied or otherwise.

'People! Huh . . . people should know what they are getting into. Better to have your eyes open – or opened, as the case may be.'

Appa tried to diffuse the situation. 'Maybe we should . . .'

Listening to his father struggle, Padhman was struck by the pointlessness of the argument, an argument based on a non-fact, a non-affair. In effect this was nonsense. But for the moment, caught up as he was in what he perceived was an insult to his judgement, he was determined to get Amma to make her point plainly. Surely, when bigotry was stated plainly it would be seen for what it was.

'Yes, let Appa explain why we worry. Let him explain.'

Amma was trying to prop up her argument with bits of Appa's logic.

'No, Amma, you explain. Is it because she is Anglo-Indian?'

'Well, they *are* different, quite different from us.'

'*Is* it because she is Anglo-Indian?'

'Don't put words into my mouth, Padhu.'

'If you admitted your prejudices, Amma, you would at least see them for what they are.'

'Prejudice-shredjudice! I have nothing of that sort. We are talking about compatibility here. Would you marry a Negro?'

'Black, Amma, black. They are called blacks now.'

'Yes, yes, black Negro.'

'No, not Negro. Just black.'

'But that is an insult! Why would you address a person by their colour? What are Indians called?'

'Coloured.'

'See Padhu, *that* is prejudice. The Negroes are called blacks and the whites are called whites and we, we are called coloured. Has anyone ever called you coloured? With your colouring – I mean you are so fair . . . nearly white.'

I'll have to leave it for another day, thought Padhman, wondering how his battle for principles had disintegrated into a farce.

Later that morning, he met an agitated Manoharan at the Post-Graduate Centre.

'Bloody white bastards! Did you notice those two? Those two – there, just walking past that Portakabin. They called me a "Bloody Paki". Do I *look* like a Muslim? Come on, tell me – do I?'

'Did you say anything back to them?'

'Not worth it. They'll always be ignorant bastards.' Manoharan kicked a small stone in the direction of the receding figures but, when he turned towards Padhman again, it was with a knowing grin.

'Heard you had a busy weekend. You're a sly fellow, Pads.'

Before Padhman could say anything, Manoharan slapped him on his shoulders, confessing that his source was none other than Maura.

'Niall and Aoife's brother play rugby together,' he added in further explanation. Another slap on the shoulder was followed by more questioning and some advice.

'Did you meet her father, the Professor? She took you horse-riding, I heard. Have you taken her to the Taj Tandoori? It always does the trick with Irish girls. A good restaurant, some exotic food, a bottle of wine and decent guys like us, and they quickly stop moaning about all their migrating men. Just remember, don't split the bill and *don't* worry about the garlic.' Manoharan winked as he revealed, 'There is a bowl full of mints at the cashier's.'

Padhman nodded uncomfortably, unable to think of anything appropriate to reply and as he beat a hasty retreat into the library, Manoharan grabbed him by the arm. 'They sometimes like to go out in pairs,' he confided. 'The Imperial Szechwan is good too. I'll tell you the next time Deirdre and me are going.' And then with a final, 'OK, see you,' he turned and walked off, neatening his well-oiled hair with a little stainless steel comb that he pulled out of his pocket.

Once inside the library in the Post-Graduate Centre, Padhman found the sight of Sunil sitting with his head buried in his books, totally off-putting. People haven't stopped hassling me all day, he thought as he tapped Sunil on the shoulder.

'The long-lost friend! Renu was going to send out a search-party tonight.'

'If that's an invitation, I'll come over for dinner.'

142

'It wasn't exactly, but we are dying to hear the uncut version so you are allowed to invite yourself.'

'Renu's waiting to grill me, is she? How did you guys find out? I was going to come across this evening and tell you about Aoife anyway.'

'Listen, Pads, instead of telling us about her, why don't you bring her along?'

'For dinner – on a Monday? Do you want to check with Renu first?'

'Is Aoife on call tonight? Are you?'

Padhman shook his head. 'Aoife's on call Wednesday and the weekend. I'm on Tuesday and Friday. What about you?'

'It will have to be this evening. I'm off today and then it's Tuesday and Friday on call just like you.'

Padhman was looking forward to introducing Aoife to Sunil and Renu, and so he was a bit taken aback when she greeted the idea with a less than enthusiastic, 'Do we have to?'

He watched her push the food around on her plate.

'Don't you want to eat it?' He was suddenly irritated with her. Hadn't she told him last week that she couldn't wait to meet his friends?

'Friends since conception.' She had laughed when he told her the story. 'It gives a whole new meaning to life-long. Is his wife nice? Tell me their names again.'

She had practised saying their names, even getting Padhman to write them down, but now she seemed more interested in creating random hollows in the mashed potato on her plate. Her reaction hardly seemed fair after his efforts with her family over the weekend. He was unsure of what he wanted to say to her. The canteen was nearly empty and the sight of two cleaners, who had started their table-wiping and chair-stacking routine at the far end of the room, distracted him for a few seconds.

143

It jogged a memory that already seemed so distant. Look at me! Three months on and here I am, grabbing a few minutes and a hurried lunch with a girlfriend who isn't behaving as she ought to. Or at least as I think she ought to.

When he turned back to the table and looked at Aoife, she seemed close to tears. His spirits lifted immediately. This was nothing to do with him. I should have known it, he thought as he mentally rapped himself on his knuckles.

He nudged her knee with his. 'The bitch has been hassling you again, hasn't she? Why don't you tell the SR, for God's sake? Aoif, are you listening to me?'

She nodded her head still looking down at the topography on her plate. She then looked up at him and shook her head. 'No, it wasn't Sister. She's off work this week. Having her veins done, can you believe it? She actually does have blood coursing though her body, the heartless bitch.'

Padhman sneaked a look at his watch. It didn't go unnoticed.

'I could go on about my miserable morning if you had the time. Larkin humiliated me in theatre again. "And why would you want to be a surgeon, Miss Gorman? Did the nuns in school tell you your needlework was good?" And when he looked up, every single person in theatre laughed. On cue, the whole bloody lot of them. And not one had the balls to look me in the eye.'

Padhman empathised with the way she felt. He also knew this was not a profession for the weak-stomached, the faint-hearted or the sensitive-souled. Not in dealings with one's colleagues anyway. He was about to soothe her feathers when she slowly broke into a smile.

'I told him the nuns had taught me how to avoid pricks. Oh Padhman, the silence was priceless! He laughed . . . eventually, much to everyone else's relief. He'll think twice before he messes with me again.'

'He'll think thrice before he gives you a reference.'

'I know.'

Despite that realisation, reliving that fleeting moment of eloquent revenge seemed to have cheered her up. Padhman hesitated. He knew better than to encourage her. Audacity wasn't on the list of virtues for a young intern. He would have to say it to her sometime. Sometime soon, but not right now. Right now, she had perked up and was asking him whether she ought to get something for Renu.

'Flowers or chocolates?'

'Chocolates,' he replied without hesitation. The last thing he wanted this evening was to get Renu into a huff. He hadn't forgotten that the last bunch of flowers he had so cheerfully bought for her had effectively brought the evening to a silent and grinding halt. He had watched, with amusement, as she turned to Sunil with her nose buried vainly in the scentless hybrids, with a plaintive, 'You never buy me flowers.' Amusement turned to discomfort when Sunil blundered with a, 'You never asked me to.' And to compound matters when she looked up, her eyebrows raised, Sunil had shrugged in reply. Padhman had watched from the sidelines, occasionally stepping in to do some refereeing during the week of domestic disharmony that followed in the Patel household.

'Yes, get her a box of liqueur chocolates. Or chocolates with nuts,' he said to Aoife. Padhman was not about to risk another big bust-up.

CHAPTER FIFTEEN

~

PADHMAN WATCHED THE six dried red chillies that he
had counted and thrown into the pan, splutter in the hot
oil, whizzing around this way and that, like little jet-
propelled torpedoes that were out of control. When the
phone rang he took the pan off the hob and crossed the
kitchen to answer it. It was Amma and she sounded upset.
Padhman listened to her for a while, a sense of helpless
gloom settling into the pit of his stomach.

Despite having been a model doctor, Grandfather had
always been a difficult patient, and increasingly over the
years – and more so in the three years since he had turned
eighty – had become unreasonable and irritable when it
came to medicines and hospitalisation. He was notorious
for random self-medication, insisting on reading his case
notes, repeatedly asking the doctors the same three or four
questions and making alterations to the prescriptions and
doses, and even disputing diagnoses. In any other patient
it would never have been tolerated but in Grandfather, his
doctors, many of whom had been his students, first saw
their old Professor, much respected and nearly venerated,
and only then considered him for what he was: an old man
fighting a hopeless battle against age. It was a cruel thing
to happen to Grandfather, he who had always declared he
would rather die than become senile. And look at us,
thought Padhman, here we are doing our very best to
keep him going, making sure his senility is total and
complete.

What of Appa? he asked his mother. Amma prefaced

her reply with a long silence. Padhman knew what she was thinking. She had said it many times to him. 'Every father should have a son like your father and every son should have a father like yours.' It was only in his early teens that Padhman had been able to work out the simple message behind what had initially been a mere tongue-twister, that Amma would throw at him whenever she was either happy with Appa or annoyed with Padhman.

But Padhman was taken aback by her reply. 'Padhu, Appa has become so short-tempered – no, no, not short-tempered . . . impatient. Not with me, but with Grandfather. Sometimes I wish they would both forget they are doctors.'

Padhman sensed a lifetime's frustration in what his mother had just said. He had once heard her explaining to her friend Nimmi what it was like being a doctor's wife. 'It's like marrying someone, knowing well that he has a demanding mistress, only to find out that *you* are expected to pander to her every demand too.'

'And you let me become one?' Padhman had spoken his mind even before he knew it.

'You always wanted to be a doctor, Padhu. Nothing would have stopped you.' Then, as if she in turn had sensed something amiss, she became all concerned.

'Are you finding it difficult on your own, son? Working so hard and then having to study and to cook and clean as well? We worry about you a lot. Are you studying? The Part One is only four months away.'

Padhman was able to answer in the affirmative and it felt good to be able to do so. He had spent every spare minute of the past week studying earnestly and he did feel that he was back on track for the exams. He owed the renewed vigour for his books to Renu, who had rather bluntly pointed out the obvious link between studying, passing the exams, getting the next job and then the next exam.

'I'll tell Appa that when I go to see Grandfather in the hospital. He has been a bit anxious about you. All those diversions . . .'

'Amma—'

She interrupted him quickly. 'Padhu, I don't want to have an argument with you right now, but we can't help how we feel. Girls like that are a diversion.'

'Not if one is serious about them.'

He could hear Amma drawing in her breath and wished he hadn't said something so provocative – especially when there was no basis to it. Why in God's name did he have this inexplicable instinct to fly the flag for Annie?

He was mentally exhausted when he finally put the phone down. At the back of his mind, even as he was establishing another truce with his mother, promising to call in the morning to get an update on Grandfather, he wondered how he was going to break the news about Aoife to Amma and Appa.

When Aoife arrived twenty minutes later, she sniffed the air appreciatively. 'Basmati rice and dal! I'm going to eat with my fingers tonight. Are Renu and Sunil joining us?'

Padhman pulled her close as she took off her coat. 'You smell delicious too.'

'Oh, Padhman, that's so terribly unoriginal. But you get points for trying,' she teased, as she walked slowly up the stairs, stripping and flinging her clothes onto Padhman as he followed behind.

'They'll be here in half an hour.' His voice was muffled by her skirt, which had landed on his face. He goose-stepped with his arms stretched out stiffly, Frankenstein fashion, to the edge of the bed.

148

'We . . . have . . . half . . . an . . . hour,' he said, his voice staccato, his fingers wriggling above her.

Padhman watched Aoife lick her fingers clean of the dal and rice.

'Renu,' he said accusingly, 'you've known her for three weeks and already you have turned her into a junglee.'

'Come on – I haven't yet taught her how to do it with the sound effects.'

'What sound effects?' Aoife had stopped to serve herself again. Where does she put it all away, Padhman wondered, pushing the bowl of fried chicken that Renu had brought towards her.

'Finish that, Aoif, the rest of us are all done. There is a neckpiece and a wing, I think. Don't waste the masala.' Padhman leaned forward and scraped the gravy from the bowl onto her plate.

'The slightly burnty bits are the best,' advised Sunil, scraping back his chair and dutifully heading for the sink.

'Padhman is trying to fatten me up.' Aoife's fingers deftly mixed the chicken gravy into the rice and dal. Padhman watched fascinated, as she picked out the red chillies from the dal and kept them safely on the outer edge of her plate. She had got the hang of it so easily, he thought appreciatively, and all of it was for him, for his sake.

'You didn't answer me, Renu. What sound effects?' Aoife was licking her fingers again.

'Oh, it's a South Indian tradition.' Renu was looking at Padhman and grinning.

'What's the joke? Am I having my leg pulled?'

'Not you, Aoif, Renu's trying to be funny with me. These North Indians have this superiority complex, you see . . .'

But Renu was not to be baited. She had served herself

149

again, a tiny bit of rice and a huge amount of dal and ate in between holding her sides and laughing as she proceeded to graphically demonstrate what she gleefully called the Southie Slurp.

'You gather it up like this, making sure your entire palm is a cup . . . see Aoife? Ignore what I told you earlier about using only the tips of your fingers. Now if you are ready, start slurping the bits that have dribbled down your wrist, and move upwards toward the scooped up portion, slurping loudly as you go along. Yes, that's it. Get your tongue to work in one long motion from the wrist to the tips of your fingers. Shall we have another go?'

Padhman watched as Aoife copied Renu expertly. The two women giggled and lapped at their hands alternately, Renu occasionally exaggerating a manoeuvre to hilarious response from Aoife. Padhman had to smile for a different reason: he had never imagined that it would take a messy scene like this to convince him that he had finally found his soulmate.

Sunil walked back from the sink and stood behind Padhman sharing the spectacle with him.

'Bastard, your Amma is really going to love her.' Sunil poked him with a yellow rubber-gloved finger. 'A little bit of coconut oil on her hair and she will be any South Indian mother-in-law's dream.'

Renu looked up from the table. 'Don't mutter, Sunil. If you have something to say about us women, say it aloud.'

'He is as bad as you, Renu. A Narad muni to the core.' Padhman knew he was going to have to face up to telling Appa and Amma about Aoife. This was the second time in the same evening that he had been reminded of the task that lay ahead.

'What's a Na . . . Narad muni?'

'Do you really want to know, Aoif? Narad muni was a man – he was also was what you Irish would call a shit-stirrer.'

'A fatwa on you, Pads! He was a saint! He was a shit-stirrer only in his official capacity.' Renu, who had started clearing the table, wagged the pickle spoon at him. It sent tiny flecks of oil onto the table, which she dabbed at with tissue that had been placed next to Aoife, to assist in the event of the meal being too spicy.

'He stirred shit for the greater good. That was his mission. And mine.' Sunil turned around from the sink where he had started washing up and looked at Padhman pointedly. That makes it three times in one evening, thought Padhman.

'What are you lot on about? Was this man for real?' Aoife looked mystified.

'It's Hindu mythology. I suppose Narad muni is as real as Noah and his Ark. Beyond that, I'm no expert.' Padhman shrugged his shoulders and looked at Renu. Maybe she would know.

'It's a convenient religion, Aoife. Details don't matter when the one basic is so simple: what goes around comes around.'

'Rubbish, Renu! That doesn't make it a convenient religion. That's just your own convenient way of looking at the religion,' said Sunil. He had nearly finished washing up.

'Exactly! That's exactly what makes the religion so convenient. You can look at it, approach it and practise it any way you please. And whether you treat it merely as a way of life or go the whole hog with all the rituals, no one can question your Hindu credentials.'

'*Jai Hind*!' said Padhman, laughing at Renu's earnestness. 'Victory to India!'

'*Jai* Renu!' said Sunil, who had removed his rubber

gloves and headed towards Padhman, palms in the air for a high five.

But later, Renu had the last word as she switched the kettle on to make coffee. 'Aoife, see these westernised Hindu liberals? Come the exams or the next job interview, they'll be the first ones on the phones to their mothers asking for ghee lamps to be lit and special prayers to be performed. You see, they access their religion on a need-to basis. It is, as I said earlier, terribly convenient.'

CHAPTER SIXTEEN

~

ONE LOOK AT Sunil's face and Padhman knew it was bad news. Bad news from India. The way Maura took him by the elbow as he came out of the examination cubicle and gently pushed him towards the nurses' station, told Padhman that the bad news was for him.

'Pads . . . it's your grandfather. My mother called. Your parents were with him . . . he died at home, just half an hour ago.' Sunil's eyes were brimming.

Padhman swallowed. I hope Grandfather got my letter, he thought. He should have got it. He must have read it. He must have seen the three photographs. His hands would have been unsteady but he would have read every line, examined every detail.

Thoughts ricocheted in his head as he, strangely enough, found himself consoling Sunil. In the background, he could hear Maura filling Micheal in with the news. A couple of nurses looked up from whatever they were doing. Someone patted him on his back. One of the nurses came and put her arms around Sunil. The other nurses shook their heads frantically.

'It was *my* grandfather,' said Padhman, feeling sorry for her. She was going to get crucified by her mates. Later at the pub, they would all probably get drunk, recounting her mortification again and again. Micheal was on the phone and he smiled grimly at Padhman while he spoke, flicking through the desk calendar, nodding his head several times, looking at his watch and then finally putting the phone down.

'Padhman, that was Morris. I've let him know about your grandfather. It's OK by him if you want to go to India. Will you be able to make it for the funeral?'

Padhman thanked him politely. He felt completely empty. In fact, he wished he could just go back to the cubicle and wait for Maura to send in the next patient.

The phone did not stop ringing when he got home. He accepted condolences, went into unnecessary details about his flight timings and agreed with everyone who called that, yes, this was indeed the most difficult part of living away from home. Everything seemed a bit unreal and he felt he was tearlessly play-acting the role of the bereaved grandson. He sat on the edge of his bed and stared in a desultory fashion at the things he had put into the small holdall at his feet. He had had no idea so many people in Dublin knew him. Or would be bothered.

It was when Aoife arrived that he broke down. She stood on her tiptoes, trying literally to give him her shoulder to cry on. She helped him up the stairs where he cried once more and briefly in a childlike fashion, before curling up into a ball on the bed.

'Cover me, I'm cold,' he said, not looking at her.

She slipped off her shoes and got into bed, pulling the duvet over both of them. They lay like that, a pair of spoons for what seemed an eternity. Padhman dwelt on the sadness that he knew was yet to come. And he wasn't even thinking about what lay ahead in the week that he was going to spend in Madras. It was the irreversibility of the loss that gripped him. I won't miss Grandfather on an everyday basis, he thought. I didn't in these months that I have been here in Ireland. But I'll never ever, ever see him again. Never ever. As obvious as that was, it was difficult to accept and Padhman pushed his face into the pillow. He thought about his father. The emotions must be different for Appa, more intense, more painful. I wonder what state I would be in if it was Appa who had died. I suppose I would have Amma to worry about. She would go to pieces if anything happened to him. If Amma went first there was no telling what would happen to Appa. It all lies ahead, thought Padhman morbidly. He shuddered involuntarily and felt Aoife stiffen, momentarily, in response.

He pushed back into her and she pushed forward against him. Can you ever really share someone's sadness, he wondered. You could only share their sorrow if you had also shared their memories, if you had shared their regrets.

She startled him when she spoke, for it was as if she had read his mind.

'I never knew your grandfather, Padhman, but I think I know how you must feel. I only have to think of not having Nana around. It all lies ahead . . . it's scary.'

Padhman turned around to hug her and they drifted into sleep, hers deadened by thirty-six hours on call, and his crammed with a million memories of growing up with Grandfather, Appa and Amma.

The sea reflected the strong mid-morning sun, the waves catching the light and blinding those who ventured to look at the horizon. Padhman had his arm around his father's shoulders as they waded into the water. The waves, which had receded as they took their first bare-footed steps onto the wet sand, were merely gathering force and came rushing towards them, the surf rising up to Padhman's knees within a few seconds. The sea was very cold, and took him completely by surprise. The water hung around for a minute or so before rolling back again, under itself, pulling back the very sand on which they were trying to steady themselves. They walked in a little further and this time when the waves returned they had to brace themselves sideways, standing awkwardly with their legs wide apart. As the surf continued to race for the shore, calmer waters milled around them and Appa took a step forward. He bent down from the waist and broke open the earthen pot that he had carried this far. Then without any ceremony Grandfather's ashes swirled into the sea, colouring the tiny eddies around them grey, circling and surrounding first Appa and then Padhman, remaining on the surface for a few seconds more before being dragged swiftly back into the depths by the immense body of water that was the Bay of Bengal.

As they waded back to shore, holding on to each other, Appa seemed momentarily a diminished man. If there was ever a ritual designed to bring home the absolute finality of death this one was it, thought Padhman. He said it to Appa and Amma as he lay across the foot of their bed late that night. Appa nodded his head. Amma, who had her eyes closed till then, opened them and, patting her pillow, signalled Padhman to come up and lie between them. There, lying between his father and mother, a comfort that he hadn't indulged in since he had left school, he began telling them about his life in Ireland.

'No Padhu, don't tell us about the hospital,' his mother said fondly. 'Start at the beginning. Who came to pick you up at the airport?'

Padhman looked at Amma. She knew very well who had come to collect him at the airport. She had asked him that question in the very first phone call he had made to Madras, the morning that he had arrived in Dublin. And even *then*, she had known who had picked him up. But it would be from answers to questions like that, that Amma would assimilate her store of related information. The first time around, that question had revealed that Renu hadn't got a driving licence yet, and that Sunil and Renu had sensibly not spent too much on their first car. Amma was not one for abridged versions of anything.

'Amma . . .' Padhman was about to tell her that they would be there the whole night if he had to repeat details that she already knew, when she interrupted him.

'Had she made a nice dinner? You know, Renu. Had she made a nice dinner for you?'

Padhman sighed inwardly. He knew the finer points were important to his mother and tonight he decided he was going to humour her. Padhman held Amma's interest as he meandered slowly through his daily routine describing the hospital, his house, his efforts at cooking and his work. His father stopped him occasionally, sometimes pointing out how much things had changed since he had done his stint as a junior doctor in Glasgow, and sometimes, concluding with a laugh that things had obviously remained the same.

'Oh, the Ward Sister held the keys to the kingdom even in those days.'

'Did you ever travel to Ireland . . . to Dublin from Glasgow, Appa?' Padhman was suddenly curious.

His father shook his head. 'But we will now. Now that we have a house, a car and a chauffeur waiting for us in Dublin.'

Amma laughed and agreed. 'We'll have to make a trip, have a holiday before you return to Madras, before you come back home.'

His parents went silent for a while and Padhman knew what they were thinking. They had suddenly, overnight, found themselves in 'after Grandfather's time' time. From here on, duty no longer would call the shots. Padhman knew that Appa and Amma had never begrudged Grandfather for the increased restrictions that his dwindling faculties had placed on them and yet, thinking about his parents' lives in the last few years, Padhman realised that his grandfather was a lucky man. Not only had he died at about the time he would have wanted, but he died well before those around him had started waiting for him to do so.

Appa and Amma had drifted into a somnolent silence, both worn out from the emotions of the day, and yet Padhman sensed that they wanted to stay awake, sharing the same space with their son. After what he now realised must have been six very long months, he was once again close enough for them to see, to touch and to hear. It was as if they wanted to get their fill of him, before he returned to Dublin. However, feigning tiredness, Padhman wished them goodnight, telling them that they needed the sleep too.

'I missed you, my son.' Amma held his face in her hands and kissed him on his forehead. 'Put on the air-conditioner if you want.' Then, as he turned to leave their room, she held his arm for a brief moment. 'Padhu . . . we can't wait till you come back.' Appa, who had his eyes closed, smiled contentedly.

Padhman felt like a guest in his old bedroom. A man in a boy's room, he thought. Six salary slips and having a woman in my life has changed me. He marvelled at the change. This wasn't a woman in his life Indian-style. This was for real. This was a woman in his life, the lover in his bed. By the time Padhman got into bed, he found himself assessing his whole life in Ireland, in terms of what Amma had said. Within a few minutes, his self-assurance had been replaced by utter confusion.

Am I going to come back to Madras? To show any doubt was so heretical that he dismissed it straight away. But he found that, within minutes, he was asking himself that question again. Behind it lay the fundamental one: what about Aoife? What about Aoife, and would she come to Madras with him? She was aware that Madras was

158

the likeliest option for him once he had passed his exams. Why, she herself, not too long back, had told him that he would never understand the pressures on Irish trainees because, after he passed his exams, he only had to step as far as his father's shoes to find his feet. Padhman began to seriously wonder if she would marry him, knowing he was going to return to India. If she did, would he bring her to Madras, where she would be a total misfit? Could he do that to her? It struck him then that the reverse would not be true.

It was easy to assimilate into a lifestyle if, in your growing years all you did was imitate it to the best of your ability and, in India, to the extent your parents would tolerate. Westernised families loved to be seen as cosmopolitan, until cosmopolitan problems arose in their own backyards. Padhman knew how quickly they could call upon their Indian identity then to extricate themselves and their children from the unsuitability of a situation.

But those near-philosophical thoughts were only a temporary respite from the morass of conflicting feelings that Padhman found himself floundering in. How could he ask her or expect her to come and live in Madras, she who loved crisp cold mornings! He dwelt briefly on the fact that he was going to have to tell Appa and Amma about her. There was no question in his mind, however, that this was not the appropriate time. Right now, he wondered whether Aoife would expect him to break loose from India, leave Appa and Amma and live in Ireland? She wouldn't – she couldn't. He would be reduced to remaining 'that foreigner' for the rest of his life! It would be easier for her in India. People were nice to white foreigners. Indians were prone to fawning over velais, though privately, they would always wonder if Padhman had converted her from toilet paper to water and soap.

Padhman pulled the thin cotton sheet over himself.

The air conditioner had cooled the room down very quickly. He wondered if Aoife had thought about the dilemma that surely lay ahead. Come to think of it, it was amazing that they had never discussed it with each other. The sub-conscious was a powerful thing, keeping at bay those all-important, but horribly difficult questions in a relationship. Maybe marriage hadn't even crossed her mind. She had never suggested living with him or ever asked him to live with her. They just very naturally floated between each of their houses, staying over as it suited them.

Padhman turned over, trying to sleep on his side. I wouldn't move in with her anyway, he thought. Not with the Professor and Millie Gorman staying right above. The day he discovered that Aoife's apartment was just the converted basement of her parents' home, that they lived directly above, towering three floors over their daughter, over their daughter *and him*, he had balked. Aoife was amused. They wouldn't be bothered, she had promised him, but he wasn't too sure. In the early days, if he knew that he was going to stay the night, he would try to engineer lifts with Aoife, leaving the Celica at the hospital, or he'd get her to pick him up from home, just so that his car wouldn't be visible, parked in their gravel drive, evidence of him having stayed overnight. Of course, it was all a sham: he knew that they knew. As Padhman propped himself up on his elbow to plump up his pillows, he thought about the chasmic differences in cultures. If the situation was reversed, he couldn't quite see Amma and Appa calling Aoife and him up for an occasional drink. In fact, he was sure that Amma, if she knew about it, would have an opinion about Professor Gorman and his wife as well.

Padhman swore loudly as he turned onto his back again. All this thinking was getting him nowhere, he thought despairingly. He looked past his desk to the window, through which he could see shadows of the enormous gulmohar tree, cast in a ghostly fashion across the walls. Grandmother had planted that tree. Padhman knew the details by rote: it was only two feet high when she planted it. It had been eaten up, nearly completely, by stray goats. It had been watered four times a day for the first three years and it first flowered when it was still a sapling, barely five feet high. What else had Grandfather told him about that tree? Padhman tried hard to remember, but was distracted by a return to his earlier thoughts. He couldn't shake off an overwhelming feeling of anxiety about the future.

Aoife should have met Grandfather. If only she had. Grandfather who, as he grew older, would give his opinion only if asked. And a singular opinion it almost always was, one that his old patients and colleagues, ex-students and family were well familiar with, one that doubled up as his advice on most things: Sort out the basics and you'll get a clearer picture. Padhman repeated it to himself, sentimentally assuming Grandfather's matter-of-fact, measured tone. 'Sort out the basics, Padhu, and you'll get a clearer picture.'

Padhman sat up and switched on the bedside lights and pulled the phone closer. Sort out the basics, that's what I'll do. He picked up the phone and dialled. If he was lucky, she wouldn't have left for the hospital as yet. His heart was in his mouth as he heard the distant ring.

He woke with the distinct feeling that there was someone in the room. He was frozen stiff, colder than he had ever been in a bed in Ireland. He pretended he was still asleep, just stirring. He was quite sure it was Amma.

'Padhu, shall I turn off the air conditioner?' Only Amma would have sensed that he was awake . . . barely awake, which was why she was whispering. If I know my mother, she knows me twice as well. Except she doesn't know about last night. She will know soon, because I am going to have to tell her. Her and Appa. But not yet . . . not yet. We are in too sad a time. I'll just have to wait till they feel better and then I'll . . . shit! I'll send them into mourning again.

This was not the way Padhman thought he would wake up. This was the morning after the night before. Sort out the basics and things will get clearer. I did it just the way you would have wanted me to do it, Grandfather. If Amma would only go away, I could go back to sleep and wake up a second time round, start over again. He knew he was thinking irrationally, for he was hopelessly wide-awake now and the night before was coming back to him.

Asking Aoife if she would marry him was not, on the face of it, the most rational way of sorting things out. But as he said to her, he was asking her *if* she would marry him. The big *if.* If she would marry him, that was the basics done and dusted. If he knew that, then he could get on with the telling, the sorting out, the coming to terms with.

'Asking me to marry you or asking me *if I will* marry you . . . Padhman, the only difference is in the tense.'

'Humour me, Aoif. There *is* a difference. This is my way of sorting it out.'

'Sorting what out?'

He hesitated before he started, struggling desperately to explain to her what he thought would be their shared, unsolvable dilemma. She listened quietly as he told her what he thought lay ahead for them. 'Which of us is going to give up everything for the other? You see, Aoif, if I knew that you would marry me and if you knew that I wanted to marry you, we would have the basics sorted out. Then we could tackle all the awkward bits . . . face the questions. One of us will have to give up a lot – everything – for the other.'

'You mean if we tried to sort out the awkward bits first, we'd never marry each other?'

'Yes.'

'You're inviting me to jump in first and then learn how to swim?'

'I'm asking you if you'll marry me.'

'I will.'

'It'll work out, Aoif.'

'I know.'

They listened to each other breathe. It was a comfortable feeling, like having their arms around each other.

'I'll teach you how to ride elephants and levitate.'

'I'll teach you to fiddle, while driving a donkey and cart.'

Then they had both laughed, euphoric and delighted with themselves. But just as quickly and suddenly, they were both mindful of the time, she panicking about being dangerously late for Larkin's ward round, and he wondering what this half-hour inter-continental phone call was going to cost.

He was almost literally shaken out of his reverie by the air-conditioner, which gave an almighty spasmodic shudder as Amma switched it off.

'Open the veranda doors as well, Amma, please.'

'I thought as much,' said Amma as she drew the curtains and unlocked the double doors to the terracotta-tiled veranda. 'You looked cold.' But as she stepped back into the room, having folded the hinged doors back as far as they would go, she was surprised, concerned.

'No wonder you were cold, Padhu. Why didn't you wear your pyjamas? You could have taken one of your old pairs or borrowed some from Appa.'

'It wasn't cold to start with,' said Padhman, laughing.

And I can't really tell you this, Amma, he thought, but I've got used to sleeping naked. As Amma marched into the walk-in wardrobe, he pulled on the pair of jeans that he had carelessly flung on the chair and walked out onto the veranda. He stretched, facing into the intense heat that lay beyond the shade. Within minutes, the fiery breeze had washed over him and he could feel his bare feet hotting up uncomfortably on the terracotta. Amma stayed inside the room, watching him. Can she see the change in me, he wondered. He smiled at her as he walked back in and gave her a hug. She tried to push him away affectionately.

'You haven't changed, Padhu. Brush your teeth first.'

'You haven't changed either, Amma.' Padhman shook his head in mock exasperation. He headed for the bathroom. 'Has Appa woken? What is the time?'

Padhman was galvanised into action when Amma informed him that it was nearly noon. Sunil's parents were expecting him for lunch and by Amma's account, at least four sets of visitors had already been to the house to pay their condolences. As he showered, he was grateful to his mother for not having woken him up.

'Appa told them that you were jet-lagged,' she said, fetching him his towel from where it was drying on the veranda. 'I wanted you to have a good rest,' she added as she left his room, closing the door behind her.

Half an hour later, showered and ready to leave, he wandered around the house and finally found Appa and Amma in Grandfather's bedroom. They sat on Grandfather's bed, their backs to Padhman, looking out of the window, out over the courtyard. They had their arms around each other and Padhman was sure that Amma was crying. How did they end up so close, he wondered. They had only met thrice before they married. He stood at the door, nearly holding his breath, wondering if he should

164

back away from what was definitely a deeply personal moment, when Amma turned around, her eyes red and her lips pursed. Before he knew it, Padhman found himself crying, crying bitterly, as Appa and Amma hushed him, both of them stroking his hair and holding him close.

Distance can warp your judgement, smother your emotions with logic and make you temporarily so detached, thought Padhman, becoming conscious of Appa's hands holding his shoulders gently. Whatever made me think I wouldn't miss Grandfather? He stayed like that for a while, slumped in his parents' embrace, the three of them in a room full of memories.

Today I will go back. Go back to my other life. That's what it would feel like. A foreign world. Not as in abroad, but as in different, totally different. How long would it be before *this* life, his Indian life, became the foreign part of his world? Padhman sat alone at the dining table. Appa had started back at the clinic, seeing patients for the first time after the funeral. Amma had just left the house. She was going to Nilgiris and then onwards to Grand Sweets. Grand Sweets. That's a grand name, he thought smiling and then – I haven't forgotten my Irish and that's grand too.

The cook and the maid fussed around him, plying him with crisp dosais and hot idilis. He ate slowly, savouring the traditional breakfast and the fact that when he was finished he just had to push the chair back and walk away. In the last few days he had found it impossible to do, see or feel anything without immediately assessing it on the sacrifice scale. The coffee when it arrived, on the veranda where he had moved to after the seventh and final dosai, was just the way he liked it, strong and robustly aromatic. The beans had been freshly roasted only that morning and ground barely an hour ago.

Tomorrow, I'll make my own breakfast and clean my own bathroom. Tomorrow, I'll work through lunch and I'll come home too knackered to study and yet I will. Tomorrow, I'll lie naked with Aoife late into the night and start telling her about this, my other world . . .

It was the flies that woke him. Flies buzzing around his mouth and around the lip of the empty mug of coffee that sat on his lap, held upright by a single finger and thumb that had somehow stayed in place, even as he had dozed off. He shuddered as he swept them away with an annoyed flick of his wrist. Through the bougainvillaea-covered garden screen that gave the family near-complete privacy from the passing parade of patients, many of whom suffered from incurable curiosity, and that also gave the house a modicum of protection from the relentless sun, Padhman could see that Appa was having a busy morning.

He walked across the lawn, through the little gate and then across the courtyard into the clinic. The ayahs were delighted to see him and they beamed at the patients as they escorted him in a guard of honour fashion to Miss Angela's successor, Miss Angela's sister's daughter-in-law, Miss Edina Rose. Miss Edina stood up to greet him. As Padhman enquired about Miss Angela, who was now bedridden and had been unable to attend Grandfather's funeral, he was aware of an audible buzz sweeping through the packed waiting room. Patients craned their necks to have a good look at him, while the ayahs unashamedly divulged all they knew. He was the foreign-returned, foreign-qualified grandson and son. The heir to the reputation that had drawn them all here, from far and wide. Will I ever be worthy of this sort of awe, Padhman fretted. I don't even have one exam as yet, he thought, as he only half-listened to Miss Edina. She seemed to be repeating something to him.

'Doctor Sir said to send you in if you came.'

A grateful Padhman headed for Appa's door. As he did so he felt compelled by politeness to acknowledge the sea of faces. They seemed to be smiling encouragingly, some heads nodded approvingly. Go on, they seemed to be saying, go on right in. A son's place is by his father. They had no doubt that it was only right and proper.

Padhman knocked and then entered. Appa was writing a prescription and didn't look up. He just nodded and spoke.

'This is my son,' he said to the patient and her family. 'The next generation . . .'

Upon hearing this, the pregnant lady, her husband and her two elderly female relations immediately stood up, the husband wasting no time in offering his chair to Padhman. The latter went through the motions of refusing and quickly retreated behind Appa's desk. But as Appa handed the prescription to the pregnant lady, her husband picked up his chair and came around to where Padhman stood. Placing the chair next to Appa's, he insisted on seeing Padhman seated, before he ushered his wife and family out of the door. At the door, he turned to look back at his handiwork and, satisfied that Padhman remained where he had been positioned, followed his wife out.

Appa looked at Padhman and chuckled. 'Don't look so worried. You won't always have to sit under my nose. You know that Grandfather's room is yours, when you return.' He buzzed for Miss Edina to send in the next patient. 'That's what he wanted, Padhu.'

Not you as well, Appa, thought Padhman. 'Could be some time away, Appa. I haven't even sat for my Part One yet.'

'Hmmm. Tough exam, very tough – but you will get it, my son. Just ignore all that nonsense about luck. It's

167

not luck as much as single-mindedness. Determination. A sense of purpose.' Appa was looking at him straight in the eye. 'Remember what you went for and you'll have the exams before you know it.'

Has my father been talking to Millie Gorman? A bit disconcerted, Padhman sat quietly through the next consultation. Appa normally never lectured, and when he did, he tended to stick to advice about the broader picture, as he was doing now. It was almost as if he had sensed that Padhman had been side-tracked. Padhman had always been receptive to his father's advice. Suddenly filled with self-doubt, he wondered if he had got it all wrong. Maybe this was the basic that he needed to sort out. He should concentrate on getting through his exams and then the picture with Aoife, India and Ireland would be clearer. Aoife will marry me. That's over and done with, he reasoned. I just need to get my exams now. That's the next basic that I have to sort out. Sometimes, Padhman found that just stating the obvious helped.

He stayed on with Appa till the last patient left, and then they walked back to the house together. Amma was waiting with Sunil's parents at the dining table. Padhman sat, as instructed, between Nimmi and Raja Patel. Amma called out to the cook to serve the lunch and then, turning her attention back to her son, she pushed a platter piled high towards him. Poppadams! Studded with cracked pepper and shavings of garlic, they glistened from having been deep-fried. Look at me, like a velai I'm calling them poppadoms instead of appalams! Padhman was surprised by himself. He even felt a twinge of guilt. Nimmi Patel, who had waited a decent few seconds, nudged a silver bowl with three leaf-shaped sections towards Padhman. It didn't escape Amma, but she waited till Appa had finished telling her about the busy clinic that he had had, before she turned again to Padhman.

'Nimmi Aunty has brought you your favourite pickles, Padhu.'

On cue, Nimmi Patel eagerly elaborated. 'Stuffed red chilli, mixed vegetables and sweet mango . . .' she paused dramatically, waiting for Padhman to finish serving himself a spoonful of each, '. . . and, son, the kheema parathas are just being reheated.'

Amma looked impatiently towards the kitchen and then got up, pushing her chair back purposefully. Padhman watched as she headed for the kitchen, deftly tucking the end of her sari into her waist. Within minutes Amma was back at the table and the food began to arrive. The appams with their crisp lacy rims and soft tender centres were placed in front of Raja Patel. He beamed happily, knowing that the sweet coconut milk and the egg curry that were just being brought out of the kitchen would also be placed in front of him. It was a rare occasion that when the Patels were over, Raja Uncle would be denied his favourite appams and curry. Padhman reached towards the platter that his mother was holding out and tore a kheema paratha into half. The crumbly, spiced mince and herb stuffing spilled out of it and Padhman turned to Nimmi Patel apologetically.

'I'll start with half, Nimmi Aunty. Amma's made prawn kurma. And ghee rice. I'll have to keep some space for that.'

'And for the appam and egg curry too, if Raja will spare some.' Appa was looking at his friend as he ladled the egg curry into the centre of his appam. The crisp upturned edges softened and began to collapse as the appam absorbed the creamy gravy. Raja Uncle gave Amma an appreciative look before he began eating.

'Padhu, I asked the cook to make a little of the ginger-garlic chicken that you like. But have that on its own with the rice and spinach dal. Some paneer tikka is just

169

being fried as well and here, try the boondhi raita with the paratha.'

Man was always meant to eat with his fingers, Padhman decided. Anyone who had switched to cutlery had lost the feel for food. How else would you know that a really well-made paratha could be teased open to reveal many flaky layers, the inner ones soft and silky almost, while the outer ones were nearly crisp, flecked with brown spots where the paratha had been pressed down against the griddle? You couldn't appreciate the well-rounded ginger-garlic flavour of the slow fried masala unless you could hold a chicken piece in your fingers and nibble at the meat and suck the spicy gravy out of every groove and crevice in the bones. Cold metal couldn't mix rice and curry like deft fingers could, drawing in from the edge of the plate any number of accompaniments: tiny bits of pickle, stir-fried vegetables and thin slices of marinated, fried fish. Padhman tore a bite-sized piece of the stuffed paratha and pressed it down on the chilli pickle and then, pinching the paratha into a scoop, he picked up a good bit of the deliciously cool raita and deposited it in his mouth. Food on a plate needed to be felt. Fingers were essential . . . the ability to touch enhanced the taste, he concluded. Amma was pushing the bowl of ghee rice across towards him and beside him Nimmi Aunty stirred the prawn kurma, waiting in anticipation. Padhman served himself a couple of spoons of the rice and onto the fragrant mound, Nimmi Aunty poured the deliciously thick gravy, fussing over the prawns, discarding smaller ones and fishing with the ladle for the very large plump ones until Padhman asked her to stop.

'But this is ghar ka khana – home-made food, your mother's cooking. Eat up, for there is nothing like it to bring back memories of home.'

As he prepared a mouthful, expertly encasing a prawn

in the gravy and rice that he had mixed on his plate, Padhman realised that he was being fortified for the journey, nourished up until the next time he returned to Madras. Like a travel vaccination, this food and the tastes it would evoke was meant to make him immune to the unsuitable influences of western culture.

Nimmi Aunty sniffed a little into her lace-edged handkerchief.

'Your grandfather . . . When you and Sunil were children he loved to see you both eat well.'

Nimmi Patel hadn't heard enough about her son and now, having reminded herself of him once again, she questioned Padhman, starting where she had left off the day Padhman had lunched with them.

'So, have they said anything to you, son? Sunil and Renu . . . have they decided to start a family?'

'Exams first, Nimmi Aunty, and anyway they've only been married for ten months.'

'Exams, my foot! Tell us how many Irish lassies you have lined up for your Amma?' Raja Patel was looking at Amma and laughing.

'A Narad muni . . . as always,' said Appa, looking at Amma, smiling, cajoling her into sharing the joke.

Narad muni – like father, like son. Padhman was amused.

Amma did laugh, but her heart was not in it. The conversation moved on, but Padhman sensed that his mother was brooding. They were to leave for the airport in two hours' time and he realised it was going to be emotional, difficult. In a way he was thankful that the departure lounge was restricted to passengers only. It kept the goodbyes brief.

To Padhman's surprise, Appa decided to leave the driver behind and drive himself. Amma was unusually quiet and Appa looked at her pointedly once or twice, but she wouldn't respond. When they were in sight of the airport, she turned around and put out her hand to Padhman. He was holding Amma's hand in both of his, so he felt the tension in her as she spoke.

'The Ewart girl – Annie – is coming to Dublin again.' Amma was looking at him accusingly. So that was what had been eating her up since lunch. And he thought it was to do with him going away. Even as he laughed, Padhman knew it was not the right thing to have done.

'Nimmi mentioned it to me today. Prabha told her. So you are still—'

'Amma, I can't stop Annie from coming to Dublin! She must be coming for the Choir Festival.'

'So you *did* know about it.'

Appa had swung into the airport car park and was cruising around looking for an empty slot.

'Amma, she had mentioned it.'

'So this was planned.'

Appa's face was black as he parked the car. Padhman wasn't too sure who his father was annoyed with. They walked on either side of Padhman, in silence towards the departure lounge.

Padhman turned to face his parents at the security barrier. 'Amma,' he began, but she interrupted him.

'That girl is most unsuitable.'

It was that, calling Annie unsuitable – that was what made me lose it, thought Padhman later, as he watched the air hostesses coming around with the duty free. It wasn't the way he had planned to tell Appa and Amma, just throwing it at them, minutes before saying goodbye. When he had very curtly told Amma that he disagreed, that Annie was quite suitable, Padhman didn't anticipate that what would in anger follow, would be a further declaration that the only reason he wasn't interested in Annie was the fact that he already had a girlfriend. And she was Irish.

Did they have to look so aghast? He tried to remember what exactly Amma had said. Something about why was he telling them now?

'Because I didn't think the circumstances were suitable – you know, with Grandfather's funeral. It wasn't the right time to tell you.'

Appa looked uncomfortable and Padhman had never seen his mother at such a loss for words.

'Her name is Aoife, spelt A . . . o . . . i . . . f . . . e. A typical Irish name. She's an intern at the same hospital as me.'

Amma had looked at him rather vacantly and Padhman felt his hackles rise. He always said the wrong things when Amma made his hackles rise. This time was no different.

'She's of the same species, you know – human.'

Padhman had said his final goodbye a few silent minutes later. Appa had hugged him mutely and when Padhman turned to Amma she kissed him woodenly, tears of anger and disappointment filling her eyes. Padhman headed for the queues at the check-in counters and then looked back to wave to them. But they had turned around and walked away, Appa with his arm around Amma's shoulders.

CHAPTER SEVENTEEN

~

PADHMAN ALMOST FELT guilty for being so happy to be back. He strode down the featureless airport corridor with its sheet glass overlooking the runways. Back, back! How strange, he thought to himself. Even a week ago, 'back' would have meant India. He nearly lifted Aoife off the ground, hugging her passionately.

'I missed you, Aoif.'

'And I missed you desperately,' she said, holding his face still and looking him directly in the eye. Linking arms tightly, they walked to the car park.

'Dinner's at my place.' Then without warning she added, 'Upstairs actually, with my parents.'

'Tonight? Why – what's up?' He groaned inwardly.

'Nothing. It's for you. I guess they felt sad for you, about your grandfather, and felt terrible that they didn't get a chance to speak to you before you left. They've promised it will be an early night, Padhman. It was my mother's idea, would you believe it? Do you want to head for your place, for a shower first?'

Padhman showered and shaved, while Aoife tried hard to get him to talk about how things had gone in Madras. He didn't even realise that he was being reticent, so lost was he in the feeling of utter happiness at being back. This was the civilised way to be. He reduced it to a very simplistic comparison. Here were Aoife's parents taking the trouble to express their concern irrespective of the fact that they, if the truth were known (and he knew it), wished he had never happened to their daughter. And what had Amma and Appa done? One mention of an Irish girl and they had turned and walked away. The way he felt at the moment, he would go so far as to say that they had turned their backs on him.

On the way to the Gormans', the blustery winds of the hour before had turned vicious and the rain was being driven nearly horizontal against the car.

'Lashing, isn't it?' he said, with a big grin on his face. Small things can give a person a sense of belonging and in an instant he felt a part of her world, just by using that Irishism. 'It's lashing and I'm knackered and don't give out to me,' he added, the grin on his face widening into idiotic proportions.

'Are you OK, Padhman?' Aoife was looking at him curiously.

'Grand,' he replied. 'Just grand.'

When they finally reached her parents' house, having driven at a snail's pace, Aoife parked the car and they raced up the twelve stone steps together. Eamon opened the door and the wind literally blew them inside.

'Everybody's in here.' Eamon put his arm around Padhman's shoulder and guided him to the sitting-room door, which he opened with his other hand. The conversation came to a halt as Padhman walked in, and Professor Gorman and Millie got up to walk towards him. Nana was there and so was Molly. To Padhman's surprise, Sunil and Renu were there too, sitting on either side of Nana.

'How are your parents, Padhman?' The Professor had taken his hand and was shaking it vigorously in both of his.

Millie Gorman had followed Padhman's eyes, and as she took her turn shaking his hand she said, 'Aoife told us your grandfather was the grandfather Dr Patel never had.' She turned to look at Sunil and Renu. 'Dr Patel and his wife were just telling us about him. Padhman, you never told us that you had such charming friends. Mrs Patel is a delight.'

Nana and Molly had joined the queue behind her and Millie Gorman moved aside. Nana gave him a heartfelt hug and Molly kissed him. As they expressed their condolences he could see, out of the corner of his eye and over their shoulders, Renu squirming uncomfortably. He held her glance for a second, willing her to see the funny side of being called a delight. She lifted her eyebrows slightly, ever so slightly, in reply.

Over dinner the conversation lingered over matters funereal. The Gormans were fascinated by Padhman's account of the immersion of Grandfather's ashes. He nearly felt obliged to spare them no detail. After all, as Eamon had cheerfully pointed out when he was giving Eamon a hand with the drinks, this was a clear signal that he, Padhman, was being welcomed into the family. This evening could be described, said Eamon, as a wake *in absentia* for Grandfather. Putting that into a cultural context, for he had been listening to the discussion on funeral etiquette that had taken place, Padhman decided that to be welcomed with a wake was a good enough welcome for him.

Padhman stared blankly at Sunil, who was sitting across the hospital canteen table from him. He couldn't believe what his friend had just told him. The sheer cunning of Amma – and to have involved Nimmi Aunty! Whether that involvement had been witting or unwitting, he and Sunil would never know. When the two mothers wanted to, they would close ranks. They had always been able to justify, at least to themselves, the convoluted reasons for their behaviour, because the root of it lay in the nobility of their intentions. 'It's for your own good' was a dreaded

176

refrain and for Padhman it had meant that even Appa and Grandfather would not come to his rescue.

'It's a month since you came back from Madras. Are you telling me that you haven't spoken to them on the phone?' Sunil looked perplexed.

'Oh, I have – every Sunday and a couple of times in between.'

'Didn't you tell them anything about Aoife then? You must have said something, discussed it a little?'

'Sunil, it's bloody complicated.' Padhman was toying with a bowl of rhubarb and custard. 'Here, you have it.' He pushed it towards Sunil who eyed it critically. Please don't say that Renu makes better rhubarb and custard, thought Padhman wearily. I don't want to know how lucky you are. I *know* how lucky you are. In fact, *you* don't know how lucky you are. Everything just fell into place for you and Renu.

'Pads, everything with you is complicated.' Sunil was tucking into the rhubarb.

Padhman ignored him. 'The first call I made when I got back, Amma never said anything about what happened at the airport. In total denial, I think she was. So I decided that if she was going to pretend that Aoife was just going to go away, I couldn't be bothered explaining.'

'Are you telling me that while you were busy thinking she was in denial, your Amma got my mother to find out everything about Aoife from Renu and me?'

Padhman shrugged. The answer was pretty obvious. Sunil and Renu must have told Nimmi Aunty everything there was to know.

'Anyway Pads, what's the big deal? So your mother knows all about Aoife. You've saved yourself the trouble and a massive phone bill.'

Padhman shook his head. It was a matter of principle. If Amma wanted information she should have asked him.

Why drag Sunil and Renu into it? And why did Nimmi Aunty have to do Amma's dirty work? And what was he going to do now? The status quo was a much easier state to be in.

'What about Aoife? Does she know the hungama she has caused?' Sunil asked.

'She hasn't caused it.'

'Don't dodge the question. You haven't told her, have you?'

'This is something I have to sort out with Amma and Appa myself. Anyway, how would telling Aoife help?'

'At least she'd know what she's up against, or as you would insist, what *you're* up against.'

'If I told you I wanted Aoife to see them in the best light, would you understand? I've told her so much about Appa and Amma and this one thing could completely cloud her judgement about them.'

'This "one thing" as you call it will not cloud her judgement, Pads. From all your accounts, her mother did not accept you with open arms either. Aoife wasn't embarrassed, so why should you be?'

'Shit, Sunil! It's disappointing when your own parents are unreasonable.'

Sunil nodded his head quietly. This was one of the threads that had bound them together for the best part of their twenty-four-year friendship. He picked up the ceramic bowl that had *Hospital Property* embossed around the rim, and proceeded to scrape the bits of rhubarb and custard together for one last spoonful. Padhman knew that the whole act mirrored what his friend was doing in his mind. It was an unconscious habit of Sunil's. His angry outbursts always tended to be preceded by furious tapping or drumming of his fingers on the nearest surface. If he was unsure of himself or trying to make up his mind, he would tip his head first towards one shoulder and then to the other, as if he were literally trying to approach the matter from all angles. And that was usually after he had assessed a situation while simultaneously arranging and rearranging anything at all that was to hand.

'OK, say it,' said Padhman. 'What's the one last piece of advice?'

'You didn't have to join your mother in her vow of silence. You announced the existence of an Irish girlfriend and then just clammed up, basically left your Amma floundering. That's unreasonable too.'

'Piss off, Sunil.'

'Actually that's exactly what I'm going to do. You're off to Galway tonight, aren't you? What time is the interview? Is Aoife nervous?' He didn't hang around for a reply, just scraped his chair back and with a declaration that he was full to bursting, Sunil hurried out of the canteen.

It wasn't that Padhman hadn't dwelt on his own silence on the matter. I'm childish, he admitted. But Amma was the one who had turned and walked away at the airport. And Appa. In fact, Padhman found Appa's silence more alarming, it being quite out of character. I am allowed to be childish if my parents don't want to be grown up, he reasoned, totally peeved with the truth as presented to him by Sunil.

When he got home that evening Aoife rang to say that she would be late. 'Another two cases to go, Padhman. And we're here twiddling our thumbs. Larkin's tearing his hair out. He can't see why the nurses need to have a break, blah, blah – you know how he can carry on. I thought the Theatre Sister was going to spit in his eye. So, I'll see you when I see you.'

Padhman stared at the phone and picked it up again impulsively. They would both be in bed. Amma would be

179

reading and Appa would be watching television, waiting for the late-night English news. But they weren't. The cook, who was delighted to be able to speak to Padhman, said they were at the Patels'.

'How is it in London, aiyyah?'

Padhman indulged her. For the cook, the epicentre of 'foreign' was London. She felt worldly just asking him that question. He looked out of his bedroom window. The sun was setting on what had been an unexpectedly mild and sunny winter's day.

'There is four feet of snow, Kannima. It's very, very cold. Even the rivers are frozen. You can walk on them.'

'Aiyo . . . yohhh!' The cook exhaled in satisfaction. It was just like what she had seen in the latest Tamil movie. 'Don't step out of the house with wet hair,' she said very firmly and then put the phone down.

Padhman toyed with the idea of calling the Patel house. The impulse that had made him call home in the first place, now seemed to present the most logical way forward. He was filled with an inexplicable sense of urgency to speak to his parents. I'll tell them something, make a statement, say something . . . anything about Aoife. Padhman placed his hand on the phone. Should he ring Kannima and ask her to tell Amma and Appa to call back when they returned? He decided against it. Aoife might call and he would be gone. He calculated the time in India. It was past eleven in Madras. Padhman could picture them so clearly. Right now Raja Uncle would be persuading Amma to have another Baileys, while Nimmi Aunty stuffed and rolled the sweet stuffed betel leaf 'beedis' that were Appa's favourite. Baileys and beedis. Padhman shook his head. That's the bloody trouble. Baileys and beedis . . . they epitomised the incongruity of growing up with westernised aspirations and Indian values. It was like Renu's grumble about being brought up on a diet of Enid Blyton and never knowing what clotted cream tasted like.

When the phone suddenly rang, Padhman literally jumped with fright. The ringing had nearly shot through his arm like a bolt of electricity. It was Amma sounding concerned.

'Kannima said you had called, Padhu. Is everything all right?'

'We must have just missed your call. She told us she had just put the phone down.' Appa was on the extension.

Padhman had no time to think. 'I'm away for the weekend. No, nothing's wrong. I just wanted to let you know that I'm off to Galway tonight.'

They waited for him to qualify what he had said. It was as if they knew what was going to follow. Nimmi Aunty must have beaten him to it. Despite that suspicion, Padhman plunged ahead. 'Aoife has an interview tomorrow. We decided to make a weekend of it. I'll be back Sunday evening.'

'Is it for a job?' Appa was clutching at straws to keep the conversation alive, but Amma hadn't yet said anything.

'She . . . Aoife's finishing her internship in December, Appa. She's interviewing for the surgical SHO's post in Galway Regional.'

'Her father's a Professor. He must have pulled all the strings.' Amma's voice was emotionless.

'It's not like that here.'

'It's like that everywhere, son. When you have lived a little, you'll know.'

'Anyway, I hope she gets it. It's a good job, a surgical rotation.' Padhman remained non-confrontational. He could barely believe they had got this far in the conversation and he was not going to nitpick about nepotism or take offence at Amma's little jibe about his naivety.

181

Appa dominated the rest of the conversation, while Padhman found himself trying to hear what Amma was thinking. When Appa finally said that the conversation had gone on long enough for an international call, Amma, sounding subdued, told Padhman to drive carefully.

'Call us when you get back,' was the last thing she said as Padhman put the phone down.

He fell backwards onto the bed, arms and legs spread-eagled and eyes shut. So this was what relief felt like. He lifted his legs off the mattress and criss-crossed them in a scissor-like motion. He held his stomach in while he did the scissors and a few seconds later, stopped and let out an explosive breath. There was no real reason for him to be so euphoric. Do Amma and Appa crave my approval as much as I crave theirs, he wondered. It's all about approval. Isn't that the reason I am lying on the bed now cycling with my legs in the air – because I think I am on the first step towards approval? Or have I started at the wrong end of the scale? Have I only just moved from denial to bitter resignation? Will I then have to hope for helpless acceptance then onwards to grudging approval and finally: the *filmi*-style whole-hearted welcome. Padhman cycled faster, his legs clawing through the air, the mattress springs providing the sound effects of the squeaky bike that he was on. It had the makings of a Tamil movie all right. Ireland would make a great outdoor location. After the poignant close-ups of Aoife in Amma and Appa's arms, the camera could zoom out, taking in Powerscourt Gardens, Sugar Loaf Mountain, the Wicklow Range.

Dream on, you fool, he thought as his legs flopped back onto the bed. He knew in his heart of hearts that with that telephone call, the battle lines had been formally drawn. Amma would spend the weekend gathering her wits about her before she launched her offensive. His inner thighs ached with the frenzied cycling. He punched his stomach. Must get some exercise this weekend. A couple of long walks, but only if the weather held. He could see the rectangular outline of the *Textbook of Surgery* as it sat, stuffed into the outer pocket of his weekend holdall. He reflected on what a strange thing reality was. Picking up the *Textbook of Surgery* was not exactly the most likely post-coital act, but that was reality for, satiated, they would both reluctantly, but matter-of-factly, turn to their waiting books. Aoife would return to her struggle with Internal Medicine, while Padhman manoeuvred the duvet over his drawn-up knees, so that the cold plastic cover on the surgical tome would not make him flinch.

Sometimes, lost in the twisted maze of inflammatory bowel disease or unable to get a grasp on the breast and the intricacies of cyclical mastalgia, Padhman would find himself drifting away from the text, studying instead the snug domesticity of lying beside Aoife and preparing for an exam. For wasn't it domesticity that was a measure of the total ease that he felt with her? But this was more than just the thrill of playing house, more than loving the novelty of being in love and what's more, actually sleep-ing with the woman in question. This was more serious, more fundamental, more profound. He couldn't put it into words except to summarise that in the last few months he had truly grown up in the most pleasurable way. The fact that they occasionally fought, disagreed and argued underlined the realness of the relationship. How-ever, both being partial to stony silences, those clever but regrettable unkindnesses remained largely unsaid and then forgotten, so that when they did pick up a few hours or days later, there was not much pique to file away.

Padhman dragged himself on his elbows up to the pil-lows at the head of the bed. As he lay there, knowing that Aoife would be at least another two hours or more, he wondered if he should nip across to Sunil and Renu's. Though his friends obviously liked Aoife, Padhman suspected that they were amazed, perhaps even concerned, at the speed and energy with which he had hurled himself into the relationship. There was no doubt that they had been taken aback at the Gormans' house, when they had been invited to be Padhman's stand-in family, the night he had returned from India. It was nothing to do with being invited, of course. It was just that, for them, observing Padhman's familiarity with Aoife's family, his knowledge of their comings and goings and everyday affairs had been a bit of an eye-opener. In fact, their surprise had heightened his realisation of that very fact.

Renu had once tried to pry out of him the sequence of events with Annie and Aoife, trying to figure out if he had messed Annie around. He wasn't successful in fobbing Renu off with his cheerful, 'Mind your own business, Mrs Patel.'

She had been equally blunt. 'Hey, I was the in-between, remember?'

Agreeing that he did owe them an account, he had proceeded in a minimalist fashion to outline what had transpired, and Renu and Sunil had accepted it without judgement. Padhman was aware of and appreciated their efforts over Aoife. Sometimes, when he was in analytical mood, he would look upon Sunil and Renu as the additional background artists, filling in the finer details, setting the scenes and adding bits and pieces to the Tableaux Padhman, doing a better job than him for unlike him, they weren't conscious of what they were doing.

By extending their friendship to Aoife so wholeheartedly, Sunil and Renu had unwittingly provided some sort of balance. If any of the Gormans were privy to the times he and Aoife had shared with Sunil and Renu, they would, in turn, have been struck by how relaxed and at home Aoife was in their company. He wondered suddenly if Aoife's parents had seen her eat with her fingers. Seen her eat rice and dal with her bare hands. Now, wouldn't *that* be an eye-opener? More likely a real jaw-dropper!

Padhman lifted the phone and placing the instrument on his chest debated his course of action for the evening. If Aoife was not yet in theatre and was able to answer her bleep, he could tell her that he would wait at Sunil's. He was about to dial the hospital when the phone rang. It reverberated through his chest and he felt his legs and arms jerk involuntarily with fright. I'm being defibrillated by a telephone, he thought as he picked up the receiver. It was Aoife.

'Larkin let me off. The anaesthetist told him I was interviewing tomorrow.'

Padhman swung his legs off the bed reluctantly. She was ready to go to Galway.

CHAPTER EIGHTEEN

~

THE CELICA WAS stalled at a gravity-defying angle behind a queue of cars, leading up the ramp into the multi-storey car park. It was obvious that the whole country had realised there were only eight shopping days to go till Christmas. In his rearview mirror, Padhman could see the woman with two children in the car behind him; he had been watching her for a while now, and she was getting increasingly agitated. She had spent the last few minutes twisted around in her seat, speaking to her children at the back, and in between had cast hurried and hopeful glances at the queue ahead. The little drama had kept him mildly interested and he watched now, as she seemed to be threatening to get out of her car. She did so and to Padhman's consternation, she walked up to him and, bending down, indicated with her hand that he should roll down his window.

'They're bursting to go.' She was looking back at her children in the car.

Padhman wondered how the hell she expected *him* to help.

'You wouldn't do me a favour, would you?' she went on. The queue's hardly moving and it could be a while. If I leave the keys in the car, would you move it along for me as the queue moves? There are toilets by the lifts, I'll rush them there . . . I'll be back in a flush . . . please?'

A Freudian slip, thought Padhman, and he nodded his head. However she wasn't even looking at him, instead was signalling urgently to the kids. He watched them disappear hurriedly around the hairpin bend that lay ahead. Why didn't she ask the guy in the car behind her, he wondered, suddenly hoping that the queue would not move at all. But perversely, it did move, in three quick bursts. Padhman approached the task as nonchalantly as he could, but by the third time, he was beginning to feel like a clockwork monkey hopping in and out of cars.

'Children can drive you to desperation,' she said, panting and out of breath when she finally returned. She bundled them into the car and came back to thank him once again, clutching her jacket around her as she spoke to him, but not ever looking at him, her eyes swinging in an arc, back and forth, from her own car to the final steep bright yellow ramp, beyond which an all-knowing machine dispensed tickets and raised barriers.

This was definitely kismet, he decided, sitting back and holding onto the steering wheel in shock. A total stranger had picked him, not the man in the car behind her, and then had repeated the same fatalistic mantra that Amma had chanted to him over the phone, only forty minutes ago.

'Children can drive you to desperation.'

When Amma had thrown that at him at the tail end of their twelve-minute conversation, Padhman had ignored it. That was Amma just expressing her annoyance. Or was it? Should he have read more into it? He looked at his rearview mirror. The woman was looking into her own mirror and touching up her lipstick. Oddly enough, he found his lips moving in sync with hers, in a goldfish fashion. He looked away. He could understand Amma's frustration. She had obviously been persuaded by Appa, against her better judgement, to take a softly, softly approach about Aoife and was consequently finding it very hard not to be confrontational. Perhaps she even thought that ignoring the issue would ensure that it would never become more than something on the sidelines.

'Padhu's having his little bit of fun, Nimmi. These white girls throw themselves on our boys, you know. We had hoped that he would have had better sense, but . . . What? Yes, yes, loneliness is a big factor. That's how most of them fall prey to . . . Yes, I agree. At least she is a doctor – a nurse would have been too much, but you know, Nimmi, what more can you do other than give them a good grounding in values? Respect for women is what he has been taught all his life, but the problem is the women there have no respect for themselves . . .'

Padhman was quite sure he was not too far off the mark. Amma was hoping Aoife was just a bit of temporary lustfulness. In fact that was exactly what she had said to him today.

'Relationships are not all about fun, you know. You have to consider suitability, adjustability, respectability and presentability.'

'If you add durability to that list, Amma, you could be talking about a Mercedes.'

'Children can drive you to desperation,' Amma had said in reply and shortly afterwards, had handed the phone to Appa.

The woman in the car behind him was honking. Realising that the queue ahead of him had begun to move again, he gave her an apologetic wave and, releasing the handbrake, began the climb upwards. Minutes later, as he parked the car, he mentally decided that he would let Amma and Appa set the pace. When they treated Aoife as a serious problem, he would give them serious battle. Till then, he would tackle it one phone call at a time.

Right now he had forty-five minutes to scout around for a present for Aoife, buy it and bring it back to the car and then meet her outside Bewley's in order to help her with her Christmas shopping.

'There is a social element to Christmas shopping,' she had warned him, 'so we won't be buying the first suitable present we see. Do you really think you will be up for it, Padhman? You'll be exhausted by lunch.'

Padhman was surprised by his own sudden fascination for all things Christmassy, and he had had to contain his enthusiasm last weekend, when he and Aoife had gone to help her Nana decorate the tree.

'You're allowed to be excited, Padhman. Everyone's a child at Christmas.' The old lady had come to his rescue when Aoife had teased him about the sheer size of the Christmas tree that he and Eamon had chosen.

He walked around the shops and was delighted with his luck at having spotted something that he was certain she would love. He decided to surprise her with the Walkman. Heading back to the car sooner than he expected, he was already beginning to recognise and relish that feeling of having done well, of having bought that perfect present. He had heard that elusive feeling being discussed animatedly on the radio on his way into work, and then had heard the radio show itself being discussed at work. Though he had barely been able to grasp the notion then, it was obvious that the satisfaction he was feeling now, having placed the Walkman, all gift wrapped, in the boot of the car, was that very same, much sought-after gratification that only came to those who had their Christmas shopping all wrapped up at least the week before Christmas.

Aoife was waiting for him at Bewley's. They walked in and out of shops, up escalators and down aisles, through a Christmas craft market via two florists, sometimes backtracking swiftly, sometimes being propelled ahead by the press of people at traffic lights, meandering in what seemed an aimless fashion through galleries, arcades and shops within shops, and all the time Padhman was constantly being assured by Aoife that this was the only way to get that special and different Christmas present. It all seemed a bit of a hit and miss affair to Padhman, but as he looked around at people while Aoife looked at things, he realised that nearly everybody else seem to have the same idea: fulfilment was more likely to come to the clueless browser. Crowds milled around indecisively at the tills, at the junction of aisles, at the meeting of departments, at the doors to the stores and the corners of streets. Everywhere he looked was a surfeit of visual offerings. He had never seen such fantastical decorations, never thought shop windows could come close to being works of art. It was the sheer excessiveness of everything, with everyone colluding to go over the top, the exaggerated fear of running out of time and an all-embracing thematic congruity that made the spirit of the season so infectious.

That evening, Padhman massaged her feet for her. Aoife groaned with relief as he squeezed her toes and kneaded her heels with his knuckles. It was an unscientific but enthusiastic attempt and he watched her face, tempering his intensity if he thought that her brows were about to furrow in pain. He had watched Appa doing this so many times. Shit! This was like Appa and Amma!

Aoife closed her eyes and listened as Padhman reminisced aloud. If Amma had been away from the house for a length of time – and if she were shopping for anything other than groceries it would almost always be a good length of time – she would bustle around the house on her return, sometimes with her handbag still hanging on her shoulders or tucked purposefully under her arm. The pattern very rarely varied. Amma would make quick visits to every room and just a cursory glance was enough for her to know if the instructions given to the servants before she left had been followed. As a child, Padhman had often marvelled at her X-ray vision and her disconcerting ability to spot if anything was amiss in the house, in his room and even in his mind.

After that brief inspection, Amma would head straight for the kitchen to conference with the cook. There, while she got the run down on all that had transpired while she was away, Amma would satisfy herself about the readiness of the dinner and the general state of affairs in that most important room of the house. Only when she had caught up with her duties would she ask for her cup of coffee, and where she was to drink it would be a signal to Appa. If she called out to the cook as she left the kitchen, to bring it to her room, Appa would, if he were sitting with Grandfather or Padhman, excuse himself and join her in the bedroom. She would wash her feet and then, making herself comfortable on the huge cane sofa that faced the veranda, she would put her feet up on her husband's lap. Amma's feet were slim and even the very slender bands of her toe rings looked heavy on her. Appa would twist the rings around and slip them off carefully and Amma would keep them safe, wearing them on her fingers. She loved to have her feet massaged but Padhman could see now that the therapeutics actually lay in the talking and listening that would ensue.

'So would you say they're happily married, Padhman?'

Padhman stopped what he was doing to Aoife's feet and flexed his fingers. 'Oh they are, but sometimes I think they're too damn dependent on each other.'

'That's part of being happily married, I suppose.' She had closed her eyes again and was nudging his fingers with her toes. 'Just another few minutes, please.'

Padhman looked at her feet, as he massaged them with what he thought were soothing circulatory movements of his thumbs. 'What about your parents? Are they happily married?'

'They are. Reasonably. They had a whirlwind romance and later they had to learn to be happy. I think they are. My mother thinks she's happy despite Nana. My father would be happier if my mother didn't feel that way. We were . . . are you OK, Padhman?'

'That could be us, Aoif. You are going to be happy *despite* Amma, and I am always going to be hoping that you don't feel that way. Hell! Will we find that we too are going to have to learn to be happy?' He hung his forehead down wearily until it touched her toes.

'Oh Padhman, don't be so dramatic. The trouble is, you're always dissecting things and analysing them. Let things just happen – and anyway, that was my parents we were talking about, not us. We're different. We will be different. Are different, will be different – there, look, I'm even talking like you now.' She was laughing at him. 'Your mother hasn't met me as yet. When she does, she is going to *love* me. So there!' Aoife pushed his head up with her toes. 'Come on, misery guts, you were doing great on my feet until you started thinking.'

Forty minutes later they were in the car with Sunil and Renu driving to Niall's house. Maura opened the door with undisguised relief. Not only were they rather late, they were also the first to arrive. They shuffled around each other in the narrow hallway, removing coats, gushing a little more than required and air kissing awkwardly. Renu, who had got the sequence out of sync, brushed lips with Niall and Padhman was amused as he caught her instinctively but surreptitiously wiping her lips with the back of her hands.

The Christmas tree, wedged into the corner created by the fireplace and a large, button-backed leather sofa, dominated the room and the uncoordinated, mismatched decorations that hung so defiantly from its branches were like a magnet demanding attention and explanation.

'I love the decorations on the tree.' Maura was on the defensive, having read the query in everyone's mind. 'They're special. They bring back memories. We were eight of us, eight children, and every Christmas it was a tradition that we would go to Mooney's Emporium and choose a Christmas decoration each. When the tree came down in January, Mammy would supervise us as we packed away our own little growing collections. She made us keep them all, even the ones that we made in school and particularly the ones that we attempted at home.'

Padhman, Sunil and Renu looked at the motley collection in silence. At about eye level, a Styrofoam apple hung close enough for Padhman to see where an attempt at a small bite had been made, the toothmarks visible on the hundreds of tiny red glass beads that completely covered the fruit's surface. Six peg dolls carelessly dressed in gold lace sat in a row on a branch nearby, and above them a miniature bunting trailed across the tree wishing everyone *A Merry Christm*. The paper triangles with the *a* and the *s* were missing, though it was clear that *a* had been completely lost while *s* had merely been torn off, for a tattered corner of that triangle still remained pasted to the silvery cord. Some of the decorations were much more expensive, and they looked out of place on this unpretentious tree.

The Waterford crystal rocking horse that hung heavily and precariously from an upper branch had, Maura told them, been bought well before Christmas, immediately after her Confirmation, with all the money she had received at that time. A black papier-mâché egg, with a winter scene delicately painted on it in gold, had come from a Russian penfriend to whom Maura had written for four years. The very realistic robin, who looked slightly uncomfortable in his designated spot, had his own little story too.

'We had come up to Dublin – it was the first wedding in the family – and all five of us girls came up with Mammy and our sister Maureen for the fitting. I was Maureen's flower girl and she bought it for me. I saw it in the window of the shop next to the dressmaker's. Of course, once she indulged me she had to buy something for the rest of the girls and then Mam said the two lads would feel left out so . . .' Maura had been smoothing down the feathers on the bird's red breast with the tip of her little finger as she spoke, but she stopped mid-sentence as the robin lurched and then toppled over.

Padhman lunged, just managing to catch him by his feet, but had to lunge again, for the feet came off in his hand and the robin continued his descent, impaling himself noiselessly, beak first, into the thick pile of the carpet. Renu's hand flew to her mouth and the three of them watched as Maura bent down and yanked the bird up, and taking the thin metal feet from Padhman's hand, rammed them cheerfully back into the bird.

'Don't worry, I've had to do this before. Now what'll you have to drink?'

Maura had placed the bird back on the tree, his tail feathers resting on a shiny bauble. The robin was unharmed, and a relieved Padhman pointed out the wispy bit of carpet fluff that the bird had picked up in its beak. He hoped Maura would let the fluff remain. He liked the idea of being linked to the bird's history and through that, being part of the rake of memories that this simple, but obviously precious collection of decorations would evoke every Christmas.

The rest of the expected guests descended on the house much later. When they did, Padhman followed Maura into the kitchen to give her a hand with the drinks.

194

'Sunil's wife is lovely,' Maura enthused. 'She's very normal, you know what I mean? She has very good English. Will you take the red, Padhman, and I'll pour out the white? Yeah, her English is great. She told me she was taught by the nuns – Irish nuns, would you believe?'

'What's "normal", Maura? What were you expecting?'

'Well . . . Oh, you know what I mean. I've been talking to her for ages. She's very intelligent.'

'That's normal enough.'

'No, that's not what I meant. I mean, she's in trousers and she drinks! Hmm, how do I explain this. Hers wasn't an arranged marriage, that's one thing, and she said she loves Simon and Garfunkel, for God's sake.' Maura placed two trays of frozen sausage rolls in the oven and turned back to Padhman. 'That makes her like us – normal.'

Padhman thought about Maura's analysis as he handed out the drinks. All these months, I must have been judged by the same count. When I discussed the lightness of her soufflé, Millie Gorman realised I was normal. Eamon thought I was a regular guy when we had that animated session about the chicanes at Monaco. The hospital crowd must have deemed me normal, that night on call, when I told them my dirty party piece. 'An Indian, a Pakistani and a Bangladeshi walked into a pub . . .' They thought I was great craic, even before I had finished the opening line. It is incredible, thought Padhman, that it is my perceived *abnormality*, my deviation from their idea of a defined norm for someone like me, which makes me one of them i.e. normal.

He peered through the tinsel-wrapped balustrades of the staircase, having spotted the edge of Aoife's grey and silver dress. As he leant closer, a very authentic plastic holly leaf pierced him hard on his nose and he yelped, holding his nose and blinking back the tears that had sprung to his eyes. He realised that Aoife's green eyes were peering back at him through the staircase.

'Padhman, are you OK? I'm here. Come on up. Hang on – just top up my glass, will you?'

Aoife was sitting on the tenth step. The house was full and when all the chair and sofa space was gone, people spilled into the hall and the kitchen, with some converging around the stairs, for it seemed to be a good place to sit down. The pairs of people sitting on the steps below Aoife squeezed their bums and swung their thighs, knees and shoulders out of the way, in what seemed a choreographed effort, as Padhman took the steps two at a time. She leant back against him as he settled down a step above her.

'You tired?' he murmured, stroking the back of her neck knowing she would say yes.

'Yes, but I plan to enjoy the next twelve days.'

There was a hidden adjunct in what she had said.

Padhman had already sensed that Aoife was nervous about the move to Galway. He was certain it wasn't to do with being apart from each other. Three hours' driving time wasn't too daunting on a weekly basis and he knew that theoretically if he wanted her, there was nothing to stop him from getting into the car after work and arriving in Galway by ten at night and leaving by four the next morning. Nothing except good sense, of course.

No, Aoife was jittery, but it was about the new job. Her nerves were understandable. Everybody agreed that it was sheer madness for hundreds of doctors all over Ireland to start their new jobs on 1 January. Year after year, the changeover happened on that singularly most unsuitable of days, but who would ever question anything that happened year after year? There would be so many tired, bleary-eyed, hungover and indecisive people on the wards on New Year's Day – and that was only counting the junior doctors. To be stuck between patients who took your competence for granted and nursing staff who, knowing well how green you were, had you under close surveillance was very nearly soul-destroying.

The last time he had circuitously coaxed her into discussing the move to Galway, hoping to allay some of her anxieties, she had been upbeat but her underlying frustration was something that was so familiar, he had merely nodded mutely, unable to dispute what she was saying.

'It's such a charade, Padhman. You are supposed to be in control and all you can think is what a dog's dinner you are making of it all.'

'Take it from me, Aoif, knowing when to wake your Registrar will be your most crucial skill.' That wasn't an exaggeration. Amongst the many things that Padhman had learnt from Appa and Grandfather was, that if you didn't realise you were out of your depth, you took your patient down with you.

Right now though, Aoife had tipped her face up towards him and all contemplative thoughts about the harsh realities of training disappeared at the sight of the shadowy valley between her breasts. He clasped her around her neck, bending down slightly towards her, as if to hear what she had repeated twice already. He had an urge to slide his fingers down into her dress and take the place of the smooth grey silk that encased her. She recognised his look and placed her hands firmly over his. This time she laughed as she repeated herself for the third time. 'What about you, Padhman? Are *you* tired?'

CHAPTER NINETEEN

~

CHRISTMAS EVE GOT off to an inauspicious start. Amma had been very direct.

'Why have they invited you? I thought Christmas was meant to be a family affair.' Amma had drawn her conclusions from that rhetorical question even as she stated it, and the annoyance in her voice was palpable.

'Has this Aoife invited you against her parents' wishes? Keep your dignity, son. Don't go if you are not welcome.'

Poor Amma, she couldn't bear the thought of him being invited. It was too forward a gesture, loaded with implications, and yet at the same time she would be outraged if the Gorman family spurned him.

'We are going to her grandmother's place, Amma. You don't need to read anything into it. It's just an invitation.'

'These people are not like us, Padhu. Foreigners, they don't invite you to their houses that easily. Ask Appa. How many months did we know the Kendals before they called us to their house? I'll tell you. Eight. *Eight* – and after all that time it was only for drinks. No eats, nothing.'

'Aren't you on call, Padhu? I thought you said you were rostered to work over Christmas.' Appa was looking for the least painful way out.

'Why should they have invited you?' Amma carried on, mentally accusing them of what in her estimation was unforgivable. These Gormans were trying to engineer things. Padhman was sure that words like 'ensnare' and 'good catch' were at the tip of her tongue.

Provoked, he snapped back. 'They are as unsure about me as you are about their daughter, Amma. I have been being invited because they are being civilised.'

Padhman had sensed that privately, Millie Gorman was delighted with the Galway rotation. She would be quite happy to see Padhman quietly fade out of her daughter's life. Two terrified mothers, cornered and helpless, they could create havoc.

'Huh! We are not unsure, Padhu. In fact, we are quite sure. Quite sure that this kind of cross-cultural relationship will have no future. It is not decent for you to fool around with her like this. And anyway, what makes them unsure about you? Do they know anything about your background, your family? Have you told them who your grandfather was? Do they know who your father is?'

'You're shooting yourself in the foot, Amma. I rest my case.'

'Don't try your newly acquired expressions on me. Do you realise how upset we are at the way you are treating this Aoife girl? Appa feels the same. You shouldn't be fooling around. Ask your father.'

Appa had remained calm and his advice was earnest and unemotional. 'It's not the right thing to do, to dally with her while you are there and then let her down. That's probably what her parents are afraid of. Do you see what I am saying, son?'

'I'm not fooling around and I won't let her down. Do we have to go on like this? All we seem to do is argue on the phone, Amma.'

Amma had been quick to note the ominous nature of Padhman's reassurance and she retreated in shock, unable to say anything more for the time being.

Other events in the course of the day slowly chipped away at the weariness that had enveloped him since that phone call. It began with Mr Morris' Christmas card. A cheque for fifty pounds accompanied the card that wished him A Merry Christmas, with a simple hand-written command: *Enjoy*. Padhman wasn't the only recipient, for Morris was known for his generosity to his team. Later on that morning, Maura handed him a small neatly wrapped present, left at the nurse's station by a patient attending the fracture clinic. It was a set of postcards called *Ireland of the Welcomes*, that opened out in concertina fashion and the gift tag stuck clumsily to the wrapping paper said *To Dr Paddy (Indian). From Mary Ann Murtagh. Thank you for your kindness. Merry Christmas.*

He had not planned to get Maura a gift, but the tiny stuffed elephant that she now held aloft in delight had caught his eye and he had bought it on impulse.

'It's for your tree, Maura.'

'I suppose you'll be wanting your present,' she said as she hugged him.

Padhman opened it happily, relieved that he had bought her the elephant. She must be relieved too, that she had something for him. He struggled to open the box. It was a coffee mug with *Paddy* emblazoned on it. They hugged again, his spirits well lifted. He was himself again by lunchtime, after Mary in the canteen placed a small, awkwardly shaped parcel on his tray, next to the plate with curried turkey and chips.

'It's only a small one seeing as you're by yourself.' The shape was a give-away, and whiffs of the alcoholic content confirmed Padhman's suspicion that it was a Christmas pudding.

When he got home that evening, Padhman placed all his presents in a row on the kitchen counter and he looked at them as he drank his coffee from his *Paddy* mug. It was such a satisfying feeling, to receive and to give. He had one more present to give and, finishing his coffee, he headed for Sunil and Renu's.

Padhman hadn't thought twice when he had included them on his list. He knew there was a danger that Sunil would laugh at him, tease him about his conversion to the Irish ways, a conversion that seemed almost traitorous, considering he had all but forgotten to wish them well for Diwali in October. Sunil and Renu had chastised him for his omission and he had laughed, challenging them instead to show him what they had done to mark the Hindu festival.

'We've lit a lamp and I've made kheer.' Renu was feeling very righteous.

'That's only because you have a mother-in-law to impress, Renu. Has she rung up to check? The first Diwali for the new daughter-in-law and all that.' Padhman watched Renu's eyes. She was guilty as hell.

'OK, Pads, you've made your point. Now are you going to have some kheer? Then you can tell your Amma how tasty it was and she will pass that on to my mother-in-law, and then the daughter-in-law and Sunil will live happily ever after.'

In fact, Padhman had gone on to finish the entire bowl, and when he complimented her, as she reached forward to take his bowl, he hadn't been fast enough to stop the small gurgle that travelled up his throat, gathering momentum, escaping out of his surprised mouth in a hefty burp. Renu shuddered and stepped back.

'I'm sorry,' he began, but from the corner of his eye he could see Sunil's shoulders shake uncontrollably. He tried not to look at Sunil and began apologising again, but Renu had turned and walked away to the sink.

'Your mothers should see you now. You are a disgusting pair.'

With no exchange of words or glances, and feeling like little boys all over again, they had crept up behind where she stood and had burped stereophonically on either side of her. Now, as he stood at their doorstep, thinking about that admittedly low juvenile prank, he wondered what they would think of him bearing a gift for an occasion that none of them would have normally celebrated. Whatever their reaction, Padhman knew it wouldn't have felt right and it would have been mean, too, not to buy them a present.

Renu was thrilled. Sunil wasn't home yet and instead of taking Padhman into the kitchen, as was their normal routine, she propelled him into the sitting room. With surprising childishness, she pointed out the small collection of presents that were neatly arranged next to the hearth: a token present for the next door neighbours, the big box for Aoife and the small box on top of Aoife's box which was his. The other two gifts were what Sunil and Renu had bought for each other.

'Did Sunil tell you what he got me? Come on, Pads, I am dying to know.' She had begun tugging at the ribbon on the present Padhman had handed her at the door.

'No, he didn't, and should you be opening that now? Tomorrow is the day.'

Renu sighed and tied the ribbon back into a bow and placed the gift next to the others. 'Well, you had better not open yours till tomorrow,' she warned in return, as she handed him the little box with his name on the corner.

'Aoife called me about half an hour back to check if we were at home. She told me she was coming to pick you up, and that she would drop by before you both left. Coffee, Pads?'

Padhman sat at the kitchen table and listened to Renu as she chatted away while the kettle boiled.

'So, you're on show this Christmas. On parade, the exotica that Aoife has attached herself to. Hope you have some decent clothes, Pads. First impressions matter, you know. I believe both her older brothers have been able to make it. Are you nervous?'

Padhman cleared his throat. 'Actually I wasn't, until now. The way you put it, maybe I should be.'

'Don't feel sorry for yourself. Whatever they put you through, it will be nowhere near as bad as what Aoife will have to face when she goes to India. *If* she goes to India. Pads . . . you aren't just fooling around, are you?'

It's never enough for me to hear anything once or twice. Everything has to be thrown at me a dozen times before the powers are satisfied. Padhman reached out for his cup of coffee, slightly exasperated. 'No, Renu, of course I'm not fooling around. I hate those words . . . *fooling around*. Look, I'll just handle things in my own way and in my own time, if that's OK with you.'

Renu was quiet and Padhman felt remorseful. Did she think he had snapped at her? He started apologising but she waved his words away.

'I'll say what I have to say, Pads.'

Padhman looked at her and sighed. 'OK, Renu, say what you have to say.' At least she was honest, and unlike Sunil who would find it impossible to set aside his loyalty and friendship and offer an unbiased opinion, Renu had a streak of pragmatism in her which gave her the ability to stand at the edge, look in and say what she thought.

'We'd hate to be ashamed of you,' she said, looking him straight in the eye. 'So, don't fool around.'

Sunil arrived home tired and ready for a shower, an early dinner and bed, in that order. 'Bloody theatre was like a production line. Someone had forgotten to turn off the switch. Every patient's family wants them done before Christmas.' He headed for the stairs from where he shouted out, 'Go home, Pads. I need my wife to minister to me.'

Padhman, who had already got up to go, strode

towards the hall. 'Bastard, you can thank me later. I only dropped in with your Christmas present.'

Sunil looked down at him from the landing and shook his head. 'I'm shattered, I'm truly buggered . . . but tell Aoife I wished her A Merry Christmas.'

This Heidi looked like a Heidi. She had come out to supervise her youngest's descent down the five stone steps into the courtyard, and the thick gold plaits that she had so carelessly flung back over her shoulders when she stepped out of the house, now whipped around to the front swaying this way and that as she stooped. Padhman watched as she waited till the boy was safely down, before she looked at her three sons collectively and recited her motherly concerns. They, having heard it all before, nodded distractedly, raring to go, the call of the white slopes they had seen from the big windows of their great-grandmother's house having deafened them to any exhortations.

Hope and resignation made Heidi's face look peculiar, and when she looked at Padhman, with the palms of her hands clasped at her chest, he wasn't quite sure if she was merely cold or if she was trying to address him in the Indian fashion. 'Thank you . . . thank you.'

I'm the genie. I have made her wish come true, thought Padhman. If I put my palms together now and bow low, I will disappear in a puff of smoke.

'Relax, Heidi. I'll make sure they stay reasonably clean. I'll give you an hour at least. Peace and a glass of port be with you!'

She grinned back at him gratefully and waved to her sons, but waited on the steps till they were nearly at the courtyard gate, and then let out a final plaintive, 'Keep your gloves on.'

Padhman let the three boys run ahead. He had wanted

to get away, get away from the house, from the family lounging by the fire and the family lounging in the kitchen, from the close scrutiny that felt he had been under. Aoife's older brothers were not unlike Eamon, charming and personable. But Seamus and Ronan were unable to conceal the fact that they needed to suss Padhman out quickly. They were on holiday and they were time-bound. They were curious, observant and paid great attention to everything he did and everything he said. It was as if they were waiting to spot some gesture or keyword known only to them, that would identify him as a potential wife beater or possibly irresponsible husband material.

Heidi's youngest was screaming for his brothers to wait. Padhman caught up with him at the place where he seemed rooted.

'Shall I carry you?'

The boy seemed unsure, but a quick look at the yards his brothers had covered made him stretch his hands upwards. Padhman was surprised at how light the four year old was, despite the bulk of his brand new chubby boots, turned up jeans, thick woollen duffel coat with varnished toggles, scarf, gloves and hat. Padhman decided to hitch the boy up on his shoulders and they set off, catching up with his brothers in a few minutes. Soon, they were crunching up the gravel that led to the front of the house and Padhman wondered how the bulbs he had planted were faring in the dreadful weather they had had since autumn. He looked up at the house and instinctively knew that, in there, they were discussing him. Padhman didn't mind, it was one of the reasons he had got up and volunteered to nanny Seamus and Heidi's boys as they got their fill of the miserly dusting of snow that had fallen overnight. Seamus and Heidi, Ronan and Ciara (who, being a long-time girlfriend and who, along with the rest of the family was waiting for Ronan to pop the question, was entitled to an opinion about Padhman) had taken in as much as they could about Padhman, and he felt that they now needed the opportunity to bounce their opinions and notions about him off each other in order to come to an initial, if not final conclusion. He felt magnanimous by leaving and therefore giving them that opportunity.

As for himself, Padhman felt that Seamus was a bit pompous, but Eamon had warned him about that. Heidi was slightly harassed by her sons and their inability to keep their noses clean. No amount of reassurance from Eamon and Aoife, that they were the image of their father when he was that age, would make her let up her continuous pleas. Seamus, who had been asking Padhman about the exams in February, had gone slightly red, but the banter continued, nostalgic, rowdy and affectionate. Ronan was the quiet one, much like his father even in looks. Padhman had stayed up talking to him for a while, the night before. Aoife had been curious about what had transpired between Padhman and Ronan. As she and Padhman showered late that night, she showed no interest in his attempt to sculpt soapsuds into conical extrusions from her breasts.

'Did he say anything about Ciara?'

'We were discussing exam techniques, Aoif. Oh look, the pointy bit fell off on this side.'

'Nana thinks he'll ask her this Christmas . . . Padhman, stop it. I'm asking you something important.'

'Why would Ronan say anything to me?'

'People say things to strangers.'

Padhman smoothed back her wet hair. 'Like we did?'

She watched the blobs of lather lose their shape and begin their smooth slide down her body. 'You mean in Slattery's?'

He nodded his head and they wordlessly held each

other, both once again awe-struck by the power of the mysterious force that had so fiercely attracted two strangers to each other. Water gathered, creating a little pool in the space created by their chests pressed so close together. They stood watching it fill up, bringing their elbows close to their bodies, trying to close all gaps created by the contours of their flesh, willing the water to rise and rise but seconds later, laughing at their foolishness, they had separated, the water and the moment washed away leaving them refreshed, ready for each other.

Today, he had showered alone, unwilling to go downstairs in his pyjamas. Maybe next Christmas, he thought to himself as he dressed, I'll know the family better. He was only ten minutes later than Aoife but she had already opened her present. She cradled the Walkman in the crook of her arm as she handed him what looked like the bulkiest package under the tree.

'I love this, Padhman. I absolutely love it. Open yours. God, I hope you like it.'

He had, and he was glad for his last-minute grab of Eamon's old waxed jacket from the utility room, for as he now lowered his excited passenger from his shoulders, Padhman realised that he had saved his warm new Aran sweater from the bootmarks, wet mud and grass that now lay plastered against Eamon's jacket.

The three brothers were looking at the slope that went down to the woods. The little one, who had squealed as he had been hoisted down, had jockeyed for position between his two older brothers and he dug his hands into his pockets as he saw his brothers do and kicked at the slushy grey mess that lay around them when his brothers did. He joined them when they turned to look at Padhman, hoping he might have some interesting ideas.

'There's not much of it, is there?' Padhman surveyed

the slope that had looked so promisingly white from the house.

'My mum thinks you're handsome. She told Daddy last night.'

'Daddy thinks you won't last.'

Padhman looked at the youngest. Would he have something to add as well? But his brothers were on a roll and unable to get a word in edgeways, he satisfied himself gaping at them as they tried to outdo each other, revealing minute details of the parental conversation.

'Are you really rich? Like very, very, *very* rich?'

'No, that's not what Daddy said. Daddy said you were a millionaire.'

'A billionaire.'

'That's what I said – very, very, *very* rich.'

'Nana Millie said we would all have to wait and see.'

'Galway is going to be good for Auntie A.'

'Why are you going to spend all your time in the car to Galway?'

Padhman looked down at their enquiring faces. 'I won't. Your Auntie A will come up to Dublin sometimes.'

'Will you make her pregnant?'

Realising they had somehow startled him, they each grabbed their younger brother by a hand, their courage swelling and trembling simultaneously. When Padhman smiled at the triumvirate that stood opposite him they relaxed and, letting go of the little brother in the middle, they carried on where they had left off.

'Ronan said you would have to marry Auntie A if you made her pregnant.'

'Ciara told Ronan that was not a nice thing to say.'

'Mum said please no weddings as yet. We couldn't travel to Ireland for another two years anyway.'

'Yes. Daddy loves Munich. That's where we're going next Christmas.'

'They have proper snow.'

'Daddy said he'd have you by the goolies.'

'No, that was only if he made Auntie A pregnant.'

So that is what they did last night. While we, Auntie A and I slept, the entire Gorman clan discussed my goolies! Padhman glanced back at the house. What could they be discussing now as they lovingly basted the turkey and tenderly glazed the ham? The boys had panicked at the sight of Padhman looking back towards the house.

'We can't go back now.'

'Not yet!'

The youngest said nothing but set off determinedly down the slope. His protests were rarely verbal. His brothers, watching his tracks, decided to create their own and soon the entire slope was criss-crossed with them. They called out to Padhman to join them.

'Go on, make giant tracks.'

'No, Paddyman. Start at that hedge and then come down this way. Walk along my tracks . . . here!'

Padhman was soon caught up in track-making, marching heavily and purposefully on what remained of the unmarked snow, eliciting cries of wonderment from the boys at the size of his footprints and the intricacies of the tread on his soles. When all the clean snow had been covered, the four of them stood at the top of the slope and surveyed their handiwork.

'Now what shall we do?'

'I really don't know.'

'You told Mum you'd keep us out for an hour.' It was a swift and pre-emptive reminder.

'I'll walk you three down to the woods.'

The boys wasted no time, well used to the instant changeability of any perfect situation, should a meal be announced or a bath be filled or worse still, a time to 'relax' be declared. The woods were very mucky underfoot and they tramped around, and having found a path, Padhman instructed them to stay on it. The boys picked up sticks, leaves and stones, discarding them as newer more interesting ones were found. Padhman heard a faint shout and looking towards the house, he could see Seamus, coming around from the direction of the court-yard, headed towards the slope. Padhman waved back instinctively and the boys, realising it was their father, abandoned Padhman instantly and headed for Seamus, their sticks and assorted trophies held high in their hands.

What has he planned for my goolies this time, Padhman wondered as he walked back slowly. If I am sensible about this, I shouldn't really take offence at what appears to have transpired last night. It would be worse if she had a family who didn't care. By the time he reached the top of the slope, he was hot and had to take off Eamon's jacket. Seamus had sent his three sons racing ahead to the house.

'All I had to tell them was that their Christmas crackers were waiting at the table on their plates. I was sent to call you. Dinner is ready.'

'The boys were a bit disappointed – you know, the snow was just a dusting. But we've built up our appetites.'

'Padhman, Aoife and you . . .'

Padhman held his breath. Here it comes, the shotgun to my head. Why does he have to take his big brotherly duties so seriously?

Seamus had stopped on the gravel and had turned around to look back at the woods. Then he began again, this time looking at Padhman. 'You must both come to us in Chicago. Come this summer – take two weeks. Heidi and I would be very happy if you did.'

Padhman felt a sense of satisfaction. He nodded his

head. 'I've never been to America. Chicago? I would love to. Thank you.'

As they walked into the courtyard, Seamus added, 'Aoife will probably need the break by then. The family are thrilled that she got onto the surgical rotation. She deserved to. She flew through medical school, you know. Did much better, was far more conscientious than Ronan or me.' He clapped Padhman on his back. 'Let's go in, they're waiting.'

'I just need to wash my hands. I'll follow right behind.' Padhman had indeed built up an appetite and even though he had been slightly put off the turkey, having first watched it thaw and then seen it being unceremoniously stuffed, he knew that this Christmas meal would be extra-special. Yesterday he had helped wrap a huge bowl of small potatoes in strips of streaky bacon. Eamon, slightly inebriated, had assured him that the ones Padhman had wrapped were to have pride of place around the turkey. He knew from the discussion at the kitchen table that the parsnips would be roasted, a spoonful of honey drizzled over to caramelise them. Individual bundles of matchstick-ed carrots had been painstakingly tied with chives. There was a debate about whether the bundles should be steamed or microwaved before they were doused in butter. He had watched Aoife and Heidi make a variety of sauces and stuffings to go with the meats. Nana Gorman had asked Padhman to taste the filling for the chocolate meringue log. He had pronounced it sufficiently alcoholic.

Padhman thought of the last meal he had eaten in Madras. In comparison to all the painstaking roasting and grinding of spices, the squeezing and extracting of coconut milk, the cutting, slicing and grinding of wet and dry masalas, the soaking and the marinating, the slow, deep and shallow frying that must have gone on in Amma's kitchen, everything being made for this Christmas meal seemed so simple, easy and straightforward. What intrigued him however was all the fuss and ceremony over the beautiful table decorations, the enormously elongated flower arrangements, the masses of candles and the place settings. Where for God's sake were they going to lay all the food?

If Padhman had known he would end up making an entrance, he might not have let Seamus go ahead. The Gormans all turned to look at him, collectively heaving a sigh of relief as he walked in. Eamon and Aoife gave him a riotous welcome blast on their little paper trumpets. Padhman noted the speed with which Seamus' boys reached for their trumpets, scrambling to retrieve the rolled up, feather-tipped instruments from various places they had ended up in: under the table, impaled on the table decorations and squashed under Heidi and then, hurriedly joining their aunt and uncle in a cacophonous finale.

Millie Gorman clapped for her grandsons and pleased, she turned to Heidi. 'Music lessons – you must think of it.' Across the table Seamus snorted.

Aoife's Nana waited till Padhman was seated and then, carving knife in hand, she looked at him before plunging the huge fork into the extremely plump turkey.

'We couldn't have started without you, Padhman.'

CHAPTER TWENTY

~

THE PHONE RANG as he put on his jacket. Padhman
looked at his watch and quickly calculated the time in
Madras. It was eleven o'clock at night, Indian Standard
Time. It had to be Amma. If it were, this would be the
third time in a row that his parents had called just as he
was leaving for Galway. The ringing continued, loud and
persistent.

The last two times he had spoken to Amma and Appa
in similar circumstances, he had driven angry and upset
nearly halfway to Galway, before he could begin to relax
and shake off the unfair grip they, particularly Amma,
seemed to have on his emotions. Given that he knew what
he was up against, it dismayed him that, time and time
again, he found himself helplessly flayed.

Amma had left no angle unexplored, no aspect of
marriage and life in India unexamined. No, everything
from religion to the requirements for malarial precautions
had been sited as good reason to abandon his foolishness.
His foolishness! From 'fooling around' Amma's euphem-
ism for living together was now 'his foolishness'. The heat
and dirt, the flies, cockroaches and the snakes, the power
cuts and water shortages, the beggars, the bureaucracy
and the work to rule in the public sector plus the escalat-
ing price of meat, would all prove too much for that poor
girl. On other occasions, Amma would confront him with
purely theoretical questions, designed to show the deep
cultural and spiritual challenge that the poor girl would
have to face. Would she go to the temple? Would she

laugh at the gods? Ganesha's elephant head? Sri Krishna's blue body? Lord Shiva's Lingam? Mother Kali's bloodied tongue? Goddess Lakshmi on her Lotus? Would she touch Amma and Appa's feet when they wanted to bless her? Would she be vegetarian on Tuesdays? Would she call them Amma and Appa? And there were other things to be considered. Where would she practise? The hospitals would be different. Patients would be wary. She would have to learn Tamil. No, no, she couldn't practise till she knew the local language. She would want her children educated in Ireland. She would want them christened, baptised and confirmed. The reasons never stopped and Amma never stopped reasoning. 'Padhu son, marriage is a compromise. But here you are, asking the poor girl to give up everything. Padhu, your marriage will be compromised from the start.' Amma had examined his foolishness from her perspective, from his perspective and from that poor girl's perspective, so how could she possibly be wrong?

Padhman walked into the kitchen and picked up the phone. Five minutes, ten at the most, he thought to himself grimly. I am going to have to start putting my foot down. If Amma repeats herself any more, things will get written down in stone and she is so dogmatic already.

'Padhu? Padhu, can you hear me? Oh yes, I can hear you now. Sad news, son – Miss Angela died yesterday. Hmm . . . very few at the funeral. Just her sister and her nieces and nephews. Nimmi and Raja came, so nice of them. Appa was quite upset. Padhu, will you let Sunil know about Miss Angela, not that Nimmi won't tell him, of course. Our other news is that Appa is going to take two weeks off next month. Dr Narayanan – you know him, his son married the youngest of those Lalwani sisters. I remember the middle one, Pinkie – no, sorry, Pinkie was the eldest. She is in San Francisco now, married to one of those motel-wallahs. No the middle one was called Bubbly – don't pretend you don't remember, Padhu. All those phone calls at all times of the day and night and you were only in school! The son, Dr Narayanan's son, has started the Polyclinic on Usman Road. They had to borrow lots from the bank, all the equipment came from abroad. Anyway, where was I? Oh yes. Dr Narayanan is going to look after Appa's patients for the two weeks. I wish we would do this every year. Appa works so hard. You must tell him to slow down, Padhu. Raja and Nimmi were suggesting that he starts with taking one half day per week. To start with, till you come back. He is his own master, after all. He needs no permission. Look at Raja. He doesn't go in on Saturdays any more. Of course, architecture is different. A building can always wait, but a woman in labour . . . I remember the day you were born. We had passes, VIP passes for the President's enclosure. Grandfather had operated on his wife the year before. No Padhu, I'm talking about the President of the Cricket Board. I think it was a hysterectomy that she had. India versus Australia, it was the last day of the Test Match. But we had to leave during the opening over. You know, secretly Appa didn't forgive you till the day you captained the school cricket team. But all that aside, our news is that we will be travelling in the second week of April. Padhu, your Appa and Amma are coming to Dublin.'

All the way up to Athlone, Padhman's mind flitted from one thought to another. At first, while caught in the exodus out of the city, he had wondered why Renu looked so down in the dumps. Was it because his parents would be in Dublin and hers hadn't any plans to come at all? She wasn't given to such childishness. Maybe she had her period. When she had opened the door to him she had looked a bit out of sorts and though she had perked up when he told her the news about Amma and Appa, she had slid back into a mopiness that was completely out of character for her. She had asked him to stay for coffee but he refused.

'I was just setting off for Galway when the phone rang. Then I thought I'd come and tell you both the news. But I have to go. Even if I leave right now it will be at least ten before I get to Aoife's.'

At the door he asked her if she was OK.

'Just a bit fed up with being so alone. We agreed that Sunil should start studying in the Postgraduate Centre. He is convinced that he can concentrate better there. He'll come home only when he's had enough of the books for the night.'

Padhman nodded his head. He almost felt terrible for having passed the exam. Sunil's failure had been a bitter blow and even now, three weeks on, his friend's utter dejection was a painful thing to behold.

'He'll get it the next time, Renu. The Part One is a bitch.'

As the traffic funnelled and squeezed itself through Kinnegad, choking up the heart of the village, turning pedestrians into interesting objects to be gaped at by the occupants of the never-ending, intercity cavalcade of motors, Padhman thought about his excited dash to Renu and Sunil's. Padhman was pleased with the news from Madras. He had said it to Renu.

'It will be great to have them here. I'll have to speak to Morris and take a few days off. Appa really needs the break and Amma . . . well, it's high time she met Aoife.' Renu wasn't quite sure about the latter.

'Renu, whatever else you can say about Amma, she would never be undignified. There will be no scenes. I am totally unafraid about anything like that.'

He was nearly through the village. Reaching *Cunningham's Funeral Directors, Headstone & Monumental*

Sculptors was a sign that he was at the end of the logjam in Kinnegad, and that within minutes he would be on the open road again. He and others ahead and behind him would put their foot down now, foolishly expecting their frustrations at being delayed by this unassuming bloody village, to be released in one fell 0–60 mph burst.

It was not until he was well past Athlone that his thoughts turned fully to where he was heading. It was quite likely that Aoife wouldn't even be home by the time he arrived. She was finding work gruelling. Padhman couldn't really understand this. Hadn't she seen her father work his butt off? Or maybe she was too young to remember Professor Gorman's early days. Surely Seamus and Ronan would have made some sort of impression on her when they were junior doctors. She with her upbringing in a medical family should have had inculcated in her that universal pseudo-mystical medical ethos that had been handed down to Padhman by Grandfather and Appa. He had learnt that there was admiration to be gained from being labelled fiercely dedicated and not much sympathy to be had from playing the overworked card. 'Soldier on' was the mantra and you could feed off the exaggerated sense of responsibility that settled heavily on your shoulders as you did, indeed, soldier on.

Of course, Aoife had chewed his head off when he had expressed that opinion a few weeks back.

'If you think this is about hard work, I have nothing to say, Padhman.' And she didn't. He tried to mollify her but she was convinced that he was being condescending. It hadn't been a very happy weekend even though they had both tried to make up to each other hurriedly on the Sunday afternoon.

It had begun to rain by the time Padhman reached Ballinasloe. The drops were few and far between, but they were big and fat and they splattered on the windscreen of his car like clear bird droppings. It was too dark to see if he was heading into a downpour or if the spitting and spotting came from the periphery of some localised rain that he was merely passing by.

Since New Year's Eve when Padhman, Eamon and Molly had set off behind Aoife, their four cars stuffed with all of Aoife's bare essentials, Padhman had lost count of the number of times he and Aoife had been back and forth between Galway and Dublin. He had kept tally at first, but after a couple of trips, designated the journey as his thinking time. Sometimes he would dwell on issues that he would have specifically set aside to think about, and sometimes an entire journey would be spent on deliberations triggered off by a chance memory from that day or from before. He would drive like an automaton, his hands and feet attached seamlessly to the car and his eyes on the road, while his mind roamed free, trying to fathom the meaning and reasons behind other people's utterances and behaviour and his own feelings and sometimes his fears and hopes. There was no telling what his mood would be when he got to Galway for it would depend on where his thoughts had taken him during the journey.

Arriving at Aoife's, Padhman pulled up the handbrake. There was great satisfaction in doing that at journey's end – the motoring equivalent of a great big sigh. He had parked the car as far back in the drive as he could, leaving enough room for Aoife to reverse in. Her Galway semi-detached was a big change from her basement apartment in Dublin, but not too unlike Padhman's.

Aoife's nose had wrinkled up the first time they had seen the house, but despite its heavily patterned carpet with the ochre, orange and brown swirls, despite the faded blue melamine presses with their dull aluminium beading, and the enormous button-backed and scalloped pink Dralon headboard that spanned out like angel's wings well beyond either side of the small double bed, the house, its furniture and contents were spotlessly clean. Aoife had paid the deposit straight away. Of course, the addition of her things had only made the house look more dreadful; the contrast between her bits and pieces and those that belonged to the house was too stark.

Padhman showered and as he towelled himself he could hear her car reverse into the space he had left. He heard her walk straight to the kitchen and then minutes later, the oven door opened and shut with an agonising screech. It really needed a squirt of WD 40. I must sort that out this weekend, Padhman thought as Aoife came up the stairs. He waited with childlike anticipation, hugging her on the landing, letting her free only when she twisted out of his embrace and walked into the bedroom.

'Baby me,' she said, slipping her shoes off and lying down on the bed. He unbuttoned her clothes, easing them off her shoulders and hips. In the bathroom he soaped her slowly and then watched the water run down her in sheets and here and there in tiny, twisting rivulets and channels. He towelled her dry on the bed where she lay languid and curled up, so satisfied with herself, knowing he would soon tire of the quiet and gentle foreplay.

When they both showered again later it was quick and efficient. They filled each other up on the day's events and it was only when they went downstairs and he was putting out the two plates and two glasses on the table for them, that he remembered. He slapped his forehead and Aoife raised her eyebrows questioningly.

'Appa and Amma will be here next month. Aoife, it was the first thing I meant to say to you. My mum and dad are coming to Dublin.'

She stopped unwrapping the doner kebabs that had stayed warm for them in the oven. 'Should I be worried?'

He looked at her lips and the way she was nibbling at

219

them. 'A little bit, I suppose. I guess you are probably half the reason why they are coming. My mother believes it's easier to tackle the known devil.'

Aoife lifted the pitta breads off the foil and on to the plates, the shredded lettuce trailing behind, while the creamy dressing marbleised by the spicy tomato sauce, oozed and dripped all over the plates. The thin slices of meat spilled out of the pitta pockets.

'I'm eating with my fingers.' It was nearly an apology but one that was rendered as a statement, with all the fervour of a newly converted devotee. Much to Padhman's amusement, Aoife now ate with her fingers at the slight-est opportunity. 'Will she want to meet me, Padhman? Will I come to the airport or will I be summoned?'

Padhman was looking for the matchbox to light the 'Rock of Gibraltar'. The geographic identity of the weirdly shaped candle was embossed in explanatory fashion across its base. The large wax lump had come with the house and had been discovered in the corner of the windowsill, above the kitchen sink. They had lit it ceremoniously the night Aoife moved in, eating their Indian takeaway in the light thrown by the 'Rock'.

'Don't be silly, neither,' said Padhman. 'We'll play it by ear, Aoif. All I know is, she is going to go back to India knowing that she doesn't really have a choice. Where are the matches?'

'Try the press over the washing machine. How long will they stay?'

Padhman was unable to answer, his mouth and throat draining dry at the sight of the innocuous little roll-ups with dried parsley-like flecks spilling out of the tops, that lay half-smoked next to the box of matches. He knew without a doubt what they were. He had tried the experimental puff or two, even three. Hell, who in college hadn't?

220

'To the furtherance of medical science,' had been Sunil's nervous toast before they had had their first go. But that was then. That's what you did when you were a medical student. You had a go at everything. You tried it and you forgot it. A few went on to dabble further, but there was always a bad egg or two in every batch.

But here . . . but now! Implications, ramifications, consequences . . . they were like crazed loops of some awful rollercoaster that made his mind reach down and heave up sickening fears from deep within his belly. What the bloody hell was she up to?

'Did you find them, Padhman?'

'It's a joint, isn't it? Marijuana. There are two.' It was hard to keep the hysterics out of his voice. 'Are you crazy?'

Aoife had turned around in her chair and she looked him in the eye calmly. Padhman licked his lips. They were obviously not hers. Thank God. He shifted his gaze away from hers and back to the cupboard.

'Cannabis. Marijuana is for Americans. Don't panic, Padhman.'

Her calmness was making him anxious. It didn't portend well.

'Padhman, *relax*!'

Padhman sat down. Wasn't that what you were supposed to say as you took the first puff? *Ree . . . lax!!* No, it was, *Hey, my ma . . . an, relaa . . . x!* Padhman gripped the table. Why was he talking nonsense to himself?

'Don't shake your head so dramatically, Padhman. It's only grass – harmless. Are you telling me you've never had a puff? Tootsie – you remember Sara Tuthill – she dropped in last weekend. It was like being back in college. She had a couple of joints on her. It's great to unwind.'

'Unwind? You could have a soak in the bath. Open a bottle of wine. Watch television. Go to bed.'

'Oh, don't be such a prude. I know exactly what I'm doing. You're not the only doctor in the house. You needn't play Nanny.'

I need to stand up and say this. I need to rise above her apparent composure. I need to say it as it is.

'Christ, Aoif, you could be struck off the Register. Your father's reputation would be in tatters. *I* could get involved. Shit! Your parents would think I knew all along. I'd never get a job. I haven't got my Fellowship yet. What would I tell my parents? Your bloody judgement is impaired!'

'This is nothing to do with you, my father, my family or your family. This is me, just smoking the remainder of a harmless joint, minding my own business. And don't throw your bloody bad language at me.'

'It's not your own business. Not when you are a bloody joint-puffing doctor.'

'For God's sake, Padhman! You didn't exactly find me stoned, did you? Save the bloodys, won't you? I'm not your average Indian woman so don't shout at me that way.'

'Leave the average Indian woman out of this. They would have far more sense anyway.' Padhman pushed his chair back and looked at her. 'Aoif, you've been silly. Just admit it and . . . and bin those bloody things.'

'No, Padhman. You are grossly over-reacting. Why don't you admit *you're* being silly and go back to Dublin?'

Ballinasloe was shrouded in darkness. Approaching Athlone, he glanced at the clock on the dashboard. One o'clock, no wonder the town was deserted. He stiffened at the sight of a Garda car approaching in the opposite direction and watched it disappear, past him and then into the night, in his rearview mirror. He considered pulling up at the first phone booth and calling Aoife. He spotted a booth ahead, past the blinking amber lights. Somebody

222

was using it. As he drove past he wondered if it really was that much warmer in there, in the glass booth, sufficiently so for that man to have stepped into it for a pee. What makes people do the things they do? There was an Irishism for it: 'just messing'. Padhman repeated the phrase again and again in his head. Is that what Aoife was doing? Just messing? Did I really blow things out of proportion? It's not even something I could tell anybody. If it circulated, that you smoked pot, bang went your reference, your job and your career.

Padhman flew through Kinnegad. It was the first time he'd driven through the village in fourth gear. The main street looked large and wide. What unyielding forces created the impasse here every day? Padhman reached out to open the glove compartment and rooted around in vain for a bar of chocolate that he was sure had been there since the last time he had returned from Galway. He was starved and he could feel a hunger headache come on. Within half an hour he began to feel nauseous and sorry for himself. Their first major fight and it wasn't about unbought flowers or whose turn it was to wash up. What was he going to tell her? Choose between the hash and me? That sounded like a B-grade script. Pathetic!

When he got home, he ate six slices of buttered toast with marmalade, standing next to the toaster, grabbing the hot slices as they popped up. Of course he wouldn't say anything. He would wait for her to come to her senses. Which she would. It wouldn't be a matter of making bloody ridiculous choices. The hash or me! No, no, nothing so stupid or dramatic. It would just be a matter of plain common sense, he said to himself as he hit the bed.

He woke up just as he finished making love to her, he and Aoife satiated, but barely able to see each other through the haze of narcotic smoke that filled the room. This was a dream for beginners. Anyone could interpret it. Padhman looked at the clock as he reached for the phone. She should be at home. He didn't want to waste a minute more, considering the weekend was already a disaster. It was a relief to hear her. She had picked up the phone in the first few rings. A good sign. She had been waiting. She sounded fine too.

'Aoif, what a mess. Shall I drive back? I've just woken up. I'm sorry about the way it turned out, but I know you'll see sense. It's a matter of principle.'

There was a long silence before she answered. 'As a matter of principle, Padhman, I don't like to be preached to.' She put the phone down without another word.

What a mess. I made it worse. No, she made it worse. So she'll have to call back. He grabbed the phone when it rang. It was Sunil.

'We thought you were in Galway. What's your car doing outside and what are you doing inside?'

'We had a fight and I drove back. No questions, OK?'

'OK. Are you all right?'

'Fine. Need to sleep, though. I got back at three this morning.'

'Come over later if you feel like it.'

For a long while afterwards, Padhman stared at the phone, willing it to ring. He dozed on and off, but every time he woke he found the unhappiness unbearable. Not that he would have cried. That was something you did when you knew you couldn't ever be together again. No, this was a different thing. This was a paralysis that gripped his mind but that pushed the rewind button, playing back again and again the events that had brought him – brought *them* – so swiftly and ridiculously to this point. He tried to talk to himself, advocating patience and faith in their relationship. I'll just have to put up with this state of mind till we are past all this, he told himself.

But advocating reason to oneself was literally easier said than done. He fretted for a week and a half, unable to shake off the sad malaise taking a firm grip on his soul, but at least he could rely confidently on work to distract him sufficiently and tire him totally so that when he did come home, he had just enough energy to sit by the phone and wait for it to ring.

He didn't find it unreasonable that he was not willing to make the next move. It was her turn and he clung to that painfully stubborn decision. The air was pure and rarefied on the moral high ground, but no one had warned him about altitude sickness. When it did strike, he began wondering if the presence of two half-smoked joints was enough to indicate an addiction, a habit or anything at all for that matter. Had he jumped to conclusions? Was that why she had reacted with annoyance rather than guilt? He wanted to do the right thing but he wasn't sure what the right thing was.

It didn't help matters that Amma had called unexpectedly during the week and, having caught him off guard, had managed to detect a certain moroseness in his manner. When she asked him casually what he was planning for the weekend – was he going to Galway? – he should never have answered, or at least not so listlessly.

'Are you having problems with that girl?' Alerted, Amma's intuitive powers rose to their full, penetrative potential. Padhman could literally see them unfurl around her, like the expansive probe that NASA had recently launched to explore deep space. He could hear alarm bells go off in her head, but they were also punctuated with happy sounds of relief.

Padhman tried to extricate himself from the confessional that Amma had cornered him in, but it was no use and he attempted to salvage the situation by telling her as little as possible.

'A difference of opinion, Amma. That's all it was.'

'It's inevitable, Padhu. Your basic values are different.'

Amma had called nearly every day since, under the guise of discussing the upcoming travel plans to Ireland. The conversation would swiftly move on to enquiring about the state of affairs, assuring him that he would be fine, particularly without that girl. Amma aggravated his sense of unease and kept the phone occupied ten minutes before he left for work and sometimes for ages in the evening, in that limbo time between dinner and bed, just the very times he was sure that Aoife might be trying to make that conciliatory call to him. In fact, if he had to go by the last phone call from Amma, Aoife was history and all would be well from now on.

As another lonely weekend approached, Padhman realised that something drastic was called for.

CHAPTER TWENTY-ONE

~

PADHMAN PUT HIS coffee down on the mantelpiece and headed for the front door. He had been languishing in front of the TV, when through the net curtains, he saw Sunil walking towards the house. Renu followed behind him trying to keep up. He wasn't really up to visitors, but of course Sunil and Renu didn't fall into that category.

He opened the door for them and wondered why they both avoided his eye. They lingered a few seconds in the hall and then shuffled into the sitting room. Sunil looked cold and he shivered as he turned to look at Padhman. His shoulders heaved in soundless sobs. Renu moved to stand beside her husband, and it was only when she put her arm out to grip Padhman's elbow, that he realised that the horrid news, whatever it was, had to do with him.

What is happening to me? Is blood rushing to my head or is it draining away? Sunil says my father is dead. Look at the way he is weeping – he must be right. He loved Appa too. I don't feel faint, Renu, you needn't hold me so tight. Or do *you* feel faint? Let me hold you then. Are you going to tell me how, why? Is my mother . . . is she all right? Was she in the car? I feel sick. I want to be sick. Let me be sick and then you can tell me.

Renu held him as he retched over and over. She wiped his face with wetted toilet paper. They made him sit and Sunil dialled Madras. The house would be filling up with shocked people. Cars would have started pulling up, parking hurriedly, haphazardly. People hastily dressed in white: friends, acquaintances, patients, colleagues would mill around dazed, asking hushed questions. When did it happen? Thank God he was alone. The car is a write-off. Has the body come home? Has the son been informed? Only child, isn't he? Will he make it for the funeral? It is a pity he is so far away. The burden will be on his shoulders now.

It wasn't only good news that travelled fast. The phone would be constantly engaged, the whole world calling the house, unaware that he, Padhman, the son of the deceased, was waiting on a sofa, in a house in Dublin, while Sunil tried in vain to get through.

When he did, Sunil asked authoritatively for his own father. 'Tell Raja Patel this is a call from Ireland.'

The cordless phone would be rushed to where Raja Uncle was. People would go quiet and move aside respectfully when they realised who was at the other end of the phone. As Raja Uncle opened the door to Amma and Appa's room gently, people around would shake their heads, an uncontrollable sob or two would break out and men would blink back tears. This would be the worst bit. The son was going to speak to his mother. What would they say to each other?

'Appa has . . . left me, Padhu. Come home, son.'

Padhman nodded his head mutely. 'I'm coming home, Amma. I'm coming.'

Padhman wished he could make the tea instead of Renu. It would give him something to do with his hands. He wished he could open the door when the bell rang, but Sunil had commandeered this task as his duty. It left Padhman bereft, with nothing to do except to begin his public grieving, a process designed to be followed through mechanically, and which began with accepting the condolences of friends on the phone and those who called at the house. A dozen or so people had come and gone in the past hour, shaking his hand and standing around. They moved on to the kitchen and hung around the front door, drinking cups of tea and some smoking their cigarettes. The talk was of faraway parents, brothers and sisters, of families that wouldn't be seen for a while. They dwelt on the sad irony of being doctors, looking after all and sundry in a foreign land, but being too far away to be of any use to their own kin.

When everyone had gone and it didn't seem like any more would call, Padhman left Sunil and Renu tidying and washing up and went upstairs. Cocooned by shock and knowing it, he hoped its effects would not wear off just yet. He had pushed the memory of Amma's pathetic, childlike plea to come home, into a compartment in the deeper recesses of his mind. His private grief welled inside him threatening to burst through, but he swallowed the scream as it arose. He wasn't ready to face this all on his own. He needed his Aoife. He had rung her. She had left for Dublin immediately. It was a three-hour drive. He would wait for her. Aoife had told him to.

'I'll be there, Padhman. I'm coming.'

When she did, he would hold on to her before he let himself go.

Amma had insisted on coming to the airport to see him off. For a couple of days Raja Uncle and Nimmi Aunty had worried about this, anxious for Amma, afraid that the emotions might all be too much for her. But Padhman, who was ready to indulge his mother's slightest whim, reasoned that ultimately Amma was the only one who could decide the way she wanted to cope.

He had been upgraded to First Class, boarded first, shown to his seat up at the very front. The captain had come out of the cockpit. He shook Padhman's hand.

'Your grandfather delivered me.'

Padhman had heard it countless times in the last two

weeks. I know, I know. My grandfather delivered you, my father delivered your son. You have a family connection with mine. I know, I've heard it all before. Nearly everyone at the funeral had begun their condolences with that obstetric detail.

'And your father delivered my son,' the captain went on. 'It is a great loss, a great loss for your family, for the profession. Let the cabin crew know if you need anything at all. Try and rest, sleep if you can. The last few days must have been most difficult. I believe you are flying on from London to Dublin?' He shook Padhman's hand again and then looking down the aisle, briefly signalled something to the chief stewardess before returning to the cockpit.

Padhman looked out through the window. It was only February but the hazy heat of the midday sun diffused everything on the tarmac. The terminal seemed far away, out of focus. The aircraft hadn't even taken off and Madras was beginning to look distant. Two hours ago, he and Amma had been ushered into the VIP lounge where they had sat, mute, in fearful anticipation of what a fresh show of grief would do to each other. Raja Uncle had headed off to sort out Padhman's check-in formalities. Amma had clung to him wordlessly when the flight had been announced and yet it was she who had extricated herself from Padhman and nudged him gently towards the curtained double doors that led directly to the departure lounge.

'Would you like a cup of tea, sir?'

Padhman turned away from the window and through a film of tears that had suddenly clouded his vision he looked at the fuzzy outline of the chief stewardess.

'Oh, I'm sorry, sir. I can come back.'

'I'll have some coffee if you have any.' Padhman could see her clearly now. She looked embarrassed. She returned

230

with coffee, a chicken sandwich, a bag of salted cashew nuts, a selection of biscuits and a dish of fruit salad. 'I thought you might be hungry.'

Padhman was hungry, but he took the coffee and declined all the snacks. He smiled at her just to put her at ease. He wasn't ashamed that she had seen him cry. Close to two hundred men had seen him weep inconsolably as he had lit his father's funeral pyre, hands reluctant and trembling. They had watched as his knees had buckled of their own accord. They had seen Raja Uncle and others rush to hoist him back to his feet. He was sure he had even beaten his chest in despair, unable to come to terms with this cruel, cruel reality, this terrible unhappiness that had been doled out so prematurely to Amma.

Padhman looked at his watch. Amma would be home now, alone. He knew her. She would have feigned tiredness and insisted Raja Uncle and Nimmi Aunty go home to rest as well. She would be sitting in Grandfather's room, looking out of the window. After the tenth-day ceremony, when the stream of condolence visits had been reduced to a trickle, she and Padhman had found time to talk to each other. 'Don't worry about me,' was what she had repeated to Padhman over and over again. Other than that, the future was too painful a subject to discuss. It was a future without Appa.

The plane had begun to taxi down towards the runway. Padhman closed his eyes wearily. At the end of this journey lay what could be defined as normality. Aoife would have driven down from Galway just to be at the airport to pick him up. He had spoken to her nearly every night, staying up as late as possible to call her, not wanting to wake her too early in the morning. It had made them both sick at heart that it had taken Appa's death to make Padhman pick up the phone and bring their fight to an

231

instant end. He admitted over-reacting, she admitted being perversely blasé about a once-off lark.

The cabin lights dimmed for take-off. Within minutes the aircraft was climbing steeply. Padhman tried to control the sudden panic that he felt rising in him. He had left Amma alone in Madras. What was she going to do with herself? What would she do when she woke up? Every day would be long, endlessly lonely. He closed his eyes, miserable at the thought of her and the desperate sadness that she would never be able to shake off.

Padhman heard his name being called out across the canteen. He was just clearing his tray and was in a hurry to leave, a half-eaten muffin still in his hand. Padhman hated being late for Larkin's clinic. He knew he would be late, when he realised it was Maura. She waved as she walked towards him, weaving her way around the tables.

'Where have you been, Padhman? Haven't seen you for weeks. Forgotten your old friends in Casualty, eh?' She wagged her finger at him and stabbed him in the chest with the envelope that she held in her hand. 'Your Department of Surgery is only a floor above us, you know, though Niall says you are only ever to be found on the road to Galway. Anyway, I'm glad I caught you. I wanted to give this to you myself. Don't look so perplexed, Padhman. It's only our wedding invitation. For you and Aoife.'

Padhman hurried off to the clinic, slipping the invitation into the pocket of his white coat. The Friday afternoon clinic didn't make for a great start to the weekend, but at least this weekend he didn't have to drive to Galway. Aoife was coming to Dublin and would probably be at home by the time he got back. They had perfected the art of spending lazy weekends with each other.

Padhman heard his name being called out again, as he

walked briskly down the neverending corridor to the Out-Patient Clinic. He waited for Sunil to catch up and they both walked some distance together.

'My mother's here, Pads. I spoke to her half an hour ago. The flight was delayed by an hour and Renu said she looks a bit jet-lagged. Mama wanted to know if she could see you today.'

Nimmi Aunty opened the door to number 33 and Padhman hugged her long and hard. She embraced him tightly with her slim arms and later held him by his shoulders at arms' length and looked searchingly up at his face, as if examining him for any worries or problems he might have etched into his forehead or mirrored in his eyes. She seemed satisfied that he was OK and then she drew his head down closer to her and kissed him affectionately on both cheeks. With his arms around her waist they walked into the kitchen. Sunil was washing up and Padhman could see Renu coming in from the back garden having shaken the tablecloth out onto the grass.

'See how your daughter-in-law treats him, Nimmi Aunty? Is this the reward your son gets for having passed his exam? She's turned him into a servant.'

'Ignore him, Mama. He loves to create trouble.' Renu flicked the tablecloth over the table, her annoyance indicated by the deftness of the flick.

'Shall I wash up, son?' Nimmi Aunty was already heading for the sink.

Renu rolled her eyes at Padhman. 'I told you so,' said the look. 'You can be a real pain sometimes.'

Padhman gave her a hasty apologetic grin. He hadn't meant to create trouble. He steered Sunil's mother away from the sink by her shoulders.

'I was only joking, Nimmi Aunty. You didn't have to take me so literally. Come into the sitting room with me.

233

We'll make them wait on us hand and foot.' Padhman looked at Renu to see if she was mollified. He winked at her as he continued to push Sunil's mother out to the hall and then he added, 'Two teas, Renu, and make it fast.'

The fire was nearly out and needed to be rescued. It was a disappointingly cold and windy August evening. Nimmi Aunty sat and watched as Padhman lifted the grate aside and began to carefully arrange a layer of coal, choosing the smallest lumps so that he would not inadvertently snuff the fire out instead. He broke off two small bits of firelighter and as he placed them on the coal he spoke to her over his shoulder.

'Is it next week that Raja Uncle will be here?'

'Yes, son. He arrives on Sunday. Sunil is taking the week off from Monday onwards. They, Renu and Sunil, are going to drive us to some Ring of something . . . I forget.'

'The Ring of Kerry. You will love it, Nimmi Aunty.' Padhman had put on another layer of coal over the fire-lighters and was watching the flames tentatively lick the coals above them, darting out through the gaps and dancing with every whoosh of wind that blew down the chimney.

'I was going to take Appa and Amma there.' He stood up and put the grate back in its place. She bade him sit down next to her on the sofa. He did, not bothering to fight back the tears that still remained to be shed. She put her arms around him and cradled him for a while, like she had done countless times before: when he had needed consoling as a child after losing at violent fisticuffs with Sunil, after a bitter argument with Amma or when he had cried that night along with Sunil when the groom left with the bride at Sunil's sister's wedding.

'How is Amma?'

As Nimmi Aunty adjusted herself on the sofa, Padhman sensed that she was going to tell him what he already knew – but the picture she painted was even more dismal than he had feared.

'Your Amma is my oldest, my dearest friend. What is it that we have not been through together? But this loss is a lonely one, a loss that cannot be shared. Such a shock, so unexpected . . . so undeserved. She can barely speak. She doesn't want to speak. She has stopped going out completely. It's six months now . . . and yet she hardly ever goes out, even to the market. We've tried, Raja and I, to get her to at least come home, to us, to have dinner and maybe watch a video or drive to the beach, but she rarely leaves her room. She always says no. You know your Amma . . . polite, very firm. I am there nearly every day and I know she waits for me to come. The servants are alert for her every signal. The cook has taken to sleeping outside her bedroom door. We don't really know what to do. Not that she is worried about you, son, not any more, now that all your foolishness with that girl is over. She knows that once you have your Fellowship, you will come back. I know how often you have been calling her – she always tells me that.'

Padhman got up to stoke the fire. He stood facing the flames and took a couple of deep breaths. My foolishness with that girl! Thank God Renu and Sunil had kept mum as requested, about him and Aoife. Amma didn't need to know as yet; she was too fragile. He had his fears about Amma's emotional state, but if he was to go by what Nimmi Aunty was telling him, and she of all people would be able to assess the situation correctly, Amma had lost the will to live her life like before. She had said it to him on the phone once or twice, crying quietly and he had listened, unable to say anything that would make a jot of real difference. Padhman was gripped by a sudden fear that he was going to lose his mother to some sort of living death. He knelt down and prodded the coals, spreading them out a bit, exposing the glowing heart of the fire. A blast of heat hit his face. Appa was gone. Amma was increasingly beyond reach. Normality would never return. When will I ever be able to take my life off hold? Padhman felt sick at heart and then again, guilty with his own impatience.

'Raja Uncle wanted to have some time, while he is here, to talk to you. He really is very worried about her. Healthwise it cannot be good for her to become so reclusive. I know you have been trying to get her to come to you for a while, but you see, she was planning that trip with your father. To do it now, to come without him, would be unbearable for her. The thing is, son, she has to be given a reason to come alive again.'

Padhman hurriedly finished the tea that Renu had brought in. The three Patels looked surprised when he got up to leave. Padhman looked at his watch pointedly – but it wasn't that late, and they knew it.

He stood at the front door. 'I'll explain some other time.'

Sunil, who had walked with him into the hall, nodded.

The lights were out and he let himself into his house quietly. Aoife was fast asleep. Padhman undressed quickly; a sense of urgency had come over him. He propped the pillows up against the headboard and got into bed. Placing the phone on his lap, he dialled, his head leaning back into the pillows, relaxed.

'Amma, Padhu here. I knew you'd still be awake . . . No, nothing is the matter. I just felt like talking to you. Did you get the photographs I sent you? . . . Do you think so, Amma? I'll have to start eating a little more I guess . . . No, I got back late today. I've just come home from Sunil and Renu's . . . Yes, she arrived here safely this morning. Still the same old Nimmi Aunty. A bit jet-lagged. She told me to tell you that she would call you in a day or two . . . What? My news? Yes, Amma, I do have news. I'm coming to Madras for two weeks. I'll give you the dates as soon as I have confirmed bookings. It's not too far away – next month some time. I'm looking forward to it . . . No, I just want to spend time at home, Amma. Relaxing. And Amma, I'm bringing Aoife with me . . . Yes. That girl. It's time you met her.'

When he put the phone down, he readjusted the pillows and slipped down to lie against Aoife. She stirred and he put his arm around her, moulding his body along hers. He closed his eyes contentedly. Bloody hell! He sat up and reached out to turn off the radio alarm. He wouldn't need it. Amma would call him first thing in the morning.